MR. ROMANCE

FRANKLIN U #3

LOUISA MASTERS

Mr. Romance

Copyright © 2022 by Louisa Masters

Cover: Natasha Snow Designs www.natashasnow.com

Editor: Hot Tree Editing

MR. ROMANCE

When you're clueless, Mr. Romance can help.

Charlie

I'm not sure how it happened, but it turns out I've unknowingly been dating three people.

Friends don't spoil other friends, apparently. My trust fund means I can afford to, though, and what's a meal here and there? Or some clothes? Or textbooks? That doesn't mean we're dating, right?

Others disagree. If I want to get through the rest of college knowing who my friends are, I need help from someone who knows all about dating and can tell me what not to do.

Someone like Mr. Romance.

Liam

When people look at me, romance is the last thing they think of... but I'm still the first person they call. Need a first date planned? A big romantic moment? Gotta beg for forgiveness? I'm your man. When it comes to romance, I've got it handled.

Not personally, though. My romantic life is... barren. All I really want is someone to snuggle with and spoil me. What I've got is planning dates for people who have no clue about romancing someone.

But now I'm somehow Charlie Martin's anti-romance consultant. Charlie, who's completely clueless yet the most accepting and friendly person I've ever met. Who's giving and generous. Who's befriended me and wants me to be happy.

I'm supposed to help him stop his friends from falling for him. The last thing I need is to fall for him myself.

AUTHOR'S NOTE

All FUKing titles stand alone and can be read without reading the others—though why would you want to? All these authors are awesome! If you're following the recommended reading order, this book is third and there's some timeline overlap with books one and two, *Playing Games* and *The Dating Disaster*. Happy Reading!

CHAPTER ONE

CHARLIE

"You're a pig, Charlie Martin!"

The words seem to echo around the café, and I blink in shock up at the pretty brunette who shouted them. Cassie's my friend. Why would she do this?

"Uh... what?"

"Oh my god, don't play dumb with me! I know you're plenty smart. How could you do this to me?"

I swallow and glance around while trying not to look like I'm glancing around. I have no idea what's going on. "Cass, I don't understand. Did I do something to upset you?"

Across the table, Lesley tosses her blond mane. "Charlie, is something going on here?"

I wish I knew the answer to that question.

Cassie stomps her foot. "Nobody's talking to you, home-wrecker."

Okay, wow. This is getting out of hand. The girls clearly have some kind of history I know nothing about, but I wasn't born yesterday. Once the word "homewrecker" is tossed into the conversation, things always deteriorate.

Sure enough, Lesley pushes back her chair and stands. "What did you call me, bitch?"

"Maybe we should chill with the name-calling," I suggest desperately, trying to head things off. I come to Food Café for lunch nearly every day. It would suck if I got banned because of my friends.

They both turn on me. Speaking up was a mistake.

"How could you cheat on me with this *slut*?" Cassie hisses. I cringe. My mom works with women recovering from domestic violence, and she spent the first eighteen years of my life drumming into me that some words only demean women and therefore shouldn't be used. And these girls who are my friends are using them all pretty freely.

"I don't think there's any need for— Wait, what?" I stand too. "Did you say I cheated on you? I didn't cheat on you."

"You're dating her behind my back?" Lesley screeches. "How dare you! I don't deserve to be treated this way!"

"What way?" I ask in genuine bewilderment. I honestly thought that by the time we reached college, girls stopped doing that whole thing where if you were friends with them, you can't be friends with people they don't like. Also, I had no idea there was bad blood between them. This is so not my fault. If they're going to have dumb rules about friendship, they need to explain them to people upfront and tell me who I'm not allowed to be friends with.

Not that I'd do that. Nobody gets to tell me who I can and can't be friends with. Mom would kill me if I let them.

"You're dating us both!" Cassie declares. "That's not okay, Charlie. I thought we were exclusive!" She snatches up my soda and throws it at my face.

What. The. Fuck.

I snatch up a wad of napkins and mop myself off before it can drip onto the shirt I spent ten minutes ironing this morning. Lucky there wasn't much left in the glass—I'd be *pissed* if she ruined my shirt.

"I'm not dating you both!" Where the fuck did that come from? "I'm not dating either of you. We're friends." Aren't we? I look desperately around the café. Everyone's stopped to watch the drama unfold, and since it's lunchtime, that means there are plenty of witnesses to my humiliation. A few people are even holding up phones. Does that mean...?

"Uh, could you not record this, please?" I ask. None of them lower their phones. "Great. Thanks."

My eye catches on my friend Raymond near the door, grinning like a loon and shaking his head. He pushes his way through the crowd.

"Ladies, I'm sorry to have to tell you this, but Charlie is *not* dating either of you. You've got the wrong end of the *stick* there." He winks, and I try not to recoil. Raymond's a relatively new friend, but we're tight, and I didn't think he'd make bad jokes at my expense instead of helping me out. Besides, technically there is no wrong end of the stick for me. I like both ends. So to speak.

Lesley tosses her hair. "Uh, no. Charlie's bi. Everyone knows that. His stick is up for grabs."

"I wouldn't say that, exactly," I protest. My *stick* is up for grabs? Really?

"He's not up for grabs," Raymond insists.

"That's right," I agree. I knew he'd come through for me.

"And he's not dating either of you."

"I'm really not."

"Because he and I have been together exclusively for over a month."

"That's... what?" Did he just say what I think he said?

Everyone's staring at me expectantly.

"I'm not dating anyone," I manage. "What is happening here?"

Raymond's expression goes slack and then slowly crumples. "How can you say that?"

"I... Can everyone just calm down?" The words are more for me than anybody else. My brain is a mess, and all these people are watching. What the fuck do I do? These are my *friends*. Or at least, I thought they were.

Instead of calming down, all three burst into a babble of accusations and threats, some aimed at me, some at each other. I shake my head and wonder if I can just walk out.

"Dudes!" The shout cuts through the rising hysteria, and I turn to see Ian, a guy I know from some of my classes. He's surveying us with hands on hips and an annoying smirk on his face. "Let's all chill. From the sounds of it, Charlie's not dating any of you."

It's nice to have someone on my side, but... "You don't think we're dating, do you?" Gotta make sure before I relax any.

He laughs. "Dude, no. You're so not my type. I just feel really sorry for you right now."

Great. That's what every twenty-year-old wants to hear.

"But I'm gonna help you out, because you kinda need it." Before I can say anything, he turns to the people I thought were my friends but apparently are more than that. This has gotta be some kind of weird misunderstanding. How can I be unknowingly dating all three of them?

How can I be unknowingly dating anyone? I mean, if I was dating someone, I'd know, right?

"Now, why do you think Charlie's dating you? One at a time," he adds when all of them start to speak. "Don't piss me off. You're making yourselves look pathetic enough as it is."

Immediately, three mouths slam shut. They all glare at Ian, which makes a nice change from them glaring at me.

"You, blond girl. You go first." He points at Lesley.

"I have a name." She tosses her hair. Until this second, I hadn't realized how often she does that.

"Yeah, but I don't know it. Don't waste time; go."

She glares at him again, but says, "We talk and text *all* the time. He asked me out to eat three times *and* paid every time. And he took me to watch the sun set over the ocean."

"He did all that for me too!" Raymond exclaims.

"And me!" Cassie stomps her foot again.

The whole café turns to look at me.

"Yeah, dude, this isn't looking good for you," Ian says.

"No way. Those are all friend things," I protest. "Don't you talk to your friends and text them?"

He shrugs. "Sure. But I don't take them out for meals and a romantic sunset at the beach."

"The beach is literally across the street, and I like the sunset. It wasn't romantic! We just happened to be together when the sun was setting, and I suggested we go watch it."

Ian seesaws his hand. "It's borderline. I'd be more inclined to give it to you if you hadn't bought them dinner."

Heat rises in my face, and I hesitate. These people are my friends—well, they *were*—and I don't want to embarrass them, but...

"That was just a friendly gesture," I mumble, avoiding eye contact. "I like to help my friends out when I can."

There's a moment of awkward silence as the implication sinks in. I feel like a dick for pointing it out, but the truth is, a lot of college students can't afford to splash out on extras like meals in restaurants, even casual ones like this. My huge trust fund means I can. My family owns and runs one of the biggest warehousing and distribution companies in the country, and that's just Dad's side. Is it so bad that I treat my friends?

"Okay, the next factor's gonna be intimacy," Ian declares, moving the conversation on. I'm grateful to him for not making things worse. "Cute guy, you said you and Charlie have been together for a month. How long since you started playing hide the salami?"

I'd normally object to having such private stuff aired in public like this—and recorded for someone to put on TikTok later—but at this point, I have no dignity left.

Raymond sniffs. "I'm chaste. Charlie respects that."

I nod, because that's true. "I do. You gotta stick to your beliefs." Plus, since we're only friends, it's none of my damn business. I did wonder why he even told me.

"Chaste?" Cassie says. "What does that even mean?"

"It means he's not having sex," Ian tells her. "What about you?"

She draws herself up. "I have sex, thanks very much. *Excellent* sex. I've been told I'm gifted."

"Good for you, but I meant have you had any with Charlie."

Cass deflates. "Oh. No. We'd only been dating two weeks."

"Only," Ian mutters. I've heard enough about him to know he considers two *hours* a long time when it comes to waiting for sex. "And you?" he asks Lesley.

She tosses her hair *again*. "We've only been dating ten days. Some of us have *self-respect*." I'm not sure who she was aiming that at, since everyone just finished saying they hadn't had sex with me. Maybe Ian? But he hasn't had sex with me either.

And after this, it's not likely he ever will. Not that I wanted to have sex with him, but I still wish he wasn't witnessing this.

Ian scratches his cheek. "Last question: Did Charlie ever directly ask you on a date, using the words 'date' or 'go out with me' or any combination of those, or did you ever have a conversation about dating or being exclusive?"

Hah! I know the answer to this. It's abso-fucking-lutely not. Because they're my *friends*. They've literally seen me picking up at parties.

The three of them look at each other, at me, and around at the crowd.

"Well... no," Lesley admits first.

"It was *implied*," Raymond argues.

"I asked him what his plans were for spring break," adds Cassie.

Ian holds up his hands. "Sorry. I can see why you'd all have read into the situation, but Charlie's not dating any of you. He's done nothing wrong here except be a dense dumbass."

For a second I think they're all going to argue, but then Raymond sighs. "I knew it was too good to be true."

"A hot, sweet guy who wanted me? I should have guessed something was up." Cassie shakes her head.

Lesley says nothing, but she looks like she's on the verge of tears, and I feel like the world's biggest asshole.

"Don't say that. You're all amazing, and I like you so much." The words tumble out as I take a step forward.

"Dude, shut up," Ian mutters.

"Just not enough to date us," Raymond snaps bitterly.

I open my mouth to say of course I'd date them—hypothetically, of course—but Ian grabs my arm, stomps on my foot, and announces cheerfully, "Well, now that we've resolved this, it's time to go! Come on, Charlie." He drags me toward the door.

"My stuff—"

"I'll get it. You wait outside. Don't talk to anyone." He shoves me toward the door, then, when I hesitate, shoves again. "Leave now, Charlie. Right now."

I don't understand what his problem is, but he *did* manage to sort out the whole dating/not dating thing, so I guess I can trust him. Flipping a wave and a hesitant smile at everyone—even the asshats who are still filming—I leave.

Ian joins me less than a minute later, my backpack in one hand and the remains of my sandwich in the other. "Here." He shoves both at me. I sling the bag over my shoulder by one strap and take a grateful bite of the sandwich. "Dude, you need help."

I chew faster, then swallow. "It wasn't my fault," I whine.

"It kinda was. You know why I stepped in?" He points back toward campus. "Let's go this way."

I trail along after him, eating my sandwich and wondering if I'll get indigestion from eating and walking. My gran always said that's what happens, but I see people doing it all the time.

"Do you get indigestion from walking and eating at the same time?"

Ian casts a disbelieving look over his shoulder. "Uh, no. Let me guess... your mom used to say that."

"No, it was my grandmother." Why does that even matter?

He shakes his head. "It's not true. She probably just wanted you to sit down and eat so she could have some peace."

Thinking back to the shit I got up to as a kid, that's extremely likely. "Where are we going?"

He slows his pace to match mine. I can't eat and walk fast. I'm still learning. "Thanks for reminding me. Do you know why I stepped in back there?"

"You already said it was because you felt sorry for me. Which, you know... life goals."

He snorts. "That's true, but I felt sorry for you because I was already pretty sure of what was going on."

"What was going on?"

"You were accidentally dating people again."

I choke on some crumbs. "What?" I wheeze, then stop walking to cough a few times. He stops too and waits, but when I look up, he's got that same "I can't believe you're smart enough to live" look people sometimes get with me. I'm not actually dumb; I swear I'm not. Just sometimes I miss things other people get.

When I'm breathing normally again, he says, "I've heard the talk, dude. You've done this before."

"I have *not*." I'd definitely know that. "Wait. Done what, exactly?"

He rolls his eyes. "Dated people without knowing you were dating."

"I absolutely have never done that."

Ian smirks.

Fuck. Have I?

"But just so I can explain how you're wrong, tell me who."

"Melissa Harding."

Mel and I were good friends for a few months in freshman year, but we never dated... I think. Though she did tearfully tell me she needed to be with someone who was sexually attracted to her, then essentially cut me out of her life.

My stomach sinks. Did she think we were dating? Oh my god, I *agreed* with her when she said that! I'm also pretty sure I was dating someone else for a few weeks then, so she might think I was cheating on her too.

Ian's not done. "Billy Winchell."

Billy and I were close for the last month of last year. He was a senior, though, and we lost touch when he graduated.

"You're wrong," I insist. "Bill and I were just friends."

"Uh, I ran into him over the summer, and he was heartbroken because you were posting pics on Insta of the new guy you were dating. He legit said to me that if you wanted to break up, you could have told him instead of doing it that way."

I sit down right there in the middle of the sidewalk. "Oh my god."

Ian pats the top of my head. "There, there. Look at it this way: you're not the total douche I thought you were."

That's... not comforting. Looking up at him, I ask, "How did you know I wasn't? I mean, for all you knew, I could have been cheating on... everyone, apparently."

He shrugs and holds out his hand. "I'm good at reading people, and today, you were radiating 'clueless and confused' vibes. Get up. We gotta go."

I take his hand and let him haul me up. "Where are we going?"

"You need help. You've got nearly a year and a half left at this school, and you can't keep breaking hearts without realizing it."

"How do I avoid it? I literally have no idea which of my friends might think we're dating." The more I think about it, the more horrifying it is. Do I have any actual friends at all? "Just checking, you're not into me, right?"

"Hard pass," he assures me. "I don't go for cute and clueless. And anyway, I'm not doing relationships. Being in love is hard work and it turns your brain weird."

That's... nice.

"But I got you covered. You need someone who understands all the elements of dating and romance and can guide you. A consultant. Come on, I'll introduce you to Mr. Romance."

CHAPTER TWO

LIAM

Matt and I don't wait for Ian to begin our workout. I learned that lesson the first time he was late and I suggested waiting. Matt laughed so hard he nearly burst something, then told me if he made a habit of waiting for Ian, he'd have spent half his life waiting. Whatever. Those two are the weirdest best friends I've ever met.

They're both good gymnasts, though, and that's what matters to me. Since I don't want to join the school gymnastics team, I was limited to working out on my own before I met them. Now we even have gym time assigned to us—though we pay through the nose for it, and the team coach appears regularly to ask if we're *sure* we don't want to join up. I don't have time for competitive sports if I'm going to graduate with my bachelor's and master's at the same time, so that's always a no from me.

I'm not sure exactly why Matt and Ian aren't on the school team. It might have something to do with what I'm pretty sure was a cult upbringing and the fact that their training resembles something from an action movie more than it does my more traditional routines. I don't ask, and they don't tell.

We're almost done stretching when the door to the gym bangs open and Ian marches in. Another guy trails behind him, looking kind of lost... and adorable. He's a tall, muscular puppy with big brown eyes and pouty lips. Damn. Is it legal for a person to be this good-looking? Like, does he have to pay a beauty tax or something?

"You're late," Matt calls cheerfully from where he sits across from me, legs spread wide as he bends all the way forward and puts his nose on the mat, warming up his muscles.

"I got delayed rescuing Charlie." Ian heads toward us, then stops when he realizes his friend isn't following. He goes back, grabs the guy's arm, and pulls him along.

"I really don't understand what I'm doing here," the guy —Charlie?—protests.

"I told you, I'm gonna introduce you to Mr. Romance. You know about Mr. Romance, right?"

Charlie nods solemnly. "The guy people pay to plan dates for them? Everyone knows about Mr. Romance. He's a legend." His gaze lands on me and Matt, bounces back and forth between us, and then settles on Matt. "It's great to meet you. I'm a big fan of your work. Well, of stories of your work."

Matt shakes his head. "I really don't think you are."

I roll my eyes and get up. "My work."

He turns his gaze to me and gives me a doubtful once-over. I know what he's seeing: short and pale, with an untamable mop of ashy-colored hair. I've tried cutting it super-short. That really showed off my bone structure, which wasn't a good thing. I used to be bony too, but thankfully gymnastics has helped me build muscle. I'm kinda ripped now.

Too bad nobody but me gets to see it.

Either way, I don't look like everyone's romantic ideal.

"Yours?" he asks.

"Yeah. I'm Mr. Romance. Liam Rigby." I start to hold out my hand to shake, then make myself drop it. Nobody shakes hands in college unless they're going for a job interview. Except me, apparently.

"Charlie Martin," he says automatically. "Really? You're Mr. Romance?"

Wow. Rude, much?

Ian groans. "Charlie, don't piss him off. You need his help."

I want to make a snarky comment and walk away, because fuck him, but I'm not dumb enough to turn down a paying job. I make a lot of money from being Mr. Romance, and I don't even charge that much. It just turns out that a lot of guys hate planning dates. Some girls, too.

This guy, though, I'm going to charge double. Maybe even triple. He's interrupting gym time and being a dick while he's at it.

"Got a big date planned?" I ask, mentally flipping through my schedule. As long as it's not for this weekend, I can probably fit him in. Unless he wants something super elaborate.

To my surprise, he shakes his head so vehemently, he almost falls over. "No. No dates. I'm not dating anyone right now, no matter what they say."

Oh-kay.

I look at Ian. "Why is he here?"

"Because he's a sweet, sweet moron." Ian kicks off his sneakers and starts stretching.

"Hey!" Charlie sounds insulted, but then pouts and shakes his head. "It might be true, but words hurt, man."

"Not to be rude"—I flick a glance at Charlie—"but I'm paying for gym time here that I'm not using. Could you tell me what you need?" *And leave* isn't said, but my tone heavily implies it.

He shrugs. "I don't know. Ian said I had to come here."

We both look at Ian. Matt, bored with the conversation, has wandered off to the pommel horse.

"He needs a guide," Ian says, then launches into a story that has to be exaggerated, about three people thinking they were dating Charlie while he was just being friends with them. I side-eye Charlie, expecting him to be rolling his eyes over the way Ian's stretching the truth, but he's nodding along, his face serious, even a little upset.

"Wait," I interrupt. "He seriously—" I stop and turn to Charlie. "You seriously had no idea these people thought you were dating?"

He shakes his head. "And Ian says there were others too."

I can't even... "Other people you were friends with who thought you were dating them?"

The puppy-dog expression says it all. Wow. This guy... if I didn't already know people who are both good-looking and intelligent, I'd think the old belief that a person couldn't be pretty *and* smart was true.

"He needs your help, dude," Ian reiterates, finishing his stretches and getting to his feet.

My jaw drops. "*My* help? I plan dates for people who

know they're going on dates! He needs a kindergarten teacher to talk him through the basics of friendship."

"Fuck you, I am an *excellent* friend," Charlie announces indignantly. "I remember everyone's birthdays and what's going on with their lives and families *and* I always answer calls and texts."

I meet Ian's gaze. "He's, like, the perfect boyfriend and doesn't even know it." Raising a brow at Charlie, I ask, "Do you also perform sexual favors on demand and sleep in the wet spot after?"

He looks confused. "Not with my friends."

Oh, boy. Sighing, I ask Ian, "What exactly do you have in mind?" I can't just leave this guy to run around campus unsupervised. Eventually he'll not-date the wrong person and get beat up. Or end up married without knowing he was even dating anyone.

"Reverse Mr. Romance," Ian announced. "Charlie does nothing with his friends without running it by you first, and you point out anything that might be problematic. Like watching the sun set over the ocean." Disgust drips from his voice, and I can't exactly blame him.

"I like watching the sunset," Charlie insists. "Why is that so bad?"

"One of my most popular dates is a beach picnic at sunset," I inform him. "My feedback survey shows that ninety percent of those dates result in the desired outcome."

Charlie blinks innocently. "What's the desired outcome?"

"Sex, dude." Ian shakes his head. "C'mon, I know you're not a virgin."

"Not always sex," I correct. "Sometimes they just want a

second date. My point is... sunset on the beach is romantic. Even more if you're sharing a meal."

From the way Charlie's face slowly flushes red, I'm guessing sunset beach picnics are something he's done with friends. Ian must come to the same conclusion, because he groans.

"At this time of year, the sun sets at dinnertime!" Charlie defends.

"So eat alone," I snap. "If I'm going to help you with this, you have to listen to me."

His face lights up. "You're going to help me?"

Shit. I did say that. "Well—"

"Please?" he begs. "I don't know what to do. I don't even know if I have friends anymore. What if they all think we're dating?" He glances at Ian. "We're still not dating, right?"

"It's been, like, fifteen minutes since the last time you asked me, and the only thing that's changed is how sorry for you I feel. More, by the way." Ian pats his shoulder. "I promise, if I ever think we're dating, I'll tell you upfront that we're dating."

"You're dating this guy?" Matt asks from behind us, and we all turn. "Don't you think I should know that? What if I don't like him?"

"You're my best friend, not my conjoined twin," Ian says. "But I'm not dating him. Or anyone. Dating makes your brain soft."

"Amen," Matt agrees.

"Please don't say that where any of my clients can hear you," I beg.

"Not to sound completely selfish, but can we get back on topic?" Charlie asks. "How do I know if my friends think we're dating?" His eyes widen with horror. "Do I have to ask them?"

I scratch my head. "Don't do that just yet. Leave it with me. That is, if you really want me to help." I hesitate, taking in his trendy clothes with the discreet designer logos, his perfectly cut dark hair, the even, orthodontically perfected teeth, and his expensive backpack. "This kind of consultation won't be cheap," I warn.

"Whatever it takes," Charlie promises, and Ian cringes. I don't blame him. If I was a different kind of person, I'd totally take advantage and fleece him. As it is, I'm going to have to work out a fee schedule for this. I normally charge a flat fee depending on the type of date, or an hourly rate for anything really fancy and custom, plus add-on fees if the client wants me to do any of the shopping and prep work. Some people just want an idea, but more than I expected want a full-service package.

But if Charlie's going to be calling me every time he interacts with his friends, it would be unfair for me to charge him that hourly rate. He might have money, but I doubt he's a Rockefeller.

I hold out my hand. "Phone?"

He digs in his pocket, then gives it to me. One glance at the screen, and I hand it back. "You gotta unlock it first."

"Whoops."

A minute later, I text myself and give it back to him again. "Okay, now we've got each other's numbers. I'll be in touch tonight with my fee schedule and terms and conditions. No hard feelings if you decide to back out."

He shakes his head, mouth set in a determined line. "I'm not backing out."

Sympathy stirs in my chest. It might be completely his fault that he's in this situation, but it's also not. He can't help being naïve. "We'll work it all out," I assure him.

Ian slings his arm around Charlie's shoulders. "See? Told you it'd be okay. Now get out of here so we can get on with it. This is costing us money." He steers Charlie toward the door.

Charlie goes happily, seemingly relieved to have a plan in place. "Thanks, Ian! Talk to you later, Lee!"

Lee? Does he mean me? "It's Liam," I call after him. "Don't talk to anyone for the rest of the day!" The last thing I need is him making this situation worse.

He disappears with a wave over his shoulder, and I sigh.

"This is either going to be amazing or a disaster," Matt observes. "I'm so glad I get to watch."

I'm sweaty and in that energized/exhausted post-workout zone when I get back to my dorm room. I love the endorphin rush a good workout gives me, but it's not exactly easy on the body. That's part of the reason I've never wanted to do competition.

Dumping my backpack on my bed, I slide into my desk chair and wake up my laptop. I've got one more class for the day late this afternoon, but I should have time for a shower and to go through any new Mr. Romance requests.

There are ten, and from the looks of it, I'm picking up some new clients off campus. That's great—this business is going to help pay my way through my doctorate and supplement my income when I'm making peanuts as a physics professor. The wider I can expand my client base, the better.

Six of the requests are for basic, inexpensive first date ideas. I built my reputation on the concept that you can still manage a romantic date if you're broke. I get repeat clientele because I customize every idea for the couple involved. The client can give me a short overview of their date's likes and dislikes or tell me their name so I can check out their social media... in a non-creepy way. The first date I ever sold was to a guy whose date loved dogs in an extreme way. My idea? Picnic at the park next door to the local dog school while they had a puppy obedience class. He came back and tipped me after, then told all his friends I was the shit.

Three of the other requests are for follow-up dates, and the final one is for something custom. I reply to all of them, the first-timers with an information form, the follow-ups with a feedback survey so I can make sure I'm on the right track, and the custom guy with an email setting up a time to call. There's a lot of planning involved in a fully custom date, but they're my favorite. Because yes, I'm a hopeless romantic.

I watch romantic movies. I read romance novels. I fantasize about the perfect date with the perfect guy. I *plan* perfect dates for everyone else... and then sit at home alone.

Okay, so that might be an exaggeration. I have friends. I go places. But there's nobody special in my life, and I really want there to be. I want more than the occasional Grindr hookup. Or I want the fairy tale where my Grindr hookup falls for me. So far, things definitely haven't panned out—one guy looked at my face and asked me to keep my hoodie on and the hood up so he didn't have to see it. No, I didn't stick around. I might not be good-looking, but I'm not hideous, and even if I was, nobody deserves that. Another guy told me I was like a Ken doll—perfectly formed but in miniature.

So no, meeting guys through Grindr isn't going great.

Being Mr. Romance is a dual-edged sword. On the plus side, I get to let all my romantic inclinations fly free *and* get paid for it. But it also means I plan the perfect dates and never go on them, like an exquisite form of self-torture.

Shaking off my shitty mood, I go take a quick shower. I need to come up with a plan of action for Charlie before tonight, and so far, I've got zilch. My business is based on the premise that people want to date and know they're dating.

I only give half my attention to my professor during class, my mind fixed on Charlie's dilemma. I feel bad for him, but at the same time I'm still struggling to believe that anyone could unknowingly date multiple people. There's gotta be something behind that, right? He can't be truly unintelligent and be in college—unless he's bought his way in and is paying people to write his papers. But Ian seems to like him, and Ian's a good judge of character.

My phone vibrates in my pocket. I usually ignore it during class, but let's face it, I'm not all here today anyway.

Charlie: Jake asked if I want to get dinner, what do I do?

Time to get to work.

Liam: Jake's a friend? How long have you known him? Is it going to be just you and him? Dinner where? Dining hall?

I wait patiently while the ellipsis dances on my screen.

Charlie: He was my freshman roommate so 2.5 years. He didn't say if anyone else was coming or where.

It's unlikely that Jake could have thought they were dating for so long without catching on, but just to be safe...

Liam: Never fucked? Has he dated people?

Charlie: I don't fuck my friends!

Charlie: He had a girlfriend all last year

Liam: You're probably safe then. Just don't suggest going somewhere special. And don't offer to pay.

The dots do their dance again, this time for ages. What's he writing? A book?

Charlie: He said we should go to Shenanigans after

The bar near campus isn't a great place for a romantic moment. For a drink or a cheap meal, yes. To pick up, absolutely. To hang out with friends, sure. But to gaze lovingly into someone's eyes? Fuck no.

But this presents an opportunity. I'm pretty good at telling when people are into each other.

Liam: That's fine. Okay if I meet you there and see what Jake's vibe is?

Charlie: Please. I've never gone without friends before, and I need them. Text you when we're there

"...don't you think, Mr. Rigby?"

Oh fuck.

I look up from my phone and smile at my professor. "Sorry, sir, what was that?"

The narrow-eyed glare I get in return isn't something I'm used to seeing from my professors. They normally all love me. But then, normally I'm a model student.

"If your phone is more interesting than this class, you're more than welcome to leave."

I slip my phone back into my pocket. "No, Professor. I'm sorry."

He glares for a moment longer, then repeats his question. Luckily, it's something I can answer, since I'm that guy who reads ahead. He seems disappointed, but the class moves on, and I let out a tiny sigh of relief.

It's only been a few hours since I met him, but I can already tell Charlie's going to be trouble.

CHAPTER THREE

CHARLIE

"WHAT IS UP WITH YOU TONIGHT?" JAKE DEMANDS exasperatedly. "You've been all jumpy and distracted."

I let out a nervous laugh and shake my head, then once more look around the bar. It's pretty crowded for a weeknight —I think someone's having a birthday or something. Jake and I managed to grab a booth in the back, but I'm worried that with the crowd and being tucked away, Liam won't be able to find us. I recheck my phone, but there's still nothing since his thumbs-up reply to my text saying we were here.

"Nothing's up," I lie. I wish Liam would get here already and tell me if Jake's really my friend or if we're in some weird poly relationship where we don't have sex with each other, just other people. I mean, I don't think we are—I'm pretty sure Jake's straight like he says he is—but then I didn't think I was dating anyone at the moment, so who knows.

I lift my soda to my mouth to avoid having to say anything else and wish fervently that it was beer. Shenanigans is strict about underage drinking, though, and my fake ID is so shitty that I may as well not have one. "I should get a better fake

ID," I announce. There's no point, since my birthday is just a few weeks away, but it gives me something to say.

Jake looks at me weird. "You should," he agrees. "What made you think of it right now?" He smirks as he lifts his beer to his lips. His fake ID is excellent. I could have gotten him to get me a beer, but that feels like cheating. Plus, if Gwen, the bartender, catches us, we're screwed.

"Gimme that." I snatch at his glass, but he pulls it out of my reach. "You're a sucky friend."

He shrugs. "That doesn't break my heart."

My gut roils at the casual mention of heartbreak. Does that mean we're just friends and he's cool with me making jokes like that, or that we're in a relationship and he considers friendship to be the lesser element of what we have?

I chug the rest of my Coke, hoping the sugar will settle my nerves, and stare fixedly across the room in an attempt to not make eye contact with Jake. It takes me a second to realize I'm actually looking at Marshall, the stock guy, and that I seem to be weirding him out. That's too bad. I like Marshall. I try to make things better with a smile, but he backs away kind of fast, so I don't think it worked.

"Seriously, man, what's going on with you?" Jake's eyeing me with what looks like real concern.

"Nothing."

"Hey, Charlie."

I startle, banging my leg on the table, then scramble out of the booth. "Liam! Hey." Fuck, now what? "Uh, have you met Jake? Jake, this is Liam."

Jake's face says he thinks I'm insane, but he smiles at Liam and gives him an up-nod. "Hey. Grab a drink and join us."

"Thanks. Can I get you guys another round?"

"I'm good," Jake says politely.

"Soda? I'll come with. Sure you don't want another?" I ask Jake. "My treat." The words are out before I can stop them, and I don't need Liam's small sigh to know they're a mistake. Things like this are why people think I'm dating them. And in Jake's case, I can't even say he needs the financial boost—his family has almost as much money as mine.

But I can't exactly take it back.

Thankfully, Jake declines. He's got an early class tomorrow, so he'll probably stick to one. I follow Liam to the bar, and we wait patiently for Gwen to finish up with a group of half-drunk, squealing sorority girls.

"So, could you tell?" I ask in a low voice, drumming my fingers on the bar.

He side-eyes me. "Could I tell from his greeting if he's into you? No. Relax, will you?"

I huff a big gust of air. "I need my friends, man. I'm a people person. Wondering who I can be myself with is killing me."

"What can I get you boys?" Gwen interrupts before he can say anything, and we order—soda for both of us. I don't know if he doesn't have a fake ID or just doesn't feel like drinking tonight.

Back at the booth, a girl I vaguely recognize is talking to Jake. She smiles at us. "Hi, Charlie."

"Uh, hey. How's it going?" I shift from one foot to the other, wishing she'd go away so Liam can use his romance radar on Jake.

"Great, thanks." She fake giggles, which has to be the most annoying sound in the world. "I'd love a drink."

"Oh. Uh—"

"I'll get it for you," Liam offers, putting down his soda but staying standing. He smiles at the girl, but it's not the same smile as when he met Jake.

She eyes him up and down, then says, "Thanks, but I think I'll get it myself. My friends are waiting." Turning to me, she smiles wide. "See you later, Charlie. Jake." She saunters off.

Jake watches her go, then raises a brow at me. "What was that?" he asks.

"She was kinda rude," I add. "Who is she again?"

Jake laughs as I slide into the booth and Liam sits beside me. "Charlie, sometimes I wonder how you don't accidentally walk into the ocean, the way you miss things. That's Danae, remember? She flirted with you all freshman year, and you never noticed."

She did? "I didn't accidentally date her, did I?"

Liam groans. Jake blinks and looks from me to him and back. "Uh, no? I think that's why she's still trying."

"Still trying what?" It sinks in, and my head snaps around to look in that direction. Danae is watching us, and she tiddles her fingers in a little wave.

I smile weakly and turn to Liam. "What would have happened if I'd gotten her that drink?"

He shrugs. "You'd either have gotten laid tonight or ended up in a relationship you know nothing about. Or both."

Great.

"Is that why you interrupted? To 'rescue' Charlie?" Jake makes air quotes like a douche. "Are you two together?"

Liam snorts. "Uh, no. We're not. And yeah, that's why I

interrupted. I'm definitely not interested in Danae for myself." He turns to me. "You're safe. Jake's your friend."

"Oh thank god!" I slump forward over the table and put my head in my hands.

"What the fuck is going on with you?" Jake asks.

I tell him about my day. It takes a while, because he keeps interrupting with his laughter. I've never heard anyone laugh that much before. At one point, he's almost crying.

"Wait wait wait... she threw a drink in your face and all you cared about was your shirt?" he gasps at one point.

Then a little later, "How did you not know you and Mel were dating? She practically lived with us freshman year!"

That doesn't make me feel better.

When I finally wind down, he looks over at Liam and shakes his head. "So you're Mr. Romance? Mad respect, man. A guy in one of my classes swears you improve his chances of getting laid by sixty percent."

"Not sure I want to know how he calculates those odds," Liam says, "but tell him thanks. Stuff like that is good for business."

"And you're gonna help Charlie be less oblivious?"

They both turn doubtful gazes on me. "I mean, I'm going to try." Liam clears his throat. "Step one is making sure his friends are actually his friends."

Jake holds up his hands. "You're good here. I love you, man, but not that way. Plus, I'm not into dicks."

Um... what? "Did you just call me a dick?"

Shaking his head, Jake says, "No. I mean *actual* dicks."

I tilt my head. "I'll never really understand that."

Liam pats my arm. "You don't have to. The important thing to take away from this is that Jake is your friend."

"Always," Jake promises. "And hey, I can help you work out who else is actually your friend and who's borderline."

A knot of stress I didn't even know was in my chest loosens.

"Yes, please," Liam says, whipping out his phone. "Let's make a list."

"A list?" I repeat. "That's kind of... formal."

He doesn't even look at me, too busy tapping and swiping his screen. "A list means you can't forget. If you do, you'll have a handy reference to check."

I scoff. "Believe me, once I know for sure who my friends really are, I'm not going to forget." That shit's gonna be burned into my brain.

"Then just humor me."

"Yeah, Charlie, humor him," Jake says. He's grinning at me with a weird expression.

"Okay, who's first?" Liam looks up expectantly.

"Artie." My current roommate is a dream come true. He's hardly ever around, meticulously tidy, and never says a word about how messy I am. He's also fun to hang out with when he does happen to come home.

"Safe, since he's been with his girlfriend for two years and they're planning to get married when they graduate. Also, he's practically living with her and you're lucky if you see him once a week." It's hard to miss the edge of sarcasm in Jake's voice. "You see me more than you see Artie, and we don't share a room anymore."

I sag a little in relief. It would have been majorly awks if my roommate was in love with me. Liam taps away at the screen, then looks up.

"Next?"

"Uh, Carson." We've been friends as long as me and Jake.

"Safe," Jake says. "I think you can probably not worry about anyone who's in a relationship and has been for a while." He glances at Liam. "Right?"

"They're lower risk," Liam agrees. "Let's focus on your single friends."

"I'd worry about Sarah," Jake announces before I can reply. "I'm not sure if she thinks you're dating yet, but she'd definitely like to."

Betrayal smacks me in the face. "Sarah? No," I protest, even as Liam notes it down. "She's my study buddy."

"Trust me, she wants to study more than statistics with you."

Frowning, I ask, "Like what else? That's the only class we have together."

Liam pats my arm again. "He means she wants to study you naked. So stay away from Sarah outside of studying. No meals. No sunsets. No friendly calls and texts." He hesitates. "Where do you study together?"

"The library." I can't believe this. Sarah wants more than friendship?

Come to think of it, she has been touching me a lot lately. I thought it was just friendly head-on-shoulder and cheek kisses, but maybe she was trying to send me a signal?

"Okay, that's good. No studying in your dorm rooms."

I nod, trying not to let it get me down. I can feel Liam's eyes on my profile.

"Charlie, this doesn't mean Sarah's not your friend. It just means she'd be open to more if you wanted it. Do you and her do other stuff often?"

I shrug. "We usually get something to eat after studying.

And sometimes I go watch her flute practice. And last month I drove her home to visit her mom when she was sick."

Jake makes a sound that might be a laugh or a groan. Liam, on the other hand, just nods.

"Did you stay and meet her mom?"

I shake my head. "Nah. I just dropped her off, and she got a lift back from her little brother."

"Thank fuck for that," he mutters, then smiles at me. "So, Sarah might think you have feelings for her. And maybe more. Stop going to flute practice and stop eating after you study."

"That seems kind of rude," I protest.

"Do you want another scene like today?" he counters.

"Okay, so no more post-study snacks." I try not to sulk.

"Look on the bright side," Jake suggests. "If you back off a bit, she'll realize you're not interested that way, and you can probably go back to being friends."

"Yeah." I study the moisture ring left by my soda glass on the table.

"Maybe we're approaching this the wrong way," Liam says after a second. "Is there anyone you *are* interested in that way? I know you said you're not dating anyone at the moment, but is there someone you want to date? If people see you with someone, that should sort out who your friends are."

I hesitate, thinking about it. "Not really. Dating's a lot of work, you know?"

Liam snorts. "Yeah, I know."

It takes me a minute to remember that he does this whole dating thing for cash. Wait, no... that sounds wrong. He doesn't date people for cash.

"It's going to be okay, man," Jake assures me. "Let's do

this list so you know who it's safe to hang out with. And then Liam can help with the rest, okay?"

Pushing aside all the downer feelings, I nod. "Yeah."

It's not that late when I get back to my room, and of course Artie's not there, so I kick off my shoes, flop onto my bed, and call my mom. I try to talk to her at least once a week. Some of my friends whine about their moms calling all the time and nagging them, but my mom isn't like that. For one thing, she's too busy as a full-time advocate and fundraiser for victims of domestic violence to call me all the time. She runs a national charity and is basically famous for giving women's rights a platform. When I left for college, she told me the onus of communication was on me, since I was the one who'd be building a new life, but that if she didn't get proof of life from me at least once a month, I'd live to regret it.

"Hello, my evil spawn," she greets me.

I scoff. "Please. We all know I'm the angelic child you didn't deserve."

"I have two words for you: explosive diarrhea."

Yeah, my mom isn't one to mince words. "It's not my fault I had intestinal issues when I was an *infant*. Maybe it was what you fed me."

She laughs. "Could be. Anyway, since you're no longer doing that—I hope—tell me how you've been."

I sigh gustily.

"Oh, that sounds like a big story. Do I need to come out there and beat someone up for you?"

"You advocate for nonviolent mediation," I remind her.

"They don't need to know that. I bet I can threaten them into... whatever it is you want. Nobody gets hurt, and I get to show off how wicked badass I am."

I wince, because hearing my mom say shit like that is weird, even if she has always been the coolest mom of anyone I know.

"There's nobody who needs to be threatened," I assure her. "And if there was, I could handle it." I think. Maybe. Have I ever threatened anyone before? I usually try to deescalate shit that might turn hairy. Not that it happens much—people like me.

"So why the sigh, then?"

I sigh again, remembering the events of the day, and she laughs. "Come on, spawn. Tell your mom all about it."

"You'll laugh," I mutter, because she absolutely will.

"Probably, but I'll still be appropriately sympathetic after."

That's not as comforting as she thinks it is.

"I was having lunch," I begin, and to give Mom credit, she doesn't interrupt or make jokes while I tell her the whole ridiculously embarrassing story. "...and then Liam and Jake went through a list of my friends with a fine-tooth comb. There are five who might not actually be my friends, Mom. *Five.*"

Mom waits for a second to make sure I'm done, then says, "Oh, baby," in a tone that puts me on guard.

"What?" Why isn't she laughing?

"Tell me this: How many boyfriends and girlfriends did you have in high school?"

I think about it and mentally count them off. "Four, if I

include those three weeks where I dated Uncle Jim's hot tattoo artist friend."

"*What?*" The word cracks like a whip, and I wince. Looks like I'm not too old now for her to be mad about that.

"Uh, ha ha, so funny story—"

"Charles Jonathan Martin, did that man—"

"Mom, please don't make a big deal out of this," I interrupt, rushing the words out so fast, they're almost unintelligible. "I went after him, he didn't know how old I was, and when he found out, he ran so fast I thought he'd break the sound barrier. And it was never more than kisses." And groping, and one hand job that introduced me to wonders I hadn't yet discovered in my previous fumbling attempts. But Mom doesn't need to hear that.

She mutters something about having choice words with her brother, which... yay. Way to make my uncle hate me.

"So, you asked about my high school love life?" I prompt, hoping to get her mind off the subject of her darling underage son having made out with a thirty-year-old. A really sexy thirty-year-old, by the way. I'm talking *smokin'*. And he *knew* things.

"Yeah," Mom says after a second, during which I'm pretty sure she texted Uncle Jim. "Okay, so did you say three? Because *that man* doesn't count."

"Three," I agree, desperate to move her along. "I mean, there were a few casual dates, but those were the ones I *dated*."

She makes a little noise of regret. "I'm so sorry to break it to you, baby, but I thought it was nearly double that number."

My heart drops like a stone. "What?" I croak. She can't mean—

"Off the top of my head, I can think of five—no, six—people you had relationships with." She sounds genuinely regretful to tell me, but that doesn't make me feel better.

"*Six?*" How is that possible? Well, I know how—now—but... holy crap. "I've been doing this since high school?" That might just be the most depressing thing I've ever heard.

"I'm afraid so."

"Are you sure? I mean, who did you think I was dating?"

"Well, let's see... your first ever boyfriend was Mike—"

"Mom! Mike and I were just friends." I'm certain of this.

She hesitates. "My poor sweet spawn. Mike's mom works in the same building as me, and every time I see her, she reminds me that you were his first heartbreak."

Oh my god. "But we were friends all through high school," I protest weakly. "How could I have broken his heart and not know it?"

She makes a humming sound. "I put it down to the way teenagers fall in and out of love every second week. You broke his heart, he was sad, got over it, and you stayed friends."

"And you never asked me about it?" Shouldn't she have? Shouldn't she have been like, "Oh honey, it's so great that you and Mike are still friends after breaking up"?

"Why would I? I was proud that you had such mature relationships in your life. Although, if I'd known *how* mature...," she adds darkly, and I know she's thinking about Uncle Jim's friend again.

"Moooooom," I whine.

"Charlie, I'm sorry you're realizing all this now, and I hope this Liam person can help you learn when someone is into you... which, wow, I'm just realizing how bad this is.

How are you my child and not able to tell when someone wants to jump your bones?"

"Nobody says that anymore," I mutter. "And anyway, Raymond is chaste. So there." I regret it as soon as the words leave my mouth.

"Okay, *one* person didn't want to have sex with you," she amends. "But the rest? Charlie, I love you, but maybe I shouldn't have defended you all those times your gran used to say you were so ditzy, you'd leave the house with no pants on one day."

I gasp. "No *pants*? That's impossible. I'd never leave home in an incomplete outfit."

"Annnnnd you've totally missed the point. Never mind, you're still my sweet spawn."

Talking to Mom is not bringing me the peace and comfort I'd hoped for.

"I'm going to study," I say. It's not subtle, and she laughs.

"You do that. I'm going to go tell your dad about this conversation."

Great.

"Bye, my precious, oblivious child."

"Bye, Mom." I disconnect the call and stare at my phone for a long moment, then open my text thread with Liam.

Charlie: Don't know if this is important, but my mom says I had more b/g'friends in hs than I thought.

I put the phone down and scrub my hands over my face. It's all going to be fine. Liam will help me fix this.

The chime from the mattress has me diving for my device.

Liam: Yeah, okay. That makes sense. Just about to email you.

A few seconds later, my email alert dings, and I open it. There's a new email from Mr. Romance, with a short cover note and a few attachments. I ignore the note and go for the docs.

And whoa... not gonna lie, my classwork isn't in as good shape as this. The first doc is titled "Job Overview & Fee Schedule," and it lays out all the things Liam plans to do to help me. He's included "assessment of current friends" and "ongoing on-call friendship assessment service," which he then defines—because yes, there are definitions and notes and explanations of everything—as me being able to call or text him when I'm unsure if an impromptu activity (like lunch) might be seen as a date. There's also an item called "learning and counseling," which is about teaching me how to know these things so I don't need to hire him for the rest of my life. That's good for me but seems dumb of him. Doesn't he want me as a cash cow forever?

Speaking of cash... I skim down the doc to the numbers at the bottom, then do a double take. Has he left off a zero or something? Those amounts are way too low, seeing he's basically going to be my twenty-four-seven help desk.

I scroll back up and look through the notes more carefully. There *is* a condition that I can't expect service between the hours of midnight and seven in the morning, and that he'll provide me with his class schedule so I'll know what times he might be delayed in replying. But still... that's a lot of hours when he's available.

Charlie: I think you've quoted me the wrong price

Liam: It actually breaks down to a very reasonable cost per hour when you consider the amount of time I'll be giving you.

I stare at the screen. Uh, no.

Charlie: No, I see that. I mean it's too reasonable. You gotta charge what you're worth, man.

The ellipsis dances for a while, stops, then starts again.

Liam: I have no idea what to say to that. What do you think I'm worth?

I swipe over to my calculator app and play with some numbers until I find one that looks respectable. Then I go back to the chat and send it to him.

Liam: Uhhhh... I'm confused. I thought you were saying I needed to charge more.

Charlie: I was. I am. Don't underprice yourself.

Liam: But that's less than the original daily amount I quoted. A lot less. Like... scarily less.

Ohhhhhh. I laugh out loud. I see where the confusion is coming from.

Charlie: No, I mean you should charge me that hourly.

I use the calculator again and work out the new daily figure, then send it to him, making sure to specify that it's daily. Then I go look at the other attachments. They're questionnaires.

He wants to know every last thing about my life and my friends and my daily routine. My mom doesn't know all this stuff. If I had a therapist, they wouldn't know.

The message alert chimes, and I switch back to that app.

Liam: I don't want to be the idiot who argues himself out of more money, but are you sure?

Charlie: You're providing a specialist service, and it's not even that much. Trust me, I'm getting a bargain.

If there's one thing I know a lot about, it's fair wages and paying people a living wage. My mom would freak if she thought I was screwing someone over. I'm privileged enough to be able to afford to pay fairly, thanks to my evil capitalist grandfather.

He's not really an evil capitalist, by the way. Mom's dad was a factory worker in the early seventies who realized that if he came up with a way to change the shape of one of the offcuts, it could be used for something else, therefore reducing the amount of raw material needed and saving boatloads of money. Or something... it's really only an interesting story if you care about manufacturing machine parts. Anyway, he invented a little machine that would do the shape-change thing, patented it, then sat back while every major manufacturer in the world threw money at him. Side story: he hired an accountant to help him manage his newfound wealth, and she ended up becoming my grandmother.

My phone chimes again.

Liam: If you're really sure?

Charlie: I'm sure I'm going to make you earn it, so you should definitely ask for it.

Liam: Fine. I'm screenshotting this in case you change your mind.

Charlie: Not going to change my mind. But I might die before I finish filling out all your forms. You forgot to ask how old I was when I lost my first tooth.

Liam: LOL did I? Whoops. Better add that in

Liam: I know it seems like a lot, but it's going to help me plan your training

Charlie: This is starting to sound like an Olympic event. What do I get if I win?

Liam: You won't have to face another scene like today. Or accidentally end up married because you never realized you were engaged

I wince. Harsh. But also... not wrong.

Charlie: Fiiiiiine. I guess that's worth the effort. Hey, what happens if I meet someone I want to date while you're training me?

Liam: ...you date them? I'll even throw date planning into your service, if you want

Charlie: Sweet. But that's not what I meant. Will it, like, interfere with my training if I'm trying to be datey with someone and not-datey with everyone else?

There's a long pause, and I grab my laptop and download the forms to start filling them in. Maybe he got interrupted. I might as well make good use of the time.

I'm only two questions in when my phone chimes again.

Liam: I'm honestly not sure how to answer this. What do you think this training is going to be, exactly?

Charlie: Who knows? That's why I'm asking.

Liam: Once I understand you better, I'll put together a bunch of scenarios you might be in with friends. You'll pick an outcome that might or might not make them think you're dating. Then I'll either explain why it was wrong and point out the warning signs or reward you with chocolate or something.

Ohhhhh.

Charlie: I'm more of a savory guy

Liam: Chips, then. Do you prefer classroom discussion, written exercises, or role play?

Charlie: Role play, baby! I am the KING of role play. I even do different voices.

Liam: You probably won't need different voices, since the character you'll be playing is you. But okay, I'll design the training around role play.

Maybe this is going to be fun after all.

Charlie: Can I use costumes and props?

Liam: To play yourself? Uh, sure. If you want.

Charlie: Yessssss. This is going to be epic.

Liam: I think you're overhyping it. Please don't get your expectations too high.

Liam: I've gotta go, but get me those forms back as soon as you can, and remember to text or call me before you do ANYTHING with those five friends, okay? Or any new friends.

Charlie: Got it.

I turn my attention back to the forms. They're less daunting now that I know they're leading to epic role plays in which I'll be the innocent college student being lured into lascivious deeds. Not that I did anything lascivious with anyone who thought I was dating them when I wasn't. Do I have a reputation for not having sex or something? That's weird, because I do have sex with people I'm actually dating.

The door opens, and Artie comes in, grinning broadly.

"Hey," I say, my attention still mostly on what I'm doing.

He dumps his stuff on his bed and kicks off his shoes. "Heard you had a big day."

I freeze.

"Oh?" Without moving my head, I glance sideways. Yep,

that grin is aimed at me. Sighing, I abandon any pretense of working and meet his gaze. "What did you hear?"

He flops down on his bed. "That you were the center of a huge scene when three people threw down about you being their boyfriend, only for it to turn out you weren't."

"That's surprisingly accurate. How many people do you think have heard it?" *Please be not many. Please be not many. Please—*

"Everyone," he assures me. "It's all over TikTok. And I think YouTube."

Great. "So clearly nobody listened when I asked them to stop filming."

"Did you really expect them to?" He leans forward, elbows on knees. "C'mon, tell me exactly what happened."

"Didn't you watch the video?" I ask acidly.

"More than once, but now I want to hear your side."

I throw my pillow at him, which he catches and puts behind himself, leaning back comfortably. He's clearly ready for story time.

There's a long silence when I'm done.

"Wow," he says at last. "When you fuck yourself, you don't use lube."

CHAPTER FOUR

LIAM

THE FIRST CRY FOR HELP COMES TWO DAYS LATER.

Charlie sent me back the forms the same night he got them, and I've been working since then on putting together a series of role plays that will help him understand the difference between friendly behavior and more-than-friendly. To be fair, this isn't entirely his fault. There's no single thing he's done that anyone could point a finger at and label outside the bounds of friendship. It's just when all those things come together *and* the recipient "friend" is already interested in him that things start to get sticky. And not in a fun way.

I stop walking toward the dining hall so I can focus on Charlie's message.

Charlie: HELP ME!!!! Gina suggested lunch and when I said I was busy, she said "too busy for me?" That's bad, right? Even I know that's bad!

Fuck. Gina's one of the five "friends" we're not sure about.

Liam: That's bad. Is she watching you right now?

I turn toward the English building. If I remember right, the class he's just finished was there. But is there any point in me going?

Charlie: No, I told her I had to use the bathroom. But now I'm trapped in the bathroom!

I laugh out loud, ignoring the side-eye I get from two girls walking past.

Liam: This is what you're going to do. Go back out there. Tell her you've got to get going and you'll see her next time. If she tries to pin you down or says anything else girl-friendly, tell her you're so grateful the two of you have the kind of friendship where you don't need to make excuses to each other. Then tell her again you'll see her next time and leave.

Charlie: Okay. I can do this. I'm grateful for our friendship. Got it.

Maybe I should go over there, just in case. But he needs to do this on his own.

Liam: Text me when you're free.

I wait, staring fixedly at my phone screen. My stomach grumbles, and a message notification from Ian pops up, asking where I am. I tap on it and tell them to start eating without me, then go back to staring at Charlie's message thread.

Finally the ellipsis pops up. I take a cautious breath.

Charlie: It worked! She looked confused but let me go. So I guess she thinks we're dating? Damn.

My sigh of relief is a lot heavier than expected.

Liam: We thought she might. This is a good first step to letting her down without humiliating her. She'll probably message or try to call later. Remember to be casual. If she straight-out asks if you're dating, say no and reiterate that you value her friendship too much for that.

Charlie: That sounds so lame. She'll think I don't find her attractive but don't want to say it.

Liam: DO NOT TELL HER YOU FIND HER ATTRACTIVE!

I pause, then add a few more exclamation points before sending the message.

Liam: I mean it. Do NOT. You're friends, and you don't think of her that way.

Charlie: Got it. No saying she's hot. She is, though.

I squeeze my eyes closed and remind myself he's paying me a shitload of money for this.

Liam: But you don't want to date her, right?

Charlie: Right

Liam: And we now know she DOES want to date you. So telling her she's hot but you don't want her isn't going to help and will wreck your friendship.

Charlie: ohhhhhh I get it. Thanks, man!

Liam: No worries. Training tonight, remember?

Charlie: I'll be there! I have this awesome wig.

I don't bother to reply. What is there to say, really? He's going to wear a wig to role play himself. That's not weird at all.

By the time I make it to the dining hall, Ian and Matt are halfway through their meals. No surprise—they eat so fast, I don't think they chew. They tell me it has to do with their upbringing. You know, the one that wasn't part of a cult.

"Where were you?" Matt asks with his mouth full as I

slide into a chair with my mac and cheese. It actually looks almost edible today, so here's hoping.

"I stopped to answer a text from Charlie," I reply, scooping up some food.

One taste, and I know.

Looks can be deceiving.

I force myself to chew and swallow, since my body needs sustenance, and vow to go with the chicken next time.

"And how is my rescue puppy?" Ian asks brightly.

"Fine. He's..." I hesitate. I feel bad talking about Charlie behind his back. "...eager to get this resolved" is what I settle on.

"He's not taking advantage of your good nature, is he?" Matt demands. "You nearly missed lunch."

"Nah." Shaking my head, I scoop up more food but can't quite bring myself to put it in my mouth just yet. I need a minute to prepare. "He's paying me more than enough for me to be late for lunch, trust me."

Two sets of eyebrows go up. They're not related, but in moments like these, it seems like they could be. "Charging him through the nose, you greedy bastard?" Ian jokes.

"Actually, it was his idea. He negotiated my rate up and told me I had to charge my worth."

Matt looks at Ian, then back at me. "Are we sure he's smart enough to be here?" he asks. "First he's dating people without knowing it, and now he insists on paying more than he has to. I think he might have a few screws loose."

I snort, take a deep breath, and shovel in my food, trying not to taste it... or feel the texture. Seriously, how does anyone fuck up mac and cheese this badly?

"He's smart enough," Ian's telling Matt while I try not to

gag. "I mean, not top-of-the-class, fucks-up-the-curve smart, but he's kind of middle of the pack. In the classes I've had with him, anyway."

"C's get degrees?" Matt asks, and Ian nods.

"Yep, exactly. And he's a nice guy. Friendly. Plus I think his mom is some kind of activist. I bet that's why he cares about paying fair wages."

I swallow—finally—and add, "He's really bummed about maybe losing friends. I get the impression he's really social. And the price thing was because it's the right thing to do. I think he's just a nice person who misses social cues sometimes."

They exchange a look.

"What?" I glance back at my food. How hungry am I, really? Will it kill me to only have two mouthfuls of lunch?

As though reading my mind, Ian pushes over the cupcake he hasn't yet eaten. "Dude, please don't eat any more of that crap. None of us have time to visit you in the hospital when you're getting your stomach pumped."

"What he said." Matt nods emphatically. "If I'd known you were actually going to eat that, I would have stopped you from getting it."

Ian slowly turns his head to stare at his best friend. "What did you think he was going to do with it?"

Matt shrugs.

"Are we sure *you're* smart enough to be here?" I ask him, pushing away the gross-and-cheese and seizing the cupcake.

"Anyway," Matt says, pretending he didn't hear me, "what I was going to say was... be careful."

I put down the cupcake without taking a bite. "What do

you mean?" Is there something I need to know about Charlie? Is he violent?

An image of his friendly face with his emotions written all over it rises in my mind's eye. No way is he violent.

They look at each other again.

"You're our friend as well as our gym buddy," Ian starts.

"And we care about you," Matt adds.

"Okay, you're freaking me out." I glance from one serious face to the other. "What do you know that I don't?" Maybe the problem isn't Charlie himself but his friends or family? Are they connected to a cartel or gang or something else I don't watch the news often enough to know about? Am I going to get a visit from someone threatening me if Charlie gets hurt?

Not likely, if his mom's an activist who cares about fair wages.

"You know this," Matt assures me.

"You're a romantic. You get attached." Ian smiles sadly at me, and I realize what they're hinting at.

The laugh that bursts out of me is long and loud and tinged with hysterical relief that a mysterious stranger isn't going to appear in my dorm room and ask me if I'd like to swim with the fishes. Sleep with the fishes? Whatever.

"Guys, I'm not going to fall for Charlie," I say firmly.

They look skeptical.

"I'm really not."

"It's just... you already think he's a nice guy." Matt gestures as if that's all it takes.

"That's not enough for me to fall for anyone. I think you're both nice guys... most of the time. And I definitely don't feel more than friendship for you."

They both make offended faces.

"Excuse you, we are a catch," Ian proclaims.

I pick up the cupcake again. "Problem number one is that you refer to the two of you as *a* catch, singular. Nobody wants to have to fight their boyfriend's best friend for time with him."

"You say that like we're weird. We're *family*," Matt protests.

I snort. "Which brings me to problem number two: your creepy cult family."

They both groan and chorus, "It's not a cult."

"What is it then?" I take a bite of the cupcake while I wait for the answer I know they're going to give.

"We can't tell you."

"Mm-hm," I mumble through a mouthful of cake and buttercream.

"It's not that we don't want to," Matt hastens to add. "But you probably wouldn't understand."

I swallow. "Statements like that don't in any way change my conviction that it's a cult."

Ian throws up his hands. "Fine. But before you distracted us, we were telling you to be careful." He looks me dead in the eye. "Be careful, Liam. I brought Charlie to you because I felt bad for him and thought you could do with the extra cash. I don't want you to end up with a broken heart."

"Guys, I might be a romantic, and I might wish I had a boyfriend, but I'm not going to fall for the first halfway decent guy to cross my path. He's a client, and maybe when I know him better, he'll be a friend. That's it."

They nod doubtfully, and I sigh. Guess they'll have to eat crow when I prove them wrong.

Charlie volunteered his dorm room for our first training session, since, according to him, his roommate is never there. But the guy who opens the door to my knock is not Charlie.

"You must be Liam," the tall, dark, good-looking guy says. "I'm Artie. I can't tell you how thrilled I am to meet you."

"You... are?"

"I really am," he assures me. "Charlie told me you saved him already. Just so you know, I am really, really, so not into him and happy to help if you need backup."

Aw. That's so sweet. Who knew people could be this good-looking and nice in real life? Maybe he has a wicked stepparent or something.

I pause in case he's about to burst into song or woodland creatures are going to appear out of nowhere, but he just stares at me quizzically as the silence stretches out.

What were we talking about?

"Great," I manage, because that'll probably cover all bases, right? It seems to work. He smiles and steps back, gesturing for me to enter.

"Charlie just went to raid the vending machine. Fair warning, he's stupid excited that you're doing role plays."

All thoughts of how pretty and nice Artie is flee my brain as I remember Charlie's promise.

"The wig?"

Artie nods, and we both laugh.

"I guess if it makes him happy, it can't hurt?" I shrug.

"I dunno, man, you haven't seen it yet," Artie warns.

"Seen what?"

We turn toward the doorway, and I have to cough to cover my gasp. Charlie's standing there with his arms full of snacks, a bright smile on his face and a long blond wig on his head.

When he said he was going to wear a wig, I pictured one of the cheap ones that come with Halloween costumes, or maybe a joke one from the discount store—you know, bright orange or neon green. Instead, he's wearing a professional-level wig, the kind they use for movies that looks completely like natural hair. Hell, it might even *be* natural hair. It frames his face and flows in waves over his shoulders to about halfway down his arms, and there's about a million different shades of blond in it.

I'm speechless.

"Seen your wig," Artie replies while I struggle to regain the power of speech.

"Oh." Charlie grins, dumps the food on one of the beds, then flips back not-his hair and preens. "Looks good, doesn't it? I bought it a few years back to wear to a Gwyneth Paltrow-themed party, and I've been able to wear it a bunch of times since."

That sentence raises so many questions, I don't even know where to begin.

"On that note, I'm gone," Artie announces. "I'll probably stay at Mia's tonight."

"Okay. Want me to save you some Funyuns?" Charlie points to the pile of junk food.

"That's cool, man. I'll get my own if I want them." Artie grabs a jacket, slides his phone into his pocket, then flicks two fingers toward me in the kind of ultra-cool wave that cannot be learned. "Great meeting you, Liam."

"You too."

He closes the door behind him, and Charlie turns to me. "Are you a Funyuns or Doritos person?"

"Doritos." If he wants to feed me, I'm not going to complain. I catch the bag he tosses my way, then nab a chair from one of the desks and make myself comfortable.

"This is going to be so much fun," he announces, rubbing his hands together as he sits cross-legged on the bed.

"As fun as the Gwyneth Paltrow-themed party?" My voice is bone dry, and he laughs.

"Seriously, it was awesome! Most charity fundraisers are boring, but the theme made it so much better. All the food and decorations were taken from the Goop site, and everyone was asked to dress as Gwyneth or someone in her life or that she's worked with."

"And you chose Gwyneth." That actually fits really well with what I know about him from the questionnaire. Charlie's completely secure in himself and tries to find enjoyment in everything. He also likes to share the good things in his life with other people, and that's where the problem he's dealing with came from. Most people can't conceive of a mere friend being so generous with their time and money, because most people haven't come from an environment where time and money are so freely available to be shared. So they assume his willingness to "invest" so much in them means he's romantically interested. It's actually kind of sad for everyone involved.

Except me, of course. I'm going to make money off this.

He shrugs. "Sure. She was the queen of the party, and who doesn't want to be queen?" He smirks. "My costume was the best, too. I even found a dress that looked a lot like the one she wore to the 2005 Oscars."

I have no idea what that dress looked like, not being a fan of either the Oscars or Gwyneth Paltrow, but I have no doubt he rocked it.

"Show me pics later, but for now, let's not get distracted." We could get off-track way too easily. "Role play."

He thrusts two fists up in the air. "Role play! How we gonna do this?"

I pull out my phone and a notebook and flip to the relevant page. "Let's start with what happened today. Has Gina been in touch yet?"

Instantly, Charlie's good mood is wiped away. "No. That's good, right? It means she gets it and still wants to be friends." Hope vibrates in his voice.

"Mm," I say, not wanting to shatter it. "What did she say when you came out of the bathroom?"

He flops back against the pillows with a sigh, his wig hair fanning out beautifully around him. "She was waiting right outside." I try to hide my wince. "She said again how she wanted to get lunch, and I told her I didn't have time, but I was so grateful we were the kind of friends who didn't need to make excuses—just like you said."

"What did she say to that?" I make some quick notes.

"Nothing. She just looked confused. So I said I'd see her at the next class, and she was all, 'oh, sure. Bye.' And I left." He blows a raspberry. "I felt like a real turd, you know?"

"I know, but it's not your fault." Well, not completely. "You've never asked her on a date or promised her anything.

Now that you know what she's thinking, it's better not to lead her on."

He nods glumly.

"Let's make our first role play practice for what to say if she does call," I suggest.

He rolls his head to the side so he's looking at me. "You still think she's gonna call?"

Fuck, yes. Or message. But she'll definitely be in touch. "I think this is good practice, and if she does call, you'll be prepared."

He hoists himself up to a sitting position, flips his not-his hair over his shoulder, and takes a deep breath. "Okay. I'm in character."

Uh-huh.

"Just a reminder, the character you're playing is *you*. So... be you. Don't be anyone else." The beginning of a headache throbs in my temples. If he channels Gwyneth or one of her characters for this...

He waves his hands dismissively. "I got this, man. I'm me. Go."

I'm skeptical, but if he says he's ready... I mimic the sound of a ringing phone.

He stares at me, then cracks up laughing. "Dude, what was *that*?"

My face gets hot, but I can't hold back my chuckle. "That was your phone ringing."

"Yeah, no. My phone doesn't sound like that."

I roll my eyes. "Fine. How does it sound?"

He purses his lips as though thinking, then begins a series of... noises. There's no other word for it. It's obviously supposed to be a ringtone of some kind, but he's definitely not musically talented.

"Please stop," I beg. "How about I just say 'ring ring' and we pretend that's how your phone sounds?"

"Sure." He shrugs, smiling ruefully. "That might be the best option."

"Ring ring," I say, in as deadpan a tone as I can muster.

He coughs a laugh, then says, "Hey, Gina! What's up?"

"Hi, Charlie. Can we meet up?"

"Sure!"

I close my eyes.

"Oops. That was the wrong thing to say, wasn't it?"

Opening my eyes again, I look at his sheepish expression and try to find a diplomatic answer.

"Not wrong, exactly. She's your friend, after all. But remember that this is the call that's coming right after she found out you're not actually dating. So you need more information."

He nods. "More information. I can do that. Let's try again."

I don't bother with the ringing again. "Can we meet up?"

"Is it urgent, or did you just want to hang out? I've got a lot on."

I give him two thumbs up, and he grins.

"I need to talk to you about today."

The grin fades to a worried expression that looks incongruous with the wig. "Uh, today? You mean class?"

My thumbs go up again. He's killing this. "No, I mean what you said after class." I'm deliberately not making this easy.

He bites his lip, then says, "What do you mean?"

"Can we meet up to talk about this?"

He hesitates, and I keep my face blank. I know what he's thinking—if a friend called and was upset about something, he'd meet up with them. After all, friends support each other, right?

"Yeah, okay."

I make a time-out sign, and he groans and puts his head in his hands. "Nooooooo. I can't just blow her off if I want her to keep being my friend. What if she wants to talk about something else?"

"You're not blowing her off," I assure him. "You're setting boundaries. What else could you say that wouldn't send the signal that you feel more than friendship?"

He sets his jaw stubbornly. "Meeting up with a friend who says they need to talk about something doesn't send signals." He crosses his arms over his chest, and I'm sure it's meant to show me how resolute he is about this, but his wig is slightly askew, and combined with his posture, it's all I can do not to laugh.

"But from her perspective, the two of you are more than friends. You've just told her you have a lot on, but now you're going to drop everything and go meet her. She's going to see that as a boyfriendly action."

"If a friend needed me, even if I was busy, I'd go see them," he argues.

I nod. "Sure. And if she needs you, you should go. But she's said she wants to talk about what you said today. That already gives you the information that she's not dealing with a family crisis or boyfriend issues or school problems."

He still doesn't look convinced.

"Look, this is just a role play, right? It's not the actual conversation you'll have with her. So humor me for now, and then we'll role play what would happen if you actually met up with her."

Charlie's nod is reluctant, but it's a nod. The wig moves a little bit more, but he doesn't notice.

"So she's just asked if you can meet up. What can you say that's not 'yes' but still shows you're her friend?"

He sighs, then says, "I really can't right now. But we can talk on the phone."

I smile and nod. "You really can't meet me?"

His eyes narrow, and I get the feeling he's inwardly cursing. "I wish I could, but I'm a phone-only friend tonight."

I break character long enough to say, "That's perfect, Charlie." Then I resume my Gina façade. "Oh. Okay. Uh, this is kind of awkward. I guess I thought we were maybe more than friends?"

The outright panic on Charlie's face makes me glad we role-played this. "Uh..." He takes a deep breath. "I value your friendship too much to risk it with anything else. I really hope you feel the same way," he adds, and I smile big.

"I do. I'll see you in class." I finish the conversation because I'm compulsive like that, then I slow clap. "That was perfect. Especially that last bit, about hoping she feels the same way."

He scowls and flops back on his pillow again, and this time the wig gives up and falls off. "Fuck," he mutters, sitting up again and picking it up. He carefully fluffs it out, then hangs it from his desk lamp before scrubbing his hands over his face. "That sucked," he announces.

"I know." I'm not unsympathetic, but I would be if he

didn't make his boundaries clear and led this girl on. "This is the kindest way to tell her how you feel, though. You don't want to just say you're not interested, do you?"

He shudders. "She might not call. Maybe what I said today was enough." I nod but don't say anything, and he squares his shoulders. "Okay, let's role play if I went to meet her."

Reminding myself to be gentle, I ask, "Can we meet up to talk?"

"Sure. Now? Where?"

"I can come to your dorm."

Charlie frowns, which is a good sign, but still says, "Okay, see you soon."

I shake my head at him but knock on the desk as though I'm Gina knocking on the door.

"Hey," he says. "Are you okay? You sounded weird on the phone."

"Yeah, I'm... I guess confused?"

"Oh? And you want me to help? Not sure you've got the right guy," he jokes.

"It's about what you said today."

"What I said?"

I can tell he's starting to realize the situation he's fake put himself in by the way his voice goes up too high on the question. It's kind of cute how he panics under pressure—so not how I thought he'd react, with how confident he usually is.

"Yeah, about us being friends."

"We are friends. Or I thought we were. Don't you consider me a friend?"

Oooh, good one. I give him a thumbs-up. "Of course I do. I just thought we might be more than that." Before he can reply, I get up from the chair and go to sit beside him on the bed—way too close. "Don't you find me attractive?" I put a hand on his thigh.

His eyes go comically wide, and he fumbles to make a time-out gesture. "Okay, I get it. You were right. Meeting up would be a big mistake."

I go back to the chair. "Sorry about that—I should have made sure you were okay with touching before I did it." I feel gross about it now.

He runs a hand through his hair. "Nah, that's okay—it's dumb, but I don't think I would have got it if you'd just said? Like, it wasn't until you were practically in my lap that I realized how limited my options were." Shaking his head, he adds, "Man, if you had been Gina... I mean, I would have had to push her away to get up, and I don't think our friendship could recover from that."

"As soon as she was in a position to be flat-out rejected, your friendship was over," I tell him. "Not many people have the self-esteem to come back from something like that. I mean, unless you were really close friends who'd known each other for years. But you see now why it's important to set boundaries, right? It protects both of you and gives her space to process, because even if you let her down gently, she's probably going to be embarrassed and wish you weren't there."

He nods emphatically. "Space is good."

Guilt twinges. "Again, I'm really sorry for touching you like that—"

"It's fine," he assures me, waving a hand in dismissal. "If we hadn't been role-playing, I might even have liked it." He laughs, but it quickly morphs to horror. "Oh shit, it's stuff like that, isn't it? That's what makes people think we're dating."

I swallow my own laugh and scratch my chin. "Well... it probably doesn't help. That kind of joke is fine between friends who get you, but we don't really know each other that well yet. If I didn't know you were, uh, that you struggle in this area, I might have taken that as clumsy flirting." Not that I'd really think he was flirting with me based on something so flimsy. But someone else might.

He opens his mouth to answer but is interrupted by a cacophony of sound. We both look toward the desk, where his phone is lit up.

"That's your ringtone?" It sounds nothing like the sounds he made before.

He leans over to look at the screen, then shoots to his feet. "It's Gina," he hisses.

"Answer or ignore," I suggest.

Picking up the handset, he casts me a glance full of agonized indecision. "Should I put it on speaker?"

"No. Let her have some privacy." It's not fair to put it on speaker when she doesn't know I'm here, and if she did know, she likely wouldn't say what she's calling to say.

He takes a deep breath, then hits Accept and lifts the phone to his ear. "Hey, Gina." There's the faintest of tremors in his voice. "Uh... what? Okay." He listens for a second, then grimaces and screws his eyes shut. "Really? Ha ha, so about that... oh. Yeah." He listens again, opening his eyes and tipping his head back to stare at the ceiling. I really wish I knew what she was saying. This is clearly not going anything like either of the role plays.

Finally, he looks right at me and says, "I really value your friendship, Gina." There's another little pause, then he adds, "I'll see you in class? Okay. Bye."

With a massive exhale, he tosses the phone back on the desk and collapses onto the bed.

"Well?"

He starts to laugh. "She said she was confused after class today, but then she talked to a friend who showed her a TikTok video."

I bite my lip. "Oh." It's my turn for my voice to tremble, though in this case, it's laughter, not nerves.

"Yeah. So she watched it and thought maybe we were just 'miscommunicating,'" he makes air quotes, "and asked me straight-out if we're dating or just friends."

"This is a good outcome," I remind him. "Maybe not the best way for her to find out, but she had control of the situation, which will make her feel better than she might have otherwise."

"I guess. She didn't sound too happy at the end." He frowns.

"Give her time to process. When's your next class together?"

"Next week."

"Perfect. She'll have time to bitch to her friends, and by the time class rolls around, she'll be laughing over it and remember what a good friend you are." I'm not entirely sure that's true, but the guy's been through enough this week already. And there are still four more people who might think he's dating them.

That's a potential total of eight. If he really were dating them all, he'd deserve an award for maintaining that many relationships at once. Or a slap in the face.

"Why don't we leave it here for the night? You got some practice with different scenarios, and you did really well."

He nods, seeming preoccupied and a bit down. "Yeah, sure. Thanks, Lee."

"It's Liam." Nobody's ever called me Lee.

"Really?" He looks me up and down. "I dunno, you just seem like a Lee to me."

I don't know what impulsive worm is eating my brain, but I find myself saying, "I guess you can call me Lee if you want."

Charlie's face lights up in a genuine smile. "Really? Thanks!"

What the hell have I gotten myself into?

CHAPTER FIVE

CHARLIE

THERE'S A PARTY AT THE FOOTBALL HOUSE ON SATURDAY night, and I'm going, of course. Their parties are epic. But for the first time ever in my life, I'm nervous about a party.

Why? Because most of my friends are likely to be there, including the ones who might think we're more than friends.

It's only been two days since the whole Gina thing, and I've stuck to going to class and hiding in my dorm as much as possible. If I avoid people, there's no chance of me saying something that might be misinterpreted, right? I even thought about skipping the party tonight, but that was just stupid. Plus, as Jake pointed out, if I didn't go, those same friends would wonder why not.

So I'm going. Here I am. Jake promised to walk over with me for support, and then Artie and Mia decided to join us. Mia gave me a big hug when she came over, which is weird for her—it's not that she doesn't like me, more that we just don't have that kind of relationship. She's Artie's girlfriend, and we're friendly, but we're not exactly friends. But apparently me proving to be the most oblivious person in the world has convinced her we should be closer.

Whatever, it gives me some of my old confidence back to have people with me as I approach the house. It's already hopping, packed with bodies, and part of me relaxes as the wall of sound hits me.

Artie and Mia disappear into the crowd, probably to find her friends, and Jake and I head in the direction of the booze. One of the reasons the parties here are so popular is because they always have good booze.

Someone shouts my name, and I wave at Peyton Miller, whose house this is. He's standing with his brother, Brady, but yells something about TikTok, and I flip him the bird. We're both laughing, though. Come to think of it, maybe that video is going to solve all my problems for me. Everyone will see it and figure out that I'm just an idiot, like Gina did.

I'm not sure if that's the best outcome for me.

I get pulled into a group of dancers, and for a while I lose myself in the press and grind of sweaty bodies and wicked beats. But when a guy I know by sight sidles up to me and smiles suggestively, panic strikes.

How am I supposed to handle hookups? What if my past hookups all expected me to call them after or something? Have I been going around sending out signals I didn't even know about? Lee and I never talked about hookups!

I smile regretfully at the guy and mime getting a drink, then slip out of the crowd while he shrugs and turns to find another prospect. Trying not to freak out too much, I avoid eye contact and stumble into the kitchen... just in time to witness some chick coming her brains out as a guy eats her out on the counter.

"People cook there, you know," I say as I grab some beer. She jerks her head back and slams it on the upper cabinets.

"Ow!"

"Sorry," I mutter, and leave them to it.

I weave through the masses of people, sipping my drink slowly and trying to calm down. This isn't the end of the world. Lee said I could date, so I'm sure hooking up is also okay. And he would have mentioned it if he thought I needed to be worried about old hookups as well as my friends.

Wouldn't he?

I step out of the flow of traffic and pull out my phone. It can't hurt to check, right?

Charlie: Heeeeeyyy, so is it likely that some of my past hookups were expecting me to call them?

Propping myself against the wall, I take a slug of my drink and scan the crowd while I await his reply. All the familiar faces are here, and I get an odd sense of comfort seeing them. Sure, last year's seniors are gone, but that's the life cycle of the college party, you know? The seniors leave, the new seniors enter a frenzy of partying as they approach the end of their college era, and the freshmen do stupid things as they experience true freedom for the first time.

Over there are the future businessmen of America, rich trust fund kids like me, but unlike me, they plan to take over corporations, utilize tax loopholes, and become carbon copies of their parents after college. I should probably hang out with them more, since I'm probably going to have to deal with them when I join the company and eventually take over from my dad. Neither of those things is appealing, though, and I push the thought aside. I can think about the heavy weight of my future another time.

By the door are the human rights avengers. That's just my name for them, but it's how I picture them. I have mad respect for that group, always campaigning to raise money and awareness for injustice... even while blind drunk at a party. They love my mom—I've had more than one of them ask for an intro on parents' day.

And in the bay window there's a bunch of beefy football players with Felix, an adorable twink who's always fawning over them. We were good friends a couple years back, but we drifted apart. He loves to flirt with the big guys, and they love the attention. Right now he's batting his eyes up at Cobey Green, the only openly bi player on the team.

I love college.

My phone vibrates in my hand, and I swipe to see the message.

Liam: Did you tell them you'd call?

Charlie: No. But maybe I accidentally sent some kind of signal?

Liam: Haha don't worry about it

I stare. That's not helpful.

Charlie: So can I hook up?

Liam: Are you asking my permission? That's weird.

Charlie: We didn't role play dealing with hookups yet

Charlie: I need to talk about this. Can I call you?

The ellipsis dances, disappears, then dances again.

Liam: Look left

Huh? Is this some kind of advice I don't understand? Like... am I supposed to change my perspective of hooking up by... considering things from a more left-leaning view? I dunno. I'm pretty liberal already. My whole family is.

Liam: Turn your head to the left, Charlie.

Ohhhhh. Duh. Look left. He meant it literally.

I look left, my gaze skimming past a bunch of sorority girls, Lee, some people from the—

Wait.

I home in on Lee, who's watching me with an exasperated expression I know well. Anyone who's spent more than ten minutes talking to me usually gets that look.

Abandoning my spot propping up the wall, I weave toward the part of the wall he's leaning against. "Hey! What are you doing here?" Wow, that sounded rude. "I mean, I don't think I've seen you at one of these parties before."

He shakes his head, but he's smiling. "Nah, not usually my thing. I'm working tonight."

That takes me a second to process. "Like, you followed me here to keep an eye on me?" I'm not sure if I admire his work ethic and the value for money I'm getting or if that's creepy. Probably creepy.

He scoffs. "No. You're not my only client."

I'm sure it's wrong for me to feel disappointment.

"But don't you just plan dates for your other clients? I mean... I didn't think you actually went on them too. Or are you, like, researching or something?" Although if he thinks he's going to find romantic inspiration at this party, he's in for a big surprise.

"I don't usually go on dates with my clients," he says, and for the first time I realize he's not looking at me. Instead, his attention is... I follow his gaze. It's focused on a group of people clustered on and around a sofa. "But sometimes there's a part of the plan that needs it."

I don't get it, and I don't think that's me being clueless. "Huh?"

He doesn't answer, just keeps watching that group.

"I don't want to tell you your business or anything, but if you sold this party as a romantic date, you're probably going to have to issue a refund."

This time he does look at me, the amused sideways glance flicking at me and then away. "No, it's not a date. This is a romantic *moment*."

A... "A what now?"

"You see that couple?" He nods to a girl sitting on the arm of the sofa and the guy standing beside her. She's leaning against him while she talks to another girl. "They've been together for a year, and she recently told him that he never gives her any romantic moments. Not dates—I plan their dates, and she loves those, but small moments that tell her he pays attention to her."

Yeah, I still don't get it.

"So, what, you're here to watch and...?"

He shakes his head. "Nope. He's determined to give her anything she wants, so he asked me for help. Said he couldn't think of anything he could do. I interviewed him for two hours, and we discovered that he does know lots of little details about her, he just doesn't consciously think about them. So we have a bunch of things planned to show her he's actually paying attention."

"He's determined to give her anything she wants?" I ask skeptically. Give me a barf bag. I like helping out my friends and spoiling my significant others, but *anything they want?* Nope.

I get that sideways look again. "It's romantic," he chides, as though he knows what I'm thinking. There's something about the way he says it...

"Wait, are you a romantic?" I blurt, and for the first time tonight, his full attention turns to me.

"Why are you surprised by this? I *am* Mr. Romance." There's humor in his tone but also something else—a thread of steel. He's not going to take it lying down if I mock him about this. Not that I would. Just because I'm not a romance expert doesn't mean I can't appreciate it in other people. And sometimes big romantic gestures are nice.

"I dunno." I shrug. "You said you were a physics major, right? And you're so organized and... listy."

He blinks at me before looking back at his client. "Listy?"

"Yeah, you know. With the lists. You have lists and forms and surveys... aren't romantic people supposed to be more scattered? Head in the clouds?"

He chuckles. "Listy. I'll have to remember that one. And

I hate to be the one to shatter your illusions, but romantic people can be organized too."

I shake my head. "Yeah, I dunno. That doesn't seem right somehow."

Before he can argue, his client perks up at something his girlfriend has said. He taps her shoulder, leans down to murmur in her ear, and then she sits up straight and continues talking to her friend while he beelines across the room to... us. Well, to Lee.

"Looks like it's go time," Lee says, smiling.

"Hey, man," the guy says. "She said it. You got—?" He breaks off when Lee holds out a white box stamped with the royal blue logo of a bakery in town, the kind individual cupcakes come in. I hadn't even noticed he was holding it. "Thanks! You're the best." He takes a deep breath and huffs it out. "I hope this works."

"It will," Lee assures him. "She's going to love it."

"Yeah." The guy straightens his shoulders, takes the box, then goes back to his girlfriend.

"Um, what—?"

"Shh." Lee's attention is fully on his client now.

The guy kisses his girlfriend's cheek and offers her the box. She looks at him in surprise, then opens it and lets out one of those high-pitched squeals that almost make me want to give up on women and switch exclusively to men. She babbles something in excitement, throwing herself at her boyfriend and giving him a big smooch, and he—now grinning—says something in return, jerking his thumb over his shoulder in our direction. Well... Lee's direction, probably. Since he never even acknowledged that I existed.

Her gaze shoots toward us, and in the next second, she's

bouncing across the room, box still in hand. "Thank you!" she cries, giving Lee a big hug. "You're amazing!"

Lee smiles and shakes his head. "This was all him," he says. "I was surprised by how much he knows about you. All I did was delivery."

I'm pretty sure that's not entirely true, but she accepts it. Before she goes bouncing back to her boyfriend, I angle my head to peek inside the box. Cupcake, as suspected. It has a mountain of pink frosting, sparkles, and a bunch of tiny blue candy butterflies all over it.

"Okay, so fill me in. Why is the cupcake such a big deal?" I ask, and Lee, assured that his job has gone off without a hitch, turns to me.

"Apparently, every time she drinks beer, she craves cupcakes. It'll get to a point at every party where she says she wishes she had a cupcake." He shrugs. "So tonight she got a cupcake."

I wait for him to say more, but he's finished. "That's it? That's her big romantic moment?"

He sighs exasperatedly. "Yes. Because by bringing her a cupcake—one with butterflies, which she loves—he's shown that he listens to her, that he pays attention, and most importantly, that when she said she wanted romantic moments, he cared enough to deliver them."

Yeah, but... "It's a cupcake, though."

"It's about what the cupcake represents."

I'm pretty sure he's not talking about the baking industry. "Okay," I agree. "Uh, can we talk about my problem now?"

"If we have to. What's the problem, exactly?" Someone jostles him from behind, and he looks around in annoyance. "Let's go outside."

He makes for the front door, but I grab his hand and tug him the other way. "Backyard," I suggest, raising my voice to be heard as the song changes and a cheer goes up.

Outside, there are almost as many people, but the sound is slightly muted. Very slightly. The covered patio is packed, but I lead Lee past the clusters of people and up the steps to the lawn. By virtue of having no seating and little light, it's less crowded there, with just a few groups standing around— mostly the smokers.

"Better?" I ask, and he nods, looking around.

"So you're familiar with the house, then."

I shrug. "The parties here are fun."

Two guys come running out of the house carrying a third one between them. "HOLD IT HOLD IT HOLD IT!" one of them is screaming. People scatter out of their way. They reach the lawn, and the third guy vomits a spectacular fountain of colorful chunks.

Thankfully, we're out of the splash zone. A wave of ewwws goes around the yard.

"Fun," Lee repeats thoughtfully. I tear my gaze away from the guys who've dumped their friend on a clean patch of lawn and are looking for a hose—Peyton and Brady have a rule about vomit: You puke, you clean it.

"What, like you've never gotten so drunk you puked?"

He shrugs. "Of course I have. Just... not for a while. I'm not sure it's fun, though."

Yeah, I kinda have to give him that. The fun usually ends when the vomit starts.

"Anyway, what do I do about hooking up?"

"What do you mean, what do you do? You hook up." He shakes his head.

"But what if I'm accidentally giving off a more-than-once vibe? The same way I give the dating vibe?"

He stares at me, then breaks into laughter.

"Lee, no," I complain. "This isn't funny."

"The dating vibe?" he gasps. "Charlie, you're not accidentally giving off a 'dating vibe.' You're doing things that are open to misinterpretation. Actions, not vibes. Unless you've been telling your hookups you'll call them or that you think they'd make great long-term partners, I think you're safe."

I bite my lip, still not convinced, and his face suddenly turns serious.

"You're not, are you?"

"Not what?"

"Telling your hookups you'll call. Are you getting their numbers?" From the look on his face, I'm guessing that would be a bad thing.

"Um..."

"Oh my god, Charlie." He covers his eyes with his hands, then sighs and looks at me. "Tell me exactly what happened."

"It was just once," I assure him. "The guy had this playlist that I liked, especially some songs by a local band, and he offered to message me the next time they were gigging nearby. So we exchanged numbers."

Lee waits. "That's it?"

I nod. "Do you think he's waiting for me to call him?"

"How long ago was this, and did he message you about the band?"

"Like, last year? Uhhh... I remember nearly freezing my balls off when I walked home, so winter, I guess. And yeah, he messaged me a couple weeks later." I smile, thinking about the gig. That was a good night.

"Did he suggest you go together? Or say anything about a repeat?"

"Nah. But I saw him there, and we waved."

"I think you're good." His voice is bone dry.

"Are you sure, though? Because—"

"I'm sure, Charlie. That guy is not pining for you."

Phew. "Thanks, man. This whole thing"—I wave my hand to encompass it all—"is a lot harder than I thought."

He clears his throat. "Yeah. Maybe we'll role play what to do in a hookup too."

I grin and waggle my brows, and he starts to laugh as he realizes what he's just said. "Oh, I know *exactly* what to do in a hookup," I promise.

"Charlie?" someone calls, and I glance over my shoulder before darting a panicked glance at Lee.

"It's Lila," I hiss. She's on the "unsure" list.

"You got this," he assures me. "Plus, I'm here. She's not going to maul you."

So why do I feel like prey?

"I thought that was you!" Lila comes up and drapes her forearm over my shoulder, leaning up to kiss my cheek. Friendly gesture or possessive claim? I stare at Lee, hoping he'll be able to somehow signal me the answer.

He's looking at Lila. An awkward silence falls, and they both turn expectantly to me.

Oh, right. "Uh, yeah. Fresh air. Have you met Liam? Lee, this is Lila. Hey, both your names start with L!"

The expectant looks turn to weird ones. That was possibly not my finest moment.

CHAPTER SIX

LIAM

CHARLIE IS HARDCORE FREAKING OUT, AND PART OF ME wishes I'm the kind of person who'd video him sputtering about names that start with L and what a coincidence it is for us to meet tonight and put it on TikTok.

But I'm not. And even if I was, I wouldn't. He's my client.

So instead I muster a smile for Lila, who's clearly wondering if Charlie's been the victim of a body snatcher. "Ignore him. He's had a few too many, I think."

Charlie seems to think this is a hint for him to let his body go slack, and Lila nearly slides off his shoulder.

"Whoops!" he yells. "Ha ha, guess the beer made me unstable."

Wow. Just... wow.

"Are you okay?" Lila asks, her brow furrowed with concern. "Do you need to leave? I can walk you home."

Charlie's spine snaps straight so fast, I wince. He's going to feel that in some muscles tomorrow. "Nah, no, uh..." He shoots a panicked look my way.

"He's fine, just tipsy. I'm leaving soon anyway, so if he

wants to go, I can walk him. It's sweet of you to offer, though."

Still eyeing Charlie cautiously, she smiles. "Well, I mean, what are friends for, right? Charlie's walked me home safely a couple times. The least I can do is return the favor." She says it casually, with no coy smiles or sideways glances. I'm pretty sure she's safe. "How do you know Charlie? I don't think he's mentioned you before."

"Friend of a friend," I say vaguely. "We just ran into each other inside and decided to get some air."

She looks between us, and her eyes widen. "Oh my god, am I interrupting?" The delighted grin that crosses her face assures me more than anything else could that she's not interested in Charlie *that way*. "I can go—"

"No, you're fine. We're not..." I trail off, my face getting hot. How unprofessional of me to somehow have given her the idea that I'm dating my client. The client who has issues with people thinking he's dating them when he's actually not. "We're just friends." I shoot Charlie a significant look. "Like you are."

His face brightens, hope filling his expression. "Really? Just friends?"

Oh my god. How exactly did so many people think he was into them?

I nod, and it's like a switch flips. He goes from being nervy and weird to his charismatic self, grinning widely at Lila.

"Lee's my boy," he informs her. "He's saving my life. You have no idea."

Lila looks from him to me, frowning again. "Charlie, seriously, are you okay?"

"I am now," he assures her. "I'm so glad we're friends."

Annnnd on that note... "I'm going to head out. Nice meeting you, Lila. Charlie, I'll talk to you later." Although knowing my luck, he'll text me again before this party's over.

"You want company?" he asks earnestly. "Lila and I can walk you back." He glances at her. "Right?"

"Totally," she agrees, smiling at me.

"I'm good, but thanks. Have a good one." I flip them a wave and head back toward the house. There's probably a way to leave without having to go inside, but I don't know it, and I don't feel like exploring—not when it's likely there are people getting it on in the shadows.

So I duck and weave and backtrack a few times through the crowded rooms, but eventually find myself on the sidewalk outside the house. I take a few deep breaths just to clear my head—the party got even louder while Charlie and I were in the backyard—then turn toward campus, pulling my phone out to check it. I'm surprised to see two messages have arrived in the past twenty minutes. I was too busy talking to notice.

They're both from my friend Spencer, letting me know some of our friends are hanging out at Shenanigans while he's working and asking if I want to join. He's a server there, and on quiet nights he can swing by our table and chat between filling orders. It's still early, and honestly, I've earned a break. Plus, with so many people at this party, the bar will be pretty low-key for a Saturday night.

I stop in front of Indelible Ink, a tattoo shop that's popular with a lot of people on campus, to text him back. Then I stick my phone back in my pocket and prepare to enjoy the walk.

"...love living in the dorms, but sometimes I wish for more space," I admit, then drain the last of my beer. We were talking about food, which led to campus food, which led to a general discussion about the downside of college life. The dorms are definitely part of that.

Keisha nods emphatically, passing me the pitcher for a refill. "God, yes. My roommate is the messiest person alive, I swear. She tries to keep her stuff on her side of the room, but as a physics major, I understand how the sheer volume of her crap makes that impossible."

We crack up. Sid grabs a napkin and pulls a pen from somewhere. "Who wants to bet I can't design an equation for that?" Keisha throws a cardboard coaster at his head.

"The problem with the dorms, aside from their teeny-tiny size," Spencer weighs in, "is that most of us get stuck with roommates we don't want. Even if we don't hate them, they're just random people, and living with a random is just weird."

I can't argue with that. My roommate is fine, but we'll never be more than polite acquaintances, and if someone gave me the option of swapping to live with a friend or even just someone I have more in common with, I'd take it.

He adds, "That's why I applied to move into the Living & Learning house next year. I think I've got a good chance of being accepted too."

"That's amazing!" Keisha claps her hands.

"It really is," Sid adds. "Only environmental sciences majors live there, right? It's perfect for you."

"I can't wait," Spencer enthuses. "It'll be so great to live with people who have the same interests as me. Imagine the study sessions!"

I frown. There's a thought niggling at the back of my brain... isn't the Living & Learning house right next door to the Delta Iota Kappa frat house? Those guys take the acronym for their frat name way too seriously and have a reputation for being loud. Some people say they're DIKs by name and dicks by nature.

"Liam? Is something wrong?"

I blink and meet Spencer's gaze. There's a tiny disappointed frown on his lips.

"No, I was just trying not to be jealous," I fib. I'm not completely sure about the frat house, and there's no point ruining this for him if I'm not. Besides, he might already know. "It sounds great, Spence. Perfect for you."

His smile returns. "Well, I don't have it yet."

"You'll get it, though," Keisha assures him. "You and Liam are the type of go-getters who achieve goals."

"Aw, shucks," I say, and she blows me a kiss.

"How's Mr. Romance going, anyway?" Spencer asks. "Do you have any serious-minded clients whose boyfriend dumped them through no fault of their own and are now looking for love with the right person? Preferably a science major. Because I'm available."

I join in the laughter and pick up the pitcher to top up everyone's glasses.

It's been a good night.

I was wrong about Charlie texting me again that night. Whether he picked someone up or went home alone, he managed it on his own. Instead, the text comes the next morning at nine. I've just dragged myself out of bed after "a few drinks" turned into not that few. Still in my boxers, I squint at my phone.

Charlie: Deke wants to get brunch what do I dooooooo?

My brain is still trying to understand when another message pops up.

Charlie: Are you there help meeeeeeee

Okay. So patience isn't one of his strong points.

Liam: I'm here, hang on

I suck in oxygen and riffle through my mental file. Right, Deke is one of the people we're not sure about. Brunch?

Liam: Did he say if it was just you and him?

Charlie: He just said hey wanna get brunch?

Not helpful. I tap my finger along the side of my phone while I think about it.

Liam: Is Artie there? Ask if you can bring him along. Or another friend.

There. That way, even if Deke does think they've got something going on, there'll be a buffer there.

Charlie doesn't reply, so I assume he's dealing with it and go to brush my teeth and take a quick, cold shower. I've got shit to do today and need a wakeup. When I get back and check my phone out of habit, there's a message waiting.

Charlie: He said fine so can you meet us at ten?

I blink. Huh?

Liam: What?

Charlie: Artie's not here and Jake's busy pleeeeeeeeeeease I said I was bringing a friend. You're my friend.

I... am?

Charlie: I know we've only known each other a few days but we've bonded over the dumpster fire that is my life please be my friend and come to brunch

A snort of laughter escapes me.

Liam: You're paying

Hey, why not? I like brunch. And really, it's a working brunch. For me, anyway.

Charlie: As long as you don't think that means we're dating jk

I send back a bunch of laughing emojis, then put down the phone and go to hunt out some clean clothes.

Deke eyes me across the table as I take a sip of freshly squeezed orange juice. The little café they chose, about a twenty-minute walk from campus, shits on the dining hall. If this is what having money to splash around is like, I'm a big fan.

"So, Liam," Deke begins, "how did you meet Charlie?"

Hello, weird question. "At school," I reply, wondering how long my waffles and bacon are going to take and whether I'll have to wait for Deke's fussy porridge order to be perfected before the server brings them.

His eyes narrow slightly. Either he's taken an instant and irrational dislike to me for reasons unknown, or he's taken an instant and irrational dislike to me because he's got a thing for Charlie.

Either way, he doesn't like me.

"Oh? He hasn't mentioned you."

Charlie frowns. He's a friendly person, and that's not a friendly thing to say.

"He hasn't mentioned you to me either." I smile. It's more a baring of teeth than anything else. "Not until this morning, anyway."

This time, Charlie's frown is aimed at me. My smile for him is more natural, and hopefully also reassuring. Before any of us can say anything else, our server brings over the fancy coffees we ordered. Because ordinary filter coffee isn't good enough for this place—instead, I get a latte, Charlie gets a cappuccino, and Deke gets something that took him five minutes to order and made our server wince.

I sip my coffee—which is incredible—and resolve to be a better person. I'm working, after all, and if Charlie considers Deke a friend, there has to be something good about him. It's up to me to find out what that is... because otherwise, he's putting it on in order to lure Charlie into dating him, and that's just too ridiculous to consider.

"Brunch was a great idea," I tell Deke. "Sorry I'm cranky. I had a late night."

Charlie smiles sunnily, all right with his world again, and we both look expectantly at Deke, who doesn't smile. Instead, he flicks his gaze between us as I lift my coffee for another swallow.

"Are you two together?"

I try not to spray coffee at him and instead inhale it, which... yeah.

By the time I finish coughing and spluttering, the server is hovering with our food. "Thanks," I wheeze, gesturing for her to put my plate down.

She hovers. "Can I get you anything? I'll top up your water in a second."

"I'm good," I croak. "Sorry about the commotion."

She retreats, her smile communicating that it's no problem.

"You okay?" Charlie asks as I gulp water.

"Fine. Sorry. Went down the wrong way." I grab my napkin and spread it over my lap, more to have something to do than because I think I'm going to spill food. My waffles look incredible—every single crumb is going in my mouth.

"So, are you?" Deke asks, and we both freeze.

"Am I what?"

He rolls his eyes. "Are you two together?"

It's looking more and more like he's not actually Charlie's friend, which I know is going to devastate him. Part of me wishes I didn't have to sit here and witness it, but at least this way I can try to cheer him up after.

I open my mouth to say no, but Charlie slips his arm around my shoulders and announces, "We are. It's new."

I snap my mouth shut so fast, my teeth click. What the actual fuck? Turning my head slowly, I raise an inquiring brow at Charlie, who smiles pleadingly at me. "Right, honey boo?"

Honey boo? "Very new," I grit out. I am so charging him extra for this. Combat pay, I'm going to call it. "You might even say *painfully* new." I pick up my fork, and Charlie pulls his arm from around me so fast, it might actually set a record. You know, if there were records for things like that.

"Oh." Deke looks between us again. "No offense, but doesn't that make this kind of weird?" His gesture takes in the table, the three of us, our food, and the whole institution of Sunday brunch.

He's definitely into Charlie, and I sigh, glad I let Charlie make an exhibition of me. At least it gives him a bit of armor to hide behind. Although, I've gotta say, Deke is taking this really well. Maybe he's poly? But if that's the case, would us eating together really be that weird for him?

"Weird?" I challenge. I'm just gonna go for it, and then maybe I can eat my rapidly cooling waffles and bacon in peace. "Why would it be weird? Unless... did you think you were dating Charlie?"

He makes a face. "What? No."

Relief—and confusion—washes over me, and Charlie grins wide and scoops a huge forkful of scrambled eggs into his mouth.

"He's my sugar daddy."

Annnnd eggs spray everywhere.

Not a good day for this table.

As Charlie takes his turn choking and sputtering, I hand him a napkin and his water glass, then turn to Deke, who's distastefully picking egg off his sleeve. It looks like only that one bit landed on him, which, frankly, has to be a miracle.

Our server is heading toward us, but I make eye contact, smile ruefully, and shake my head. She retreats with a tiny frown, but this is more important.

"I'm sorry, what now?" I ask Deke. "Did you say Charlie's your sugar daddy?" Oh my god, this can't be for real. I bet Charlie set this up—it's a prank.

Beside me, Charlie gasps, trying to get his breath back, his face red and wild-eyed.

Okay, not a prank. He's not that good an actor, despite what he thinks of his role-playing skills.

Deke nods. "Well, yeah. Of course."

"Of course," I echo, then turn to Charlie. "Care to weigh in?" I can kind of see how he came to that conclusion, but at the same time, wow.

Just wow.

"Why would you think that?" Charlie bursts out. "What the fuck? I mean..." He slumps back in his chair and runs a hand through his hair. "What the fuck?" he repeats.

Now Deke looks puzzled, and maybe a little hurt. "What would you call it when one guy buys stuff for another guy all the time but they're not dating?"

Charlie's jaw drops. "But we don't have sex!"

I wince as people at the nearest tables turn in our direction. "Inside voice," I murmur.

"A sugar daddy-sugar baby relationship doesn't have to involve sex," Deke says stiffly. "I'm straight."

I blink. Called that wrong, and shame on me for making assumptions. Although from the way Charlie's reacting, he made the same one.

"It's about companionship," Deke's explaining, flags of color high on his cheekbones. "One party pays for everything, and in return they get good company."

My stomach sinks. The idea that he was essentially paying for Deke's friendship isn't going to make Charlie feel any better.

"Uh," I interrupt, hoping to steer this sinking ship away from more rocks, "obviously there's been a miscommunication. Can I ask, what kind of things did Charlie pay for? Meals, obviously." Because that seems to be his MO. But maybe Deke interpreted that wrong, the same way others thought it meant they were dating.

Deke shrugs. "Sure, meals. And some clothes. Concert tickets. Some of my textbooks."

My head turns so fast, I might actually have whiplash. "Textbooks?" I accuse Charlie. Holy crap, I wish someone would shell out for my textbooks! Those fuckers cost a bomb.

"I like to help out my friends," he protests weakly.

"What's going on?" Deke asks, frowning, and I actually feel sorry for him. It's not his fault Charlie is ridiculously, obscenely generous. And now he's going to lose his sugar daddy.

"We're friends," Charlie croaks. "I thought we were friends." His mouth tugs down at the corners, and his whole face is so tragic, I almost want to cry for him.

I look back at Deke. "Charlie likes to support his friends however he can, including financially," I say as diplomatically as I can manage. "He doesn't consider your... uh, your... relationship"—fuck, it's the only word, but somehow it sounds sordid right now—"to be a sugar one."

Deke stares back at me, then looks at Charlie, who nods miserably. "Oh."

Awkward silence descends. This is painful. Worse still, it would be so insensitive of me to start eating, and my waffle is getting cold.

Deke clears his throat. "Uh. So... I do consider you a friend. I mean... we get on, right? We have a good time when we hang out. It wasn't like I was just there for the money." He cuts himself off, wincing.

Charlie stares at his plate.

Mentally bidding farewell to my waffle, I say, "I think we all need some time to, uh... Look, we're gonna go. Let's give it a while and see how everyone feels then. Come on, Charlie." I hustle him out of his seat, then turn back to Deke, who's half standing and looking completely awkward. "Stay and eat. There's no point in everything being wasted. We've got the check." A huge part of me wants to stick him with it, but this isn't exactly his fault, and I don't know what his financial situation is. Before I started Mr. Romance, there's no way I could have afforded even one meal here, let alone three, and even now I don't like to splash out that kind of money.

He tries to smile at me, but it comes out more of a grimace, and nods. "Thanks. And... sorry."

Charlie follows me silently to the cashier, who's watching us with avid curiosity. We've given the whole place a real show. "Hey, can we settle up for table six? Our friend is going to finish, but we gotta go."

"Of course. I hope everything is okay?" she fishes as she taps the screen in front of her.

"Just peachy." I reach for my wallet when she prints the receipt and tucks it in a little leather folder even though I'm standing right in front of her, but Charlie grabs my arm.

"Don't," he mutters, and his set face deters me from arguing with him. Instead, I step back and let him pay. It's not like I wasn't going to invoice him for the expense, anyway. Just... later. When this whole thing isn't so raw.

It takes forever for the transaction to go through, but finally we're out on the sidewalk.

Charlie inhales a deep lungful of winter air. It's a balmy winter day, typical of Southern California.

"You okay?" I ask quietly.

He shakes his head but says nothing.

"Do you want to go back to campus?"

For a moment, I think he's not going to respond, but then he shakes his head again.

Okay. Where to go? Inspiration strikes.

"What about a walk on the beach?"

Something loosens in his posture, and even though he still doesn't speak, he turns in that direction and starts walking. I catch up to him in a few steps and keep pace. I'm not actually sure if he wants my company or not, but until he says so outright, I'm not going to leave him alone. He asked me to come along this morning.

Plus, part of this might be my fault. Maybe I should have told him to fob Deke off. Sure, that would have just delayed the inevitable, but at least he wouldn't be feeling this way now.

Although, it could be worse. He could have taken someone else to brunch with him or gone alone. At least he's got the comfort of knowing I'm just someone he hired who offered a confidentiality agreement and who he never has to see again if that's what he wants.

It takes about ten minutes to get to the beach, and neither of us says a word the whole time. But when we're finally standing on the white sand, the waves crashing before us, occasional joggers passing by, Charlie says, "What the fuck is wrong with me?"

"Nothing," I reply quickly, then pause. "Well, I'm sure whoever pays your credit card bill would complain that you're too generous."

He doesn't seem to hear me. "I thought he was my friend. But I was *paying* him to be my friend. That's so fucking pathetic."

"You're not pathetic," I insist. "And you weren't paying him to be your friend. I'll bet you guys got friendly and started hanging out before you paid for anything. It's just that when you did—because you're a caring and generous friend—he misunderstood what that meant." I sigh. "I didn't see this coming, and I'm sorry. I should have anticipated it so you weren't blindsided."

Charlie gives me an incredulous look. "You should have

anticipated that someone would think I was their sugar daddy?"

When he puts it like that... "Well, uh..."

His laugh is big and loud and takes over his whole body, and I can't help joining in. A few people who pass us smile indulgently, and when our laughter finally dies down, Charlie sighs. He's smiling still, and it seems like the sigh is a release of his stress.

"Let's walk," he says, turning in the direction of campus. It a gorgeous day for a stroll on the beach, and let's face it, brunch didn't take as long as I expected. I spare a mournful thought for my waffles.

"Okay, so tell me where I went wrong here." Charlie's tone is determined. "Like, we thought he might be into me because of all the usual reasons, but how did that turn into... this?"

"Not a fucking clue." I spread my hands. "I don't think most people automatically think sugar relationship when a friend pays for something. It would be more common to think the friend is super cool, or even that they might be into them, like what you've got happening now." I bite my lip and consider it. "My guess is this is a combination of Deke being straight, thus not wanting to date you, and maybe having seen or heard about a sugar relationship in his circle of family or friends. Like, for most people it's a thing of fiction, but if someone he knows has been in one..." I shrug. "It wouldn't seem unnatural to him."

"I guess that makes sense," Charlie agrees, but he sounds dubious. "So this is a fluke, right? Just bad luck. It's not likely to happen again?"

If anyone else had asked me that, I'd immediately scoff and say "No way!" But let's face it, Charlie's kind of special.

"Can we talk about what you bought for him?" I suggest. "The clothes, for example. How did that happen?"

He shrugs. "I dunno. We were at the mall, and I was buying some stuff, and he had a couple shirts, and I just... paid for them all together."

Er. Coffee, sure. Shirts? Nope.

"And did he offer to pay you back?"

"Yeah, I guess. But I told him not to worry about it." His sigh this time is frustrated. "Why is it such a big deal? I have money, and I like for my friends to be happy. Do you know how many students at this college are fucking stressed about money? Like, they eat only at the dining hall because their meals are covered there and they budget for entertainment and talk about how glad they are their parents got them new shirts for Christmas because theirs were getting worn out. I don't have those problems, and I just want to make things easier for my friends."

I don't say anything, because I'm one of those students. My parents have good jobs, and Mr. Romance is definitely helping, but I'm still going to graduate college with debt. I do spend money on stuff that's important to me—like gym time—but since meals at the dining hall are paid for, why would I waste cash on eating somewhere else? Every cent I don't spend on frivolous stuff now means dollars I won't have to repay later.

"It's really generous of you," I start cautiously. I feel like I've said that a few too many times already this morning. "The thing is, it's not a common attitude. People aren't used to it. Especially people who have to budget. For them, you don't spend big sums of money randomly on yourself, much less on friends. So they see it as a sign that there's more than just friendship between you." I give that a moment to sink in, then add, "Like brunch today, for example. Deke asked if you wanted to go to brunch, right? But I'll bet he did it with the full expectation that you'd pay, and you had that same expectation."

"Well, yeah." Charlie side-eyes me. "Is that not normal?"

I shake my head. "That's the sugar daddy thing. He wanted something, so he told you about it and you made it happen. It's different again from the dating thing. I bet none of the people who thought you were dating suggested you go to expensive places."

He thinks about it. "I guess not? Mostly it was my idea. Like they'd say 'let's go to the dining hall' and I'd suggest somewhere else. Why is this all so hard?" He pouts. It's freaking adorable, and I kind of want to slap him for that.

"Life is hard." It's a cliché, but seriously, what the fuck am I supposed to say?

"So what am I supposed to do?" he asks. "Not pay for anything for anyone? Ever again in my life?"

Oh-kay... "You're being dramatic now," I chide. "We have a plan, remember? I'm going to train you in all this stuff."

He brightens. "Role plays?"

"Yeah, role plays. But maybe no more wigs. You don't really need them."

The shit-eating grin he gives me is my only warning. "Aww, Lee, are you saying I'm as hot as Gwyneth Paltrow all by myself?"

I sputter for a second, then shake my head in exasperation. "Gay, remember? Gwyneth Paltrow doesn't get my motor running, so she's not a good basis for comparison." Yes, I'm avoiding the question.

No, he doesn't let me get away with it.

"So you don't think I'm hot?" He bats his lashes and goes full pouty lip.

I roll my eyes and give in. "You're plenty hot, you idiot."

Laughing, he loops his arm around my shoulders and yanks me close. "Thanks, Lee. You're the best boyfriend ever!"

Which reminds me... "About that." I shrug free of him, only regretting it a tiny bit. What? He's sweet and hot and it's been a while since I've been held up against a man like that.

He widens his eyes innocently. "I know, we're not *really* boyfriends. You're the best fake boyfriend ever? And thank you so much for helping me save face back there?"

"You're welcome, but you gotta be careful with that kind of stuff. I'm safe, but what if you'd said it to one of the people who think..." I trail off as I realize he's not walking beside me anymore.

Turning, I see him about ten paces back and retrace my steps. "Charlie? You okay?"

He stares at me with a dumbstruck expression. "It's the perfect solution," he whispers, and I get a very, very, *very* bad feeling.

"It's probably not."

"It *is*," he insists, a slightly maniacal gleam in his eyes. "It really is."

I brace myself.

"We should be fake boyfriends for real!"

Yep. I was right.

"That doesn't even make sense," I point out, scrambling

for a polite way to ask him if his brain works at all. Maybe he got really drunk after I left last night and the alcohol is still affecting him.

He doesn't seem drunk, though.

"You know what I mean. It's the perfect solution. Word will get around that I've got a boyfriend, and anyone else who thinks they're still dating me will realize they're not. And anyone in the future who might have thought they are won't, because they'll know I'm dating you!"

I manage to puzzle my way through the sentence and then look into his hopeful gaze and feel like a turd. Because I have to crush that hope.

"Let's sit down for a second," I suggest. He looks around.

"Where?"

"Uh... here." I gesture to the dry, soft sand behind us. We've been walking along the compacted wet sand near the water, but there's yards of space on the dry sand for us to sit.

Although judging by Charlie's horror, that's not going to happen. "Our clothes will get all sandy!" he protests.

"It'll brush off?" I didn't mean for it to sound like a question, but it comes out that way. "Don't you come and watch the sun set on the beach all the time?" I distinctly remember that coming up.

"Yeah, but I bring something to sit on. I'm not going to ruin my clothes!"

Okay then. We won't sit. I can't resist adding, "They're just clothes. They keep you warm and prevent you from getting arrested."

Charlie shakes his head, aghast. "Oh, my man. No. Abso-fucking-lutely no. Although..." He scans me up and down, and for the first time since we met, I feel judged. "Okay, I get it. Those clothes, I would be okay with ruining."

I plant my hands on my hips and narrow my eyes. "Excuse me? Are you being a snob because I'm not wearing designer labels?"

He gives me a superior look as he unzips his jacket. "You see this T-shirt? I got this at Walmart. It's not about designer, Lee. It's about *style*. That"—he waves at my jeans and sweater, which okay, they may be my nicest but I've had them for years and they were never trendy and it's possible the colors don't really go together—"is not style. Ooh, we should go shopping!"

"Hell, no!" That's it, I'm done. Time to nip this in the bud. "No shopping. Ever."

CHAPTER SEVEN

CHARLIE

"Aw, c'mon, it'll be fun. And anyway, it's necessary. Nobody will ever believe I'd let my boyfriend dress like that." I try not to sound condescending and offensive, but from the look on Lee's face, I've failed miserably. And okay, I get why. But he dresses like a colorblind seventy-year-old who didn't look in the mirror before leaving the house. Take that sweater, for example. As hideous as it is, if he pushed the sleeves up and wore a shirt under it, it might be... well, it would still be hideous, but at least it would look like the kind of hideous sweater a twenty-year-old might wear. Not me, but other twenty-year-olds.

Lee doesn't look convinced, so I fall back on my best puppy-dog look.

He sighs. "First, I'm not your boyfriend, not your fake boyfriend, and that's not a thing we're going to do."

What? "Noooo," I whine. "It's the perfe—"

"It's not the perfect solution. I'm sorry, Charlie, so sorry, but think about it. If you start announcing that I'm your boyfriend, anyone who thinks they're dating you is going to think you've been cheating. Either on them, or on me. It's going to lead to a confrontation or a lot of nasty gossip. Do you really want that?"

The scene in the café rises from my memory, and I wince. Yeah, I'd be okay with never having to go through something like that ever again. Especially knowing how hurt everyone was. I don't want my friends to be hurt. Even if there isn't a scene, they'd still be hurt... and there would be the added bonus of people whispering and side-eyeing me. And maybe Lee, too. He doesn't deserve that.

I blow out a breath. "It really did seem like the perfect solution."

Lee pats my arm. "I know. But you also have to think long-term. If you tell everyone I'm your boyfriend, what's going to happen when you meet someone you actually want to date? They might not be impressed if you tell them to wait while you break up with me, you'll be back in five minutes to ask them out."

I feel compelled to say, "I wouldn't want to date anyone who was okay with that."

"I didn't think you would. Plus, if you're fake dating me, your hookup potential will be limited. Not everyone wants to fuck a guy who's already got a boyfriend." He makes a sympathetic face. "I know the plan is going to take longer, but aside from this morning, it hasn't been too bad, right? Gina figured it out on her own, and Lila really is just your friend."

"And the role plays were fun," I concede. His whole face twitches, but he makes an agreeing noise.

"Sure. Fun. Lots of fun." He looks me straight in the eye. "Are you okay?"

I think about it, worrying my lip with my teeth. His gaze

drops to my mouth, and something about it makes me bite just a little harder. "Maybe I'm being a tiny bit dramatic," I concede finally. "This thing with Deke was a shock. I hate the idea that I've been buying friends."

"But you and Deke were already friends," he reminds me, and even though I knew that, hearing it again does help.

I nod. "Yeah. I'm okay. Just... can we not tell anyone about this? They're going to turn it into a joke, and even though it would be all in good fun, I'm not in that place yet where I can laugh about it."

He mimes zipping his lips. "Confidentiality guaranteed," he reminds me, and I grin at him. I know he's not actually my friend, that I'm paying him to be here and listen to me and give advice, but when I finally get a clue and understand how not to make people think we're dating, I'm going to keep Lee.

Which reminds me... "So, am I allowed to buy my friendship consultant new clothes?"

Lee snorts and turns to continue walking up the beach. We're near campus now, the entry to the street just up ahead. It's busier here, with some students taking advantage of the mild winter day to enjoy brunch picnics on the beach. "No, you can't buy me clothes."

"Why not? It's a work expense."

The side-eye he gives me almost makes me laugh out loud. "A work expense? How do you figure?"

Someone I vaguely remember meeting last year—was it in class or at a party?—waves at me, and I wave and smile back, but don't stop. "Well, like today. You came to brunch with me and had to wear brunch-appropriate clothing. Which, honestly, that outfit—"

"Are you about to insult my clothes again?" There's a thread of laughter in his voice.

"Yup. I really, really am. 'Clothes' is a good word, because 'outfit' was stretching things."

Now he laughs outright. "C'mon, I'm wearing jeans and a sweater. They're in muted colors and have no holes or anything."

Oh, the poor, deprived man. I do feel better knowing how little he cares about his clothes, though. It's pretty clear that he's amused by my hatred for them. "That's not the scale you should use to rate your clothes," I inform him. "Let me buy you—"

"No."

"But—"

"No. You're supposed to be practicing appropriate friendship gestures, remember? This is not one of them."

I consider a way around that. "Okay, so then what if I pick the clothes but you pay for them? You can give me a budget and everything." Actually, that's kind of exciting. I've never had to worry about the price tag before. It'll be a cool challenge!

He doesn't answer, and I glance his way as we climb the beach toward the exit. Is he thinking about it?

My excitement ramps up.

"Maybe," he says finally. "We'll see."

"My parents used to say that when they meant 'no,'" I inform him, then grin. "But I always turned it into a yes."

He rolls his eyes so hard, I wouldn't be surprised if he's given himself a headache.

We emerge from the sand, and I take a second to brush myself off while he watches with a little smile. I like his smile.

In fact, I like his whole face. It's not classically good-looking—the angles are too strong for that, not quite put together the way modern beauty dictates—but his strength of character is there, the smart-ass part of him that takes no shit, and the dreamy romantic in his eyes and soft mouth. I don't think I've ever seen a face so perfectly reflect someone's personality before.

"So, I'm not allowed to buy you clothes, but I did promise you brunch." I tip my head toward the food truck that makes bank selling breakfast burritos every weekend. "How about it?"

I clearly hear his stomach rumble. "You're on," he declares, then gestures to the Bean Necessities coffee cart. "You can even get me a fancy coffee, since I barely got to taste the other one."

"Deal."

My dad suggested I take an intro to economics class because it would be helpful when I'm working for the family company. I ignored the feeling of dread and anxiety that thought gave me and signed up for the class, because when I graduate and start working, I'm going to do the best job I can.

Halfway through the lecture on Tuesday, I'm not so convinced that's possible. Economics is the most boring thing on the planet. If the world needs it to work, then we should be working harder on the whole space travel thing, just so we can get away from Earth and find a more interesting planet.

Trying not to yawn—the professor hates that, even though he's doing his level best to make us—I slide my phone out of my pocket and debate which social media app to scroll through. Then I notice I have a new email, so I check that instead. It's from Mom, asking if I've decided yet what I'm going to do for spring break.

If you come home, you'll have to share the house with Aunt Melanie. Dad and I are going to be at a conference in Geneva, and your aunt is staying here while her apartment is painted.

My whole face scrunches up in instinctive reaction. Aunt Melanie is the most annoying person who ever lived, no exceptions, don't come at me with suggestions. I'm a hundred percent convinced that she's the reason I don't have siblings. My dad probably didn't want to take the risk that I'd have to grow up with someone as annoying as her the way he did.

I wouldn't have minded having a brother or sister—or one of each. Not if they were like Aunt Melanie, of course. But if they were normal, sure. Most of my friends have sibs, and they talk about them being *the worst* but then have a ton of stories about cool things they did together. I figure it's a mixed bag—you gotta take the fun times with the times you want to drown them. And apparently older siblings can be great sources of advice. Jake's older brother was the one who told him where to get his fake ID from. If I had an older brother, maybe my fake ID wouldn't suck so much. And maybe I wouldn't have friends who think they're dating me, because my brother—or sister—would have told me I was being dumb.

Hmm, I wonder if Lee has brothers and sisters? Maybe that's why he's so good at the romance thing. He's had people to observe and give him tips.

I flip across to the message app and send him a text.

Charlie: Do you have brothers and sisters?

While I'm waiting for him to reply, I check the time. If I remember right, he's at a study group. So... he might answer, or he might not.

Liam: Sister five years younger. Why?

Oh. That's a bust, then. It's unlikely that a fifteen-year-old has enough dating experience to have guided the Mr. Romance empire.

Charlie: Just wondering where you get all your romance experience from

He sends a shocked face emoji, then follows it up a second later.

Liam: What the hell kind of romance experience do you think I could get from my sister? I don't know what happens in your family, but mine's not like that.

I start to laugh, turn it into a coughing fit when people turn to look, then make a sheepish face at my professor. "Sorry. Uh, swallowed the wrong way."

He doesn't look convinced but resumes the lecture. I count slowly to five to give everyone time to fall asleep again, then look back at my phone and send Lee three laugh emojis.

Charlie: That's so not what I meant! I thought maybe you had older sibs who had given you advice

Liam: Ohhhh that's a relief. No older sibs, but my mom's brother and sister are only 10yrs older than me. So I grew up hearing their stories. Plus I have an addiction to romantic books and movies.

So he has a cool young aunt and uncle. Lucky him—all I have are Aunt Melanie... and Uncle Jim, but he lived in Chicago until I was a high school senior, so it's not like we were close.

It doesn't really surprise me that Lee's into books and movies—

Wait.

Charlie: Romantic books and movies? You mean like porn?

Liam: ...

Liam: Since when has porn EVER been romantic?

Charlie: Not like PORN porn, but that other porn. You know, the books with the half-naked people on the covers. My mom collects them for the women at the shelters she works with.

Liam: Not porn, Charlie. Romance novels.

Isn't it the same? Like, you call it porn on the screen and romance in a book? I ask him.

Liam: No. Porn books are called erotica. Romances have an actual story, and the characters end up happy together at the end.

Charlie: Like a happy ending?

Liam: Depends on what you mean by that. NOT the kind found in dodgy massage parlors

That's so disappointing.

Charlie: So those covers are all promise and no delivery? There's no sex in those books?

Lee takes a long time to reply, though I can see he's typing.

Liam: There is sex, sometimes a lot of sex, but it's secondary to the story. The main point is for the characters to fall in love and end up happy together.

I bite my lip to keep from grinning. People don't grin in this class.

Charlie: Now we're talking! How much sex? Is it good? There's gotta be a reason people read these books instead of watching porn

Liam: I feel like you're missing the point. People read them mostly for the romance. The sex is a bonus.

Charlie: I bet people skip to the sex scenes and ignore the rest

Liam: Some probably do

Charlie: do you?

I almost hold my breath waiting for his response. I don't know why I care.

Liam: No. I read the whole book.

Liam: The first time, anyway.

I blink at the screen, trying to make sense of that. Wait, is he saying he reads these books more than once? Why would you read a book more than once?
Duh. For the sex.

Charlie: Should I read one of these books?

Maybe they'll help me understand the whole cupcake thing.

Liam: If you want? It's not like required reading or anything.

True, but reading about sex can never be a bad thing.

Charlie: Can you recommend one for me?

Liam: That's a harder question to answer than you think. Yes, but we need to talk more about your likes and dislikes. Another time. Aren't you in class?

Charlie: Yes. This conversation is keeping me awake and sane. I like boobs and dicks, if that helps you recommend a book for me.

Liam: Not exactly what I meant.

Charlie: I want to read your favorite. What's that called? Where can I buy it?

Liam: I have many favorites. Let me think about this and decide which one you'll like best. Are you into sports? What movies do you like?

That's an interesting question. I like most sports to watch, but I'm really not competitive enough to play. I tried when I was younger, and I used to feel bad for the players on the other team when they got frustrated. Which led to my team getting frustrated when I'd "accidentally" give away the ball or whatever. Then I'd get upset because everyone else was upset. It was better all round when I quit team sports.

But I don't think that's what Lee's asking.

Charlie: I'm VERY into athletes. Especially the flexible ones. Movies... I like stuff that's not real life. Sci-fi, fantasy, superhero stuff. Period movies that in no way resemble history.

Liam: Okay, that gives me an idea. Paperback or ebook?

Charlie: Paperback.

I like ebooks for my textbooks, but when I'm reading for fun—which is rare—I like paperbacks. Sometimes I miss details, and it's easier for me to flip back and forth through actual pages to figure out what's going on.

Liam: Leave it with me. I gotta go. I'm supposed to be contributing to this group.

Charlie: Role play tonight?

Liam: Yep, but we're going to change it up. Bye

Charlie: Change it up? What's that mean?

Charlie: Lee?

Charlie: Well, fuck.

CHAPTER EIGHT

LIAM

I'M STILL AMUSED BY CHARLIE'S TEXTS WHEN THE TIME rolls around for our role play. This time when I knock on his door, he yells that it's open, and I let myself in. He's leaning over his desk looking at something on his laptop, and I'm ashamed to say I take shameless advantage of the opportunity to perv on his ass. The tight jeans he's wearing hug every inch of him, and it's a pretty spectacular sight.

Then he straightens, and I jerk my gaze away before he turns and smiles brightly at me. "Ready? I'm so pumped. And no wig, like you said." There's a hint of a pout on that last sentence, but I pretend I don't see it.

"Great. So tonight we're going to work on what to say in a few different scenarios where people might misinterpret your generosity."

He throws himself onto his bed, bouncing lightly. "Bring it. Oh, wait... did I tell you I saw James today and he was acting weird? He met me and Jake for lunch and kept looking at me funny, and then he raced to pay for his first before I even had to work out how I was going to handle it." There's a slight crease in his forehead, and I know he still hates that he can't treat his friends.

"Sounds like he might have seen the video. That's good. He might be weird for a while, but then he'll relax and things can go back to normal. What about Sarah? You had class with her yesterday, right?" When he didn't text me in a panic, I assumed it went well, but from the way his face falls, it didn't.

"She ghosted me. Didn't turn up to class, and when I messaged to see if she wanted my notes, she never replied. But on my way out, I heard someone say they were meeting up with her to share notes, so..." He shrugs.

"That might not mean anything. Maybe there's another reason she didn't come to class, and she happened to see that other person beforehand. Maybe she's been busy and hasn't seen your text." I settle in his desk chair.

"And maybe she's avoiding me because she saw the video or heard the rumors and we weren't really friends like I thought."

I shrug. "That's possible too. But don't freak out. Give her time to process and then just see what happens. You've done nothing wrong, Charlie. This is all just a huge miscommunication."

He doesn't look convinced, so I change the subject. "C'mon, let's get started. I'm a newish friend, class is over, and we're walking out together, okay?"

Determination settles over his face. "Got it."

"So... wanna get some lunch?" I start him off easy.

"Sure," he says, but it's hesitant and he shoots me an uncertain glance. I nod and smile encouragingly, and he perks up.

"Where should we go?"

"Food Café does the best sandwiches. I go there for lunch all the time," Charlie enthuses, throwing himself into the scenario.

I hesitate and bite my lip, which I'd have done if this was real, because Food Café is expensive. From everything I've heard, the food's worth the price, but I'm still not going to pay fifteen dollars for a sandwich.

Charlie notices my reticence. "My treat." The words are no sooner out of his mouth than he realizes what he's said and closes his eyes. "I am the *worst*."

I chuckle. "You're not the worst. It's actually a really nice offer for you to make. But remember that at this stage we barely know each other, and offering to buy me an expensive sandwich could send the wrong message."

He takes a deep breath and sets his jaw. "Okay. Let me try again."

"Pick it up from after you said Food Café and I hesitated. How can you recover from that without me having to say out loud that I can't afford it?"

"Or, actually," he says, sounding completely natural and even a little apologetic, "could we go to the dining hall or the student union? My next class is in an hour, and I don't want to waste time walking there and back."

I give him a thumbs-up and pretend to be relieved. "That's fine with me."

Charlie breaks character. "This is a losing scenario," he whines. "They have to use their credit at the dining hall *and* we don't get good sandwiches."

I nod. "Yep. This time. But when you get to know them better and they're actually a friend, it won't be as big a deal to treat them to lunch sometimes. By then they'll know you and understand it's a gesture of friendship. The biggest issue here is mixed messages. You're generous and flirty from the moment you meet someone, and they're seeing that as a sign of interest. Wait until after they're definitely your friend and have seen how you normally are with friends before you pull your wallet out."

"I'm not flirty," he mutters.

"Maybe that's the wrong word," I concede. "You're very, uh... warm. Sociable. Outgoing. And you're communicative with your friends. Next time you meet someone new, let them set the pace."

He looks confused.

"Don't be the first one to call or text," I explain. "Wanna try another role play?"

We get through two more, and he does a lot better than I expected. I think part of that is because he's prepared. It's going to be interesting to see how he goes in a real situation. He still slips up once or twice, and I *hate* having to point it out as a flaw. He's a sweet, open, friendly guy, and I'm telling him not to be. There's something seriously wrong with that.

Finally, he flops back on his bed, eyes closed, and declares that we're done. "My brain has finished braining."

I swallow back my instinctive response and smile indulgently at him. "You're doing great. Let your brain rest." The thick dark fans of his eyelashes against his skin make something stir inside me... as does the sliver of tanned skin on display where his shirt has ridden up. This time, it's not snark I swallow down, but lust. "I'll just get out of your hair, then," I say, my voice just a tiny bit raspy as I stand and grab my backpack.

His eyes open, and he sits up. "What? No. It's still early,

and if you go, I'll feel bad about not studying. Stay and hang out with me."

I freeze. "Uh..."

Face falling, he says, "I guess you've got work to do."

Oh, the agony. I actually *don't*. I mean, there's always something that can be done, but I cleared the evening to work with Charlie, so there's nothing I *have* to do. But somehow, I don't think it's the best idea to hang out with my client in his room when I'm thinking about how sweet and sexy he is. It seems like a test of my professionalism.

He gives me a pleading look with those big brown eyes, and I sigh. I've always liked tests.

"No, I can hang out for a bit." I sink back into the desk chair, but he's not having it. He slides over and pats the bed beside him.

"Sit here. It's more comfy. Wanna watch a movie? I'm halfway through rewatching all the MCU movies while I wait for the new one." His hopeful smile is a potent weapon.

"Sure," I agree, moving to the bed while he grabs his laptop. "What are you up to?"

"I just finished *Ant Man*, and since the only way to watch is release order, that means *Captain America: Civil War* is next."

"Go for it." We settle in, and as the opening credits roll, I add, "This is really the only Captain America movie worth watching."

Charlie gasps, and I brace myself for the outrage, but when I glance over, he's smiling. "Right? Don't get me wrong, there were scenes in *The Winter Soldier* that were badass, but this is definitely better."

Turns out, Charlie's a talker during movies, keeping up a

steady, quiet commentary on what's happening—though he does mostly pause for dialogue. It's kind of endearing, though it might not be if I hadn't already seen the movie.

But it's lucky all round that I've seen this movie before, because it's a lot harder to concentrate than I thought it would be. Watching a movie on a laptop screen means getting pretty close. Maybe that's a bonus for couples, but for me, feeling the warmth radiating from Charlie's big body and knowing a tiny movement would have me pressed against his side is... torture.

"I wish I could do that." Charlie sighs beside me, and I force myself to focus.

"Do what?"

He waves at the screen. "All that backflipping, rolling, somersaulting shit. I know a lot of it's CGI, but some of the stunts are real. People can actually do this stuff."

I don't know what devil takes control of my tongue, but I say, "I can do this stuff."

His head whips around. "Really? You can do *that*?" He points to the screen, where Spider-Man is doing his thing at an airport.

"Well, not the web thing," I joke. "But if you take out the bit where he's flying through the air... yeah."

He sits up straight. "No fucking way! That's awesome. Is that what you and Ian were doing at the gym?"

I shrug, a bit uncomfortable and wishing I'd kept my mouth shut. "Basically. It's a great way to keep fit and flexible, and it's fun."

"How long did it take you to learn? Are you, like, on the school team? Does the school even have an acrobat team?"

"They have a gymnastics team, but I'm not on it.

Competitive sports take up a lot of time, and that's not what I came to college for," I add, forestalling whatever he was going to say that put that indignant expression on his face. He closes his mouth and nods.

"As long as it was your choice," he grumbles, and I discreetly pinch myself. Hard. I am *not* going to let Ian and Matt be right about this.

But I'm really starting to see why so many of Charlie's "friends" fall for him.

"It was totally my choice. I did competitive gymnastics right up into middle school, and then I quit. It's a lot more fun without the constant drilling and pressure to win."

He nods, his usually sunny expression back. "Yeah, I get that. I like casual games of most sports, but I'm no good when it gets competitive. Life should be more about fun and less about winning." Then he blanches. "Don't tell anyone I said that. I've got friends on most of the sports teams here, and they all think I'm rabidly invested in them winning."

I snort. "Your secret's safe with me."

"Could I maybe come and watch you one day? I'll stay out of the way. I won't even talk."

Hesitating, because I'm not sure if that's something he's capable of, I hedge, "Let me check with Ian and Matt. We share gym time, and we've never had someone watch before." Except the gymnastics coach, who likes to glower at us with his arms crossed and mutter about wasted talent. "You should see them, though. They can do some whacked-out shit. I think they learned it in their cult."

He blinks at me. "They were in a *cult*?"

Whoops. "No... sorry. That's just what I say to tease them. I think it was more like a commune? And they can come and go at any time. As far as I can tell, it's just a bunch of families living together on the same land and home-schooling their kids until they go to high school." And the fitness and acrobatic stuff. But if I add that, it'll make it sound like a YA fantasy movie where kids are raised to be super soldiers. "It's really not a cult." I think. "Please don't tell anyone I said that."

He raises his right hand and gives me the Vulcan salute. "Scout's honor."

I narrow my eyes. "You were never a Scout, were you?"

"Nah." His grin takes over his face. "Mom didn't like the organization's attitude toward queer people. But my honor's good anyway."

I'm not quite sure what to say to that, so I just smile and go back to watching the movie. But it's safe to say that I need to put a lot more effort into professional distance.

Charlie: Where are you

Charlie: Need you

Charlie: Gina's blowing me off. She won't even look at me.

The three messages pop up so close together that I've barely finished reading the first one before the third is on the screen.

Liam: What happened?

Charlie: Went to class. Thought things would be ok after her call last week? But she came in, saw me, and turned the other way. She's sitting on the other side of the room and won't even look at me. I fucked this up so bad.

Fuck. I glance at my watch. If I remember right, his class just started. By the time it's done, I need to be at the gym.

Liam: You didn't fuck this up. She's probably embarrassed. Give her time to process.

Liam: Are you okay?

It's only been a week, but I already know him well enough to know he's hurting over this.

Charlie: I feel like the worst person ever.

Charlie: Are you free? I'm skipping class.

Sighing, I close my eyes for a second.

Liam: Yeah, sure. Come and have lunch with me.

Liam: At the dining hall.

Charlie: I can't talk you into Food Café? It's a business lunch, so I can pay.

I snort a laugh.

Liam: I'm eating with Matt and Ian before gym. So, no.

There's a pause, and I start walking again.

Charlie: Can I come to gym?

I've already asked the guys about this. Part of me was convinced he'd forget all about it, but just in case he didn't, I checked. After exchanging a long look and making some doom-and-gloom comments about me needing to protect myself, they said it was fine. Matt even made a joke about how good it would be to show off his awesomeness.

Liam: Yes.

He doesn't reply, and I assume that's because he's busy sneaking out of class, but when I get to the dining hall, he's already there, sitting with Matt while Ian raids the salad bar. I go there first.

"How's it look?" The salad bar is usually not too gross, although sometimes the school's definition of "fresh" is different from the rest of the world's. But today things actually look good, which is a relief. I don't like to eat anything too heavy before gym.

"It looks like you've got a new BFF," Ian retorts. "Tell me again that you aren't falling for him?"

"I'm not," I protest, glancing over my shoulder just in case Charlie might have overheard from all the way across the very noisy room. "He's having a bad day, is all. And he's paying me a *lot* of money to be helpful and supportive. Which was your idea, remember?"

The side-eye Ian gives me says louder than words that I'm not fooling anyone, and I concentrate on filling a plate.

Back at the table, Matt and Charlie have their heads bent together in intense conversation, ignoring their food. They both look up when Ian and I join them, and Matt gives me an up-and-down look before I sit.

"Yeah, you're definitely right," he tells Charlie.

Uh-oh.

"Right about what?" I ask warily.

"Your clothes," Charlie says with a beautiful smile. "I told Matt we're going shopping."

I groan. "*Thinking* about it."

"It's probably a good idea," Ian muses, biting into a piece of carrot. "Your clothes are bad."

I look down at my sweatpants and hoodie, unzipped to show a plain gray T-shirt underneath, then over at him. "We're wearing almost the exact same thing."

All three of them laugh. "Workout clothes don't count."

"Whatever." I roll my eyes, secretly relieved that Charlie's mood isn't too low.

He changes the subject then, asking about gymnastics and how the guys got into it. Their story is kind of vague—started learning when they were little, both their older brothers were into it. After the second time they dodge his questions, he shoots me a little smirk and mouths, "Cult?" I cough to keep from laughing.

Once we make it to the gym, he stretches with us—as much as he can in his jeans—making jokes about our flexibility, then settles off to the side with our hoodies and water bottles. I half wish I'd never said he could come, because now that he's here, watching me, I'm stupidly nervous.

"Liam, did you want the vault? You said you wanted to work on your landing, right?" Matt says, and I force myself to stop being an idiot. I'm paying through the nose for this gym time, and yeah, I want to work on perfecting my landing. A simple handspring vault with a somersault on the dismount is something I can practically do in my sleep, but when I make it a double somersault, I rarely manage to stick the landing, and the perfectionist in me hates that.

"Yeah, thanks. Half an hour, and then we can switch?" I suggest, because I know there's stuff he wants to work on too.

He gives me a thumbs-up, and then he and Ian start squabbling over who gets to use the bars first. I ignore them and line myself up for a run at the vault.

It's the weirdest thing, but from when I was little, it's taken just one step for me to be able to block out the world around me. It was great when I was competing, because the spectators were never a distraction for me. And that's no different now. From the second I begin my run, everything else disappears. There's just my feet pounding the mats, my arms pumping, the air streaming past me. I hit the spring-board perfectly, and then I'm airborne, instinctively flipping my body up into the handspring position, reaching for the right spot on the vault to launch from. Contact... and then the dismount, my body flipping up again, drawing my knees to my chest, one rotation, two... releasing in time to land... and stumble.

"Damn it!" I snap, jerking myself upright.

"Holy fucking shit!" Charlie's shout rings through the room, and I turn to see what has his attention.

He's on his feet, staring in my direction, and I look over my shoulder, but there's nobody there.

"Oh my god, Lee, you're fucking amazing!"

Oh. My face gets hot. "Uh... I fucked up the landing," I mutter.

"Lee?" I hear Matt say. "Since when does he answer to Lee?"

I flip him the bird without looking and bask in Charlie's admiring gaze.

"Why aren't you in the Olympics?" he asks seriously, and Ian and Matt crack up.

"I'm nowhere near good enough for the Olympics," I tell Charlie. "But even if I was, that level of competition isn't what I want."

"I'm so impressed," he says. "When you said you could do all that Spider-Man stuff, I was impressed, but this... wow."

I'm starting to get embarrassed now. What I did wasn't *that* special, and I didn't even stick the landing. I feel like I should try something more complicated to live up to his expectations, but that's a surefire way to injure myself... and besides, what *I* want is to practice my landing until I can nail it every time.

"Well, thanks, but prepare to be bored out of your skull while I repeat that about twenty more times."

He shakes his head, eyes shining in his open, honest face. "I could never be bored of watching that."

I am not falling for him. Shoving aside every emotion except determination, I grin at him and head back to my starting point. Time to do it all over again.

CHAPTER NINE

CHARLIE

I HOVER AWKWARDLY OUTSIDE LEE'S DORM, WONDERING if this is a huge, stupid mistake. Probably. But Artie's not home tonight, Jake has a date, and I really don't want to be alone right now. Like... really. I was lying on my bed, and it felt like the walls were closing in on me, echoing over and over again how lonely and alone I am (because those are two separate things).

There are a million places I could have gone, starting with one of the other dorm rooms on my floor. I'm friendly with everyone in our building, and they're used to me occasionally wandering in to say hi. But none of them know what's going on with me—though they might have an inkling if they've seen the TikTok—and I want to talk to someone who can actually understand. Because what Gina did today hurt. A lot.

And it kills me that she probably did it because she's hurt, and I did that. Maybe not on purpose, but doesn't that just make it worse? I always considered myself to be a relatively good person, but apparently I'm the kind of asshat who walks through life hurting people without even realizing it.

So... yeah. Really need to talk to someone who gets what I'm going through. Which left me with the options of Mom, Ian and Matt, or Lee.

It was no contest.

Well, it was no contest when I raided Artie's stash for a bottle of vodka and stuck it in a bag to bring with me. Now that I'm standing outside Lee's dorm, doubts have settled in. Like... am I taking advantage of his good nature? Sure, I paid him a hefty retainer, but "occasional drinking buddy and agony aunt" wasn't on the list of services we agreed on.

I can't just stand here all night, though, so I pull out my phone and text him.

Charlie: You busy?

Liam: Not really. What's up?

Charlie: Can I come over?

Liam: I guess? Is everything ok?

I don't answer, just head for the door to the building. It's conveniently propped open, much like the door to our building usually is.

I'm halfway across the small lobby to the stairs when I realize I don't actually know what room Lee's in. The dorm came up in conversation, but not his room number. I pull out my phone to ask just as someone comes down the stairs.

"Hey, do you know what room Liam Rigby is in?"

The guy looks up from his phone. "Huh?"

"Liam Rigby," I repeat.

He glances over his shoulder. "Uh, 306, I think."

Close enough. I thank him and head up the stairs. If 306 isn't right, maybe whoever does live there will know.

But my luck must be improving, because when I knock at room 306, Lee opens the door. He's frowning at his phone, but that quickly fades when he sees me.

"Charlie. That was fast."

"I was outside when I texted," I admit. He steps back to let me in.

"Is everything okay?"

I look around the room, which is a lot like mine and every other dorm room on this campus. "Your roommate's not here?"

He closes the door. "He doesn't have any Friday classes, so he usually goes up to LA on Thursdays to stay with his girlfriend for the weekend."

"Cool." I hold out the bag with the bottle. "I brought this. Because I really want to blot out everything that's happened to me this week."

Taking the bag, he lightly shoves me toward one of the beds—I'm guessing his, since an open laptop is on it—and peers inside. "Well, I can keep you company while you drink this—some of it, anyway—but I've got a full day tomorrow, so I'll only have a couple of shots myself." He raises a brow at me. "Okay with you?"

I nod, and when he turns to the desk and opens a drawer, I climb onto his bed and crawl up to bury my face in his pillow. It smells good, comforting... a lot like him. Like soap and hard work and good intentions. If those things have a smell. Whatever, I already feel better just being here. Maybe I am an oblivious asshole friend, but Lee will help me fix it.

Cool glass touches the back of my neck and then withdraws, and I roll over and sit up. Lee's holding out a tumbler with a small amount of clear liquid in it. As I take it, he picks up another from the desk, then clinks them together. "To resetting our brains," he suggests, and I seize on that.

"Yes. That's what I want. A reset where I'm not a shitty person." I knock back the vodka, only wincing slightly. Artie likes the good stuff, and it's probably a crime not to savor this, but savoring won't reset my brain fast enough.

"You're not a shitty person," Lee says. He brings the bottle over to the bed and nudges my legs. "Move so I can sit."

When we're arranged side by side, leaning against the wall, he says, "Shitty people rarely admit to themselves that they're shitty. You're a good person who's unfortunately ended up in a weird situation because you're too sweet." He pulls a face. "And kind of oblivious."

I sigh and hold out my glass for a refill. "I've always been that way. Mom got me tested for a bunch of stuff when I was little, but I'm completely neurotypical. Just not the brightest spark."

"You're fine," he insists. "And one day you'll look back on all this and laugh. It just sucks right now."

I slam back the second glass of vodka—although he's definitely being stingy with the pours—and slump down to lean my head on his shoulder. "Maybe."

We sit quietly for a few seconds. He's warm against my side, his shoulder surprisingly comfortable—probably padded by all that muscle I saw on show today. After the fifty billionth time he flipped through the air like a fucking acrobat, he got hot and sweaty enough to take off his T-shirt, and holy shit, his clothes are a crime for more than just being ugly. They also do *not* do justice to the body they're hiding.

Incidentally, the next time the Olympics are on, I'm totally watching the men's gymnastics events. Someone should have told me sooner how fucking awesome they are.

"You were awesome today," I tell Lee. I already said it earlier, but it bears repeating. "Now I'm jealous of you as well as all the stunt people in superhero movies."

He chuckles. "No need to be jealous, believe me."

I poke him in the side with the hand that's not holding my empty glass. Which shouldn't be empty, but this is more important. "Of course there's a need. You're an athlete who runs a successful business and you're acing school. You're like the trifecta of things to be jealous of. Meanwhile, I somehow haven't mastered basic friendship."

Huffing, he takes my glass and pours me a tiny bit more to drink. "You've mastered basic friendship. The problem is that you're a super-advanced friend and nobody else can function at your level yet."

"Ooh, I like that explanation." I accept my glass back and lift it to eye level. "I'm pretty sure that's not a standard shot, Lee. Or even half of one."

"It's better if you draw out the anticipation," he explains, and I'm not sure if that makes sense, but it sounds good.

"Oh. Okay. I guess you're the expert on stuff like that. Hey, how did you start the whole Mr. Romance thing anyway?"

He leans into me slightly. "It was Matt's idea, actually. Toward the end of freshman year, a bunch of us were eating in the dining hall, and one of the guys was bitching because he finally asked out the girl he'd been crushing on for months and she said yes, and he had no idea how to plan their date."

"What's wrong with dinner or a club?" I ask, genuinely curious.

"Absolutely nothing. But he was so fucked-up over her that nothing was good enough. It had to be something special and unique like she was."

"Uh-huh." He must be able to hear my eye roll, because he laughs.

"Right? But after hearing him whine about it for fifteen minutes straight, I asked him what she liked—and earned everyone else's enmity when he told us in great detail—then suggested a few ideas."

"And everyone was impressed by your genius," I conclude.

"No, they all mocked me for being a romantic sap. But he couldn't think of anything else, so he used my ideas anyway, then boasted about how amazingly the date went and that I was a genius."

"I knew your genius would come into it somewhere."

"Anyway, that's when Matt joked it was too bad I hadn't charged him for the idea. One of the other guys said he'd pay if I'd give him a good date idea, and I was about to tell him he could have it for free, but Matt jumped on the idea and basically negotiated the fee for that first official job. And it kind of snowballed from there."

"Do you like it?" I don't know what makes me ask the question. I mean, it's his own business, and he's a self-confessed romantic. He's probably going to like it.

But he sighs and nudges me off his shoulder. I straighten

and turn to face him as he draws up his legs and props his forearms on his knees.

"I like it and I hate it. No, I love it and I hate it. I love being able to indulge my inner romantic. I *live* for shit like this, you know? It's the ultimate movie moment, the one that makes you sigh. But then some random couple gets to enjoy my hard work, and I... don't."

It takes my brain a few seconds to muddle through that, and then I frown. "Why don't you? You're Mr. Romance. You must have guys lined up for miles to date you."

He grimaces. "That's sweet of you to say, but no. Guys who are interested in romance usually have an idea of who their romantic hero is already, and I don't fit the mold." Before I can ask why not, he continues, "It's fine. I get along okay with Grindr and some other apps, and I keep reminding myself that I've got time. This is college—my whole life is ahead of me." He sighs, eyes fixed on his hands. "I wish I could have kissing now, though. Not everyone on hookup apps is okay with kissing, and I just want to drown in kisses."

My hand lifts to turn his face toward me, and I lean in and capture his lips. We're kissing before I even realize what I've done, and then... I don't want to stop. He stiffens with surprise, but then melts into the kiss, his mouth softening under mine. He tastes like vodka and... chocolate? and somehow of the same hard work and good intentions I smelled on his pillow. He tastes like Lee. The only places we're touching are where our lips connect and where my hand is on his cheek. It's not enough. I want to feel all of hi—

He yanks back, breaking the kiss and the moment.

"Fuck. I mean... I'm sorry," he gasps. "We shouldn't do that. I didn't mean... I wasn't trying to hint anything."

It's like cold water in my face. "No, I... I'm the one who should be sorry. I just kissed you without..." Holy crap, I never even bothered to see if he'd be okay with it. I just forced a kiss on a friend who was trying to be supportive and give me a shoulder to whine on. If my mom ever hears about this, she'll *kill* me. "I should never have done that. I am *so* sorry. I respect your right to consent and—"

"No, wait." He holds up both hands and takes a breath. "I think we're on the same page. It was a great kiss, but you're my client and we're friends..." He hesitates on that word, so I nod emphatically. He's my friend. Me paying him for a service doesn't change that, and when I no longer need his professional help, we'll still be friends. If he wants to. "...yeah, so it was a mistake. But we can put it behind us. Blame the vodka?" he asks hopefully.

I hesitate, and his face falls.

"If you want to end—"

"No! No, no, no," I rush out. "No ending. Just... if you want to blame the vodka and pretend this never happened, I'm good with that. Totally good. Your call. And again, I'm so sorry for just kissing you randomly without even a sign that you'd welcome it. That's not me, and I have no excuse. But, uh... it was a great kiss. And you said you wanted more kisses in your life. So, you know..." I shrug, kind of not believing I'm really saying this. "I could give you kisses."

His jaw drops. "What?" he rasps.

"You know. You want kisses. I liked kissing you. We're friends, right? I could be your kiss supplier." I stop and think about it. "Only not as weird as that sounds. And since we'd both go into this knowing we're not dating, there's no chance of a misunderstanding, right? It would just be kisses between friends."

He starts to laugh, and it has an edge of hysteria that makes me think I might have pushed him over the edge. I'm not sure why, though. It's a perfectly reasonable plan.

It must sink in for him that I'm serious, because he stops laughing suddenly and stares at me. "You're not joking?"

I shake my head. "Nope. The more I think about it, the more I like the idea. I don't want to date anyone right now, with this whole stupid mess, but that doesn't mean I don't want to make out. It's fun, you know? And you want kisses that your hookups aren't willing to give you. Why shouldn't we help each other out?"

He pinches the bridge of his nose. "Just to be clear, are we talking about only kissing?"

My cock, already vaguely interested after that kiss, stirs. He's definitely on board with anything Lee might want to do. "Whatever you want. Not gonna lie, I'd be up for the whole fuck buddy experience, but if you prefer to keep it to kisses only, I'm cool with that. I like the occasional cuddle too." It's the one thing I really miss when I'm not in a relationship. Kissing and cuddling with hookups can be complicated, and yeah, sometimes they're just not interested. But I like cuddles and slow, sexy kisses.

Lee's face is pink now, and he's chewing on his lip, and I can't help wondering how he looks when he comes. I didn't anticipate our friendship heading in this direction, but I'm into it.

If he is, that is. I better not get too excited, because a "no" from him would end it all.

"I think the vodka's gone to your head," he says finally. "We'll just pretend this never happened."

Disappointment stabs me in the chest. "We can totally do that," I agree, trying to sound like I don't want the complete opposite. "Uh, just so you know, I don't think this is the vodka talking. If you don't want to do it, no problem, we'll never talk about it again. But if you're just worried that I'm not thinking clearly, we can wait until tomorrow and see how we both feel then."

He says nothing, his eyes flicking around the room. That's a good sign, and I seize on it.

"Is it just that you think I'm drunk, or are you worried how this will affect our friendship?"

"That's part of it," he admits. "Plus, you're currently paying me, which is a bit weird."

"Pffft." I like the way that sound feels in my mouth, so I do it again. Maybe I am just a tiny bit tipsy. "I'm not paying you for *that*. And technically, I've already paid you, so there's no pressure for you to do anything that makes you uncomfortable. If I cross a line, you can walk away. But"—I hold up my hands—"now isn't the time to talk about this. Let's wait until tomorrow. We can both think it over and, I dunno, come up with stuff we need to discuss beforehand." Look at me, being all mature and shit. Although the only stuff I think we need to discuss is his favorite brand of lube. Unless he just wants to kiss, in which case, do those kisses have to be confined to mouths only?

He nods. "Yeah, okay, Let's leave it for now." There's something in his tone that says he thinks I'll forget all about this—or "forget." But I don't call him on it. I've tested enough boundaries tonight, and tomorrow is soon enough to show him how wrong he is. "Hey, I nearly forgot—the book I ordered for you came."

I blink like an idiot. "You ordered me a book?"

Getting off the bed and going to his desk, he says, "Yeah, remember you asked me to recommend one for you? Well, it arrived today, thanks to the power of Prime two-day shipping."

"I didn't mean for you to buy it for me," I protest as he turns back with a cardboard Amazon envelope in his hand. "How come you get to buy me things but I'm not allowed to buy you clothes?"

"Because this cost me fifteen bucks. You have my permission to buy me clothes to the grand total of fifteen dollars," he says dryly, like he thinks I can't do it. Sure, it's not my preferred budget range, but I could probably shop for under fifteen dollars. I bet I can put together a whole outfit.

Wait... "Does that include tax?"

He rolls his eyes and pushes the envelope into my hands as he climbs back on the bed. "Yes."

Okay, that's harder, but I can still do it. I set my jaw, ripping into the mailer. "Our shopping trip is going to be epic."

"That's not the word I would use," he mutters, but I'm barely listening. The book in my hands has all my attention, what with the broody-looking horned guy on the cover.

"*Demons Do It Better*," I read, a grin spreading across my face. "Are you sure this isn't porn?"

"It's not porn. I thought you might like this because it's got some low-key paranormal stuff, but it's also funny and has a save-the-world plot." His voice is casual, but trying-too-hard casual, so I turn the book over and skim the description. It doesn't sound too bad.

"And there's sex in it?" I double-check, because I trust him to pick something I'll like, but mostly I'm here for the sex.

He smacks my arm. "There's sex in it. But it's fine if you don't like it. I won't be offended or anything."

I wave my new book at him. "I'm pretty sure I'll like it. You like it, and I like you, so therefore I'll like it."

Laughing, he takes the book away from me and puts it with the vodka bottle. "That's not how it works." His hand hovers near the bottle. "Did you want more?"

I shake my head vehemently. "Nope." I'm going to need a clear head and no headache tomorrow to convince him we should be... whatever we decide we want to be.

"Okay." He hesitates. "Wanna watch a movie?"

I grab his pillow and make myself comfortable. "Sounds good to me."

CHAPTER TEN

LIAM

THIS MIGHT JUST BE THE WORST FRIDAY MORNING OF MY entire life, and I can only blame it on myself. And maybe a little bit on Charlie's "let's be kissing buddies or more" idea.

I definitely blame it on the text he sent me at seven asking if we could have lunch together. What does that mean? Has he come to his senses and wants to make it clear to me that there will be no more kissing? Or does he just not want to eat lunch alone? Maybe he has no memory of our conversation last night at all.

Or maybe he remembers everything and still wants to do it.

I don't know which scenario freaks me the most. Because yeah, kissing and sex with Charlie would be great. More than. That kiss was phenomenal, and neither of us was bringing our A game. Plus I really do miss kissing, and it would be nice to have a regular hookup who didn't make me jump through hoops and wasn't a dick to me. But on the other hand, Charlie's a client, he's a friend—though a new one— and, if I'm being completely honest, he's someone I could fall for. A lot. Easily. I might already be teetering on the precipice. So introducing sex and kisses and cuddles to that scenario is just dangerous.

Too bad I really want to.

Of course, he might not want to. This is how I've spent the whole morning, cycling through what I want, whether I should want it, and then what he *might* want. I'm going to have an ulcer before lunch at this rate... lunch that I'm not having with Charlie, since I don't get a break on Friday until midafternoon. Instead, I eat a power bar or whatever while I'm walking between classes. He didn't reply after I told him that, so that's just one more thing to add to my list of shit to stress over.

Around me, people start packing up their things, and I realize class is over and I haven't absorbed any of it. I can't even say what was discussed. Fuck. I've never let a guy impact my coursework before, not even in middle school when I had my first ever crush on Theo Hurst and spent way too much time wondering if kissing felt as wonderful as it looked on TV.

I dig in my backpack for my sad little lunch as I let the crowd sweep me out of the building. My next class is a web design elective I took for funsies and because I thought it would be useful to be able to build my own site for Mr. Romance instead of sticking with the template I use now. And it has been fun, but I hate that it's not located conveniently in the same building as all my physics classes.

"Yo! Lee!" The shout cuts through my thoughts, and I look up to see Charlie weaving through the crowd toward me, a widely grinning Jake at his side.

Why is Jake grinning? Did Charlie tell him about the

maybe-sex-buddy thing? Oh my god, has it turned into a joke? Is Jake amused that I could ever believe Charlie might want me that way?

I grind my molars and tell myself to stay calm. I don't know for sure that's what happened. And even if it is, at least I know for sure they're not here to mock me about it. Charlie would never do that.

Anyway, he should be so lucky as to be sex-buddies with me. I read a lot and I *know* things. I've been complimented many times on my bedroom skills, thank you very much.

I wait for them to reach me. "Hey, what's up? I have class." Probably not the most gracious opener.

"I know," Charlie assures me. "I brought you lunch, since you don't have time to stop." He thrusts a wrapped sandwich at me with one hand and a takeout coffee with the other. I can smell the hazelnut syrup from here, so either he remembered my order from last week or he's a really good guesser.

"Charlie—"

"I decided to use my fifteen-dollar shopping allocation to feed you," he interrupts. "Jake's my witness that I didn't spend more than that." He jerks his head toward Jake, who puts a hand over his heart.

"It was fourteen fifty-seven, including tax," he informs me. "I paid for the tip, just in case that would have broken the rules."

I can't stop the laugh from erupting. "Okay, fine. Thank you." I take his offerings, then hand the coffee back so I can unwrap the sandwich enough to eat. "I gotta go, but I really appreciate this."

"Text me when you're done with class, because we gotta talk," Charlie says solemnly. He shoots a sideways glance at

Jake, sees he's busy watching a group of girls, then leans in and adds, "I'm completely sober and ready to continue our conversation from last night."

Oh. My. God.

Well. At least now I know where he stands?

I muster a weak smile. "Sure. Later. We'll talk." I just have to work out what I'm going to say.

Charlie steps back, and I force my feet to move, walking away from him... away from temptation. In an attempt to distract myself, I take a huge bite from my overpriced sandwich.

It's fucking amazing.

Once more, I pace the three steps that will get me across my dorm room, turn, and pace back again. Pacing might help some people to relieve stress, but they probably had more room to do it in.

Finally, I suck up my courage and pick up my phone.

Liam: Hey, you wanted to talk?

Charlie: Yep! You done with classes? Can I come over?

I look around the room. It seems smaller all of a sudden, and I know Charlie's presence isn't going to change that. Plus, the beds are really prominent. Which could be really good if we...

Liam: Sure

As soon as the message sends, I wish I could take it back. Because I'm still not convinced this is a good idea. Having sex with a client is something only a sex worker should do. It's definitely not going to help my professional reputation. Who's going to want to buy date planning from a guy who sleeps with his clients? "Oh honey, I really want a romantic date for my birthday. Go have sex with Liam and arrange it, would you?" said no one ever.

I almost send a follow-up suggesting we meet somewhere else, but instead, I put my phone down and make myself do some Mr. Romance work. With spring break coming up in a month, I've started getting requests for short romantic trip ideas.

The knock at the door comes so much sooner than I'm prepared for. I take a deep breath and call, "It's open," spinning my desk chair to face the door. This is it. I'm still not entirely sure what I'm going to do, but I'll soon find out.

Who am I fucking kidding? If he wants to fuck, I'm going to be all over that.

Charlie comes into the room with his usual exuberance toned down a few degrees, and the nerves in my gut ramp up. At lunchtime, it was pretty obvious what he wanted, but maybe I misread him? Or he's changed his mind.

"Hey—"

"I want to give you kisses," he blurts, then shakes his head. "I mean, I want to kiss you. And more. I'm sober, and I've been thinking about this all day, and I definitely want it. If you do. It's fine if you don't, though. We'll still be friends. But if you do, we'll also still be friends. And no matter what, this has nothing to do with the whole professional thing. So... yeah. Can I kiss you?"

The wave of affection that rushes through me is worrying. I already know I have more feelings for Charlie than I really should. Sex is going to complicate that, and the kisses and cuddles he's promising will just make things even worse. But... he's looking at me so hopefully. And it's college, right? Everyone gets their heart broken in college. It'll be a growth experience for me.

"Yes," I blurt.

His face lights up, but he doesn't move. "Yes?" he confirms. "I can kiss you? You want to make this a one-stop friendship?"

A one-stop... I laugh. How is he this adorable?

"Come here and kiss me, you idiot." I stand up as he bounds across the small space, and in the next moment I'm leaning up to take his mouth with mine. Part of me has been worrying that the vodka was responsible for how good our kiss felt last night—even though I didn't drink much—but that's definitely not the case. The second our lips meet, the world falls away.

His body presses along the length of mine, warm and hard and bigger than me, the way I like it. His lips are soft, his tongue sliding along mine as he changes angles slightly. It's hot and wet and all-encompassing.

It's that moment, the precursor to the storm, where I feel desired and needed and know the person I'm with wants me desperately but also cares about what I want. It's the movie moment, where the sexual tension and emotional longing leap off the screen.

It's a feeling I've never truly had before, and I could weep to know that Charlie, who doesn't want a relationship, is the one who's giving it to me.

He breaks the kiss, pulling back and searching my expression. "Okay?"

My smile comes naturally in the face of his concern. "Yeah."

"It just seemed like you..." He shakes his head. "Never mind. So... we're doing this?"

I swallow hard. If I'm going to back out, do the sensible thing, now's my chance. "We're doing it." Whoops. Guess I'm not backing out. "Uh, but we don't make this complicated, right? We're friends who fuck."

"And kiss and cuddle," he reminds me. "I want affection as well as orgasms."

Sounds good to me. I nod. "We're doing it, then."

Our lips meet again, and this time there's a whole lot more intent there. This kiss isn't tentative. It isn't sweet. It's hot and carnal, and I can't wait to get in his—

I break away. "Wait... uh, so... I prefer not to bottom." We probably should have addressed this before deciding sex was going to happen.

"Great!" He reaches for me again, but I hold up a hand.

"No, I mean, I like to top. Exclusively. So... how do you feel about that?" You'd think in this day and age, people wouldn't make stupid, stereotypical assumptions based on my height and the fact I like romance, but my experience is that people *are* stupid.

Charlie frowns, and my heart sinks. His hesitation lasts a beat too long as he clearly tries to choose the right words. "I feel really horny," he says finally. "I'm vers. Well, I've never bottomed before, but I want to. Guys just never wanted that from me." He gives me pleading eyes. "Take my ass cherry?"

Despite the distinctly unsexy phrasing, my dick throbs in my pants. It really likes the idea of fucking Charlie. My brain, on the other hand, is racing a mile a minute.

"You've never—"

"Nope. Not with a person, anyway. I have some great toys. That's how I know I love bottoming." His gaze drops to my lap, where there's no hiding how into this conversation I am. "So you'll fuck me, right? But face-to-face. I want to see your body and think of the bad things I can do with it."

Heat rises in my face, but I'm flattered, not embarrassed. And definitely turned on. I want to hear all about those bad things... later. In the meantime, why are we sitting here, fully dressed?

"I'll fuck you," I say, as though it's not what I'm dying to do. "If you're sure."

Charlie scrambles up and yanks his shirt over his head. Guess that's all the answer I need.

I get up too, but before I start stripping, I grab my lube and find a condom. It's kinda lucky I've even got any, considering the dry streak I've been on. When I turn around, I'm greeted by the sight of Charlie's naked body, and oh holy fuck, I must have been a very good boy in a past life. He's not as muscular as me, but his long body is toned and sexy as fuck, with a smattering of dark hair in all the right places and a thicker bush above the long, flushed cock that's pointing at me.

"On the bed," I croak, and he gives himself a pump and obeys. I've never taken my clothes off so fast in my life.

He pulls me down onto the mattress in a tangle of limbs,

finding my mouth with unerring accuracy, and it's such a Charlie thing to do, making sure I get my kisses even when we're both naked and hard and leaking precum, that my heart fills to bursting. I roll him under me and settle between his legs, then reluctantly pull away from his mouth and set to exploring his body.

As my lips skim the side of his neck, his collarbone, and pause to tease his nipples, his hands are sliding up and down my limbs, along my back, and settling on my ass.

"Your body is *insane*," he murmurs, breath hitching as I bite gently, and to give him a bit of a thrill, I flex. His chuckle turns to a moan. "I know you're trying to be funny, but all I can imagine is how your muscles are going to look while you're driving into me."

"God, Charlie, you can't say that." My already hard-as-nails cock pulses impatiently against his thigh, and he shifts slightly so it's rubbing against his.

"They're all gonna ripple," he whispers, "every time you thrust. All tense and tight, and I'm gonna feel it so hard. Then every time I see your muscles after, I'll remember how they looked when you pounded me." He pumps his hips, our dicks dragging along each other, and I jerk back... but not far enough to lose contact.

"Do you not want foreplay?" I demand. It's his first time bottoming. Shouldn't I make it special?

"Just looking at you is all the foreplay I need."

It's such a hokey line, but he says it seriously, his face flushed with arousal, lips wet from kissing me, his big brown eyes warm and hazy with lust, and nobody's ever given me a memory like that before.

"I'm gonna do you so hard," I breathe, reaching for the

condom. He grabs the lube, and even though I want to protest and take care of him, I let him prep himself. This time.

He's done really quickly, though. "Are you sure that's enough? I don't want to hurt you."

"I want to feel it," he murmurs, lying back and stretching out with a wicked little smile. The planes of his body call to me, and I lightly smooth my hands over his torso, loving the way he shivers in response.

"Believe me, you'll feel it. But—"

"Lee, I promise I'll stop you if it hurts. But don't make me wait more."

I can't resist that. "Pull your legs up."

Grinning, he obeys, exposing his slick pink hole to my gaze. I swallow and wonder how he feels about rimming.

"Leeeeeee," he whines.

Not now. He doesn't want to wait.

I line my cock up and slowly push forward. His body resists at first, and I look at his face, trying to judge if it's too much. He's got an expression of extreme concentration, and affection floods me.

Then the ring of muscle gives, and I'm in. An explosive breath escapes him.

"Okay?" I ask, trying not to grit my teeth against the desire to plunge in. The hot clasp of his ass around my cockhead is... indescribable.

"Yessssss," he hisses. "More."

I ease a little deeper, muscles trembling with restraint at the sight of his hole sucking me in. "You're so fucking hot," I manage. "Wish you could see this."

He moves, propping himself up on his elbows, and I groan as his muscles tighten around me in response. I'm only halfway in, and I don't know how long I'm going to last. "Ohhhhhhh that is so..." He trails off. "I want a picture. That's better than any porn."

He... what?

"Move, Lee. I want to see—" I thrust home, and he yelps and falls back. "Again. More. We'll film it another time."

"Are you o—"

"Do me hard, Lee!"

Ignoring the reaction of my dick to those words, I ease slowly back, wanting to be sure he's really okay, but Charlie's not having it. He raises his torso from the mattress and reaches forward, grabbing my hips to push me back, then yank me forward. "Harder!"

I pump into him, and when he collapses against my pillow and breathes, "Yessss," I pick up the pace even more, bracing myself on my knees and forearms and going to town on his ass.

"Jesus, this is *great*," Charlie gasps. "I definitely like bottoming. I—"

I change my angle slightly, trying to brush against his prostate, and from the sound he makes, he likes that too.

"Yes, Lee, again! Harder!"

Someone pounds on the wall beside the bed and yells, "At least *try* to be quiet!"

I'll die of embarrassment later. Right now, all I care about is how fucking amazing Charlie's body feels around me. I'm not going to last much longer.

Shifting my weight to one arm, I reach between us and grab his dick. The head is slick with precum, and from the way he moans when my hand closes around it, this won't take much. I jerk him in time with my thrusts, and he gazes up at me hazily.

"Lee... yes... unnnnghh!"

As his cum sprays between us, I give myself permission to let go, and two thrusts later I stutter to a stop, filling the condom deep inside him.

Collapsing onto his chest, I try to breathe again, surrounded by the scent and warmth of Charlie.

I leave Charlie snoring softly and go back to working at my desk. I'll wake him soon and suggest we get something to eat, but for now, he can rest. I kind of like the domesticity of him sleeping in my bed while I'm doing other stuff. Which is totally a couple-y thing, so no, it's not true. I'm just being considerate. It's rude to wake someone who's sleeping. Especially after they've just given you the best orgasm of your life. That's my story, and I'm sticking to it.

I get through all the Mr. Romance inquiries and have started on an assignment before Charlie stirs. The snoring fades out, he makes a little snuffling noise, and then his hand kind of pats across the mattress. I watch, amused, as he frowns before blinking his pretty brown eyes open and lifting his head to look around.

"There you are," he grumbles, his voice husky from his nap. "Why aren't you here? And why are you wearing clothes?"

I glance down at the briefs I pulled on. "I don't think these really count as clothes," I counter, getting up and going back to join him on the bed. He pulls me close with a contented murmur, kissing my shoulder, then draws back to study my briefs.

"Yeah, you're right. 'Clothes' is the wrong word. Maybe 'rag'?" he muses, and I pinch him.

"Fuck you, *not* a rag. They're only a couple months old." I got a new ten-pack for Christmas.

"That's not why they're a rag. They don't make the most of what you've got to offer." The way his eyes sweep over me has my cock plumping up again. "Your package deserves more," he says earnestly, and I crack up. It's hard to believe I can feel this comfortable and be laughing so hard while semi-aroused, but I am. And I love it.

"My package will just have to cope with what it's got," I advise. "C'mon, get up and let's go get dinner."

"Can we come back here after and watch a movie and eat junk food off each other?"

I freeze halfway to my feet. "Uh... what kind of junk food?"

He shrugs, scrambling out of the bed and reaching for his clothes. "Not sure. Depends what the dining hall has for dessert. Or maybe we should stop at the convenience store or a vending machine." He lightly slaps my behind. "We'll work it out, but you gotta get moving. I'm starved."

The first test to my sanity comes when we get to the dining hall and run into Matt and Ian. Literally run into them, because Ian's talking on the phone and stops suddenly in the doorway.

"Can't you put him on a leash?" I ask Matt, rubbing my nose where it collided with the back of Ian's hard skull.

Ian flips me the bird and continues arguing with whoever he's talking to as we enter the dining hall. Matt says nothing, squinting at me instead.

"You okay?" I ask him. "Did you hit your head on something?"

He shakes his head slowly, still staring.

"Ooh, mac and cheese," Charlie says.

"No!" we snap, even Ian. Charlie blinks.

"Okay. Uh, why do we hate the staple of American families?"

"We don't. But the dining hall interpretation tastes like vomit," Matt warns.

"After it lay in the sun for a few days and a cat shit in it," I add.

Charlie gags. "Thanks for that description. Remind me again why we didn't go somewhere else?"

"Because I'm a cheapskate, and I won't let you pay for my food. Try the chicken schnitzel. That's usually okay." It's what I'm going to get for myself, along with the baked potato. I burned a lot of calories today.

I smirk at the memory.

"Oh my god, you had *sex*!" Matt shouts.

Heads turn.

My face catches fire.

"Would you shut up?" I hiss, just as Charlie says,

"Yep, we did. Hey, that eggplant parma looks half decent."

"Is that a code word?" Matt asks. "Did you eggplant his parma?"

Kill. Me. Now.

Ian ends his call and says, "Dude, gross. I thought we'd decided Liam was the one who liked to do the eggplanting." He frowns. "That sounds wrong. Like you're planting eggs or something. I just meant that you give off a total toppy vibe."

Why aren't I dead yet? Why hasn't the floor opened up to swallow me whole, or lightning incinerated me?

"He is," Charlie informs them happily. "He eggplanted my parma real good."

That's why. Clearly the universe isn't done humiliating me.

Trying to pretend they don't exist, I step up to the counter and ask the server for the chicken and a baked potato. He passes me a plate, then winks and says, "Good for you. It's always the short guys you gotta watch out for."

"Thanks," I say. I meant for the food, but it unfortunately sounds like I'm thanking him for the compliment about my sexual prowess.

I flee to the salad bar.

By the time I join my so-called friends at a table, the heat has mostly receded from my cheeks. At least, they no longer feel hot enough to fry eggs on.

"Sit next to me," Charlie says, patting the chair beside him. I slide into it without a word, feeling my friends' eyes boring into me, and start eating. Maybe if I don't look up or participate in the conversation, they'll forget I'm here.

"Are we going to talk about this?" Ian asks.

"Talk about what?" Charlie sounds so completely curious that I slide a glance his way. He's got to be faking it, right?

Not according to the expression on his face. I already know he's not that good an actor.

"About you and Liam hooking up," Matt explains. "We want details."

I shovel in a forkful of bacon-and-cheese-smothered potato.

"Oh. No, of course we're not giving you details," Charlie declares. "That's gross. I thought you two were better than that."

Trying to hold in my laugh, I nearly choke on potato. It ends up as an awkward cough, but fortunately I keep my food in my mouth. Because we've already attracted enough attention tonight without me spraying bits of half-chewed potato across the table.

"Say what?" Matt asks.

"You should have more respect for your sexual partners than to gossip about private details with your friends." Charlie's lecturing tone is weirdly hot. "Consent applies to more than just the sex act itself, you know. Everyone has a right to privacy."

The sight of Matt and Ian with their jaws dropped is the best thing I've seen all month—well, other than Charlie's face when he came.

I swallow my food and say, "Thank you, Charlie, for being a decent human being. Although I'm pissed about the eggplant parma comment."

He looks genuinely surprised, then remorseful. "I'm sorry. I thought it was funny."

Sighing, because it *was* funny, even if it made me want to die, I concede, "I probably would have laughed more if it wasn't *my* eggplant being discussed."

"Understood." He nods. "But if it comes up again, I don't

have any issue with you discussing my parma." Looking down at his plate, he adds, "Though not while I'm eating it, please."

"That sounded too weird."

"Way too weird," he agrees.

"This whole conversation is weird," Matt interrupts. "Could we get back to the fact that you two fucked and how weird *that* is?"

"No," I say, then when he and Ian both give me the same "are you shitting me" look, I roll my eyes and add, "It's not weird. We've decided to have a one-stop friendship." I shamelessly borrow Charlie's expression.

Ian nods slowly. "Just a couple of bros helping each other out?"

I shrug. "Something like that."

They exchange glances, and I know that as soon as they manage to corner me alone, I'm going to get a lecture about not getting my heart broken. *You're a romantic, Liam, this won't end well for you,* blah blah blah. Charlie, thankfully, is oblivious to the undercurrent, happily working his way through his eggplant parma—which I may never be able to eat again.

"How's it work, exactly?" Matt demands. "You hang out, get each other off, then go home and forget about it?"

"We kiss and cuddle too," Charlie interjects. "It's full-service."

Matt and Ian both slowly turn to look at me.

"I can't believe you don't know how friends with benefits works," I say in a desperate attempt to change the subject, my voice higher pitched than usual.

Matt shrugs. "I get the theory, but I've never practiced it.

Too much chance of *complications*. People might get *feelings*."

"Stick to your one-nighters, then," I advise, pretending not to notice his heavy-handed hints. "So, Ian, who were you talking to before?"

Ian pauses just long enough to give me a glare that says he knows what I'm doing and I'll pay for it later, then says, "My brother. Well, both our brothers. They want to see us over spring break."

"That's nice." I know they're close to their brothers, who, if I understand right, both moved to live in rural Illinois a few years back.

"Is it, though?" Matt mutters darkly.

Charlie and I exchange a bewildered look. "It's not?" he ventures. "Do you not get on with your brothers or something?"

"We do, but they want to go to Joy Universe. Connor's boyfriend has connections there and can get us accommodation at a super bargain price, but he can't take off from work over the summer, so it has to be spring break." Ian rolls his eyes.

"Do you not like his boyfriend?" Charlie asks.

"Kieran? Nah, he's great. But who wants to go to a theme park in Georgia for spring break? I mean, Disney's driving distance from here, but nooooo, they want us to fly across the freaking country."

"Ian gets airsick," Matt explains. "Really bad. Like, last time we flew together I came very close to murdering him just so he'd shut the fuck up about his misery and I wouldn't have to smell vomit anymore. The time before that, he vomited all over me. Twice."

"You're the loser who didn't move out of the way," Ian mutters.

I'm enjoying this way more than I should be. "There's nothing you can take for it?"

They both shake their heads. "The only thing that's been effective is unconsciousness, but unfortunately, we've yet to find a drug he can take that will kick in before takeoff, when the hurling starts, but still leave him able to board the plane. Because we tried once to carry him on unconscious, and the flight attendants freaked out."

Charlie frowns in confusion. "Why'd they freak out?"

"Because they thought Ian was being kidnapped," I explain.

The confusion changes to skepticism. "No offense, but why would anyone want to kidnap Ian?"

"That's what I said!" Matt exclaims while I laugh.

"Thanks, dude." Ian shakes his head at Charlie. "After I helped you out and everything."

"It's a serious question," Charlie protests. "You're not famous, not super rich... so why would anyone bother?" He studies Ian doubtfully, and I almost choke on my laughter.

"Okay, the conversation is getting weird again. Does anyone want dessert?" Ian stands and waits for us to reply.

My laughter dies as I remember Charlie's request for us to eat dessert off each other. "Uh, see what they have. But I might take mine to go." I'm aiming for casual, but it's a dismal failure when my voice cracks.

Ian glances from me to Charlie, who's grinning wide, and shakes his head. "I don't want to know."

CHAPTER ELEVEN

CHARLIE

FULL-SERVICE FRIENDSHIPS ARE THE BOMB. SERIOUSLY, I don't know why I've never done this before. I get all the sex and affection I want, without the awkward dating politics. Instead, I'm just hanging with one of my bros. If I'd known how awesome it was, I'd have hooked up with a friend years ago.

Although... maybe not. I can't see myself having sex with any of my other friends. Sure, they're doable, but the thought of actually doing them is kinda awks. Not fun and natural like it is with Lee.

It's only been ten days since we started having sex, and no lie, it's been the best week since I started college, top five of my life. Everything is going better for me now. Is regular sex like vitamins? Does it improve your overall wellness? Someone should do some research into that.

"Hey, Charlie, happy birthday!"

"Thanks, man!" I call to a guy I had two classes with last year. "You coming to the bar later?"

He grins. "You bet."

"See you there." I wave and keep on toward Lee's dorm. I've been getting that all day, and even though I'm not sure how all these people know it's my birthday, it doesn't suck. The best part about birthdays is having people make you feel special all day. And since it's my twenty-first, I deserve to feel super special.

I'm keeping it low-key, though. No huge party or anything. I'm just going to hang out at Shenanigans with my besties, and some others might drop in over the course of the night. Classes tomorrow, so nobody wants a blowout.

But first, I'm going to hang out with Lee. And yes, that's a euphemism. He promised me a birthday bang.

It's a little earlier than he asked me to come by, but if he's busy, I can just hang out. He's getting used to doing work and shit while I lie on his bed and scroll through my socials. Even when we're focused on different things, he's good company.

I knock twice on his door, and he calls for me to come in. To my surprise, instead of being at his desk, he's curled up on the bed with his laptop.

"Whatcha doing?"

He puts the device aside and gets up. "Happy Birthday." I get a big, hot, sloppy kiss, the kind that makes me happy and horny.

"You already said that," I murmur. I got a sexy video call from him this morning, and we met up for coffee between classes.

"It's worth repeating. Today is all about you." He kisses me again, and my cock perks right up. Then he pulls away. "Let me just clear off the bed."

"I'll do it!" I grab his laptop, glance at the screen, then

stop. "You're watching a movie?" I study the frozen scene. "Isn't this that queer rom-com that came out last summer?"

"Yeah. *Gay-timatum*." His cheeks go pink, and it makes me smile.

"Let's finish watching it." Still holding the computer, I climb onto the bed and make myself comfortable.

"No, it's fine. I've seen it before." He's standing awkwardly, and I pat the mattress beside me.

"I haven't seen it, though. Are you far in?" I meant to see it when it came out, because I strongly believe that we need more queer rep in entertainment and this movie was a big studio effort by Joy Inc. But I was sick the week it released, and then one thing after another came up, and I never ended up going.

"About fifteen minutes." He gets on the bed and settles in beside me. "Are you sure you want to watch this?"

Instead of sex, he means. Which... I would rather have sex, but I can tell he likes this movie, and friendship is a two-way street. We can have sex later.

"Yep. If it's only fifteen minutes, it's not a big deal to restart it. I want to see the beginning." I click to go back.

"Charlie—"

"Shh. Movie."

His mouth snaps shut with a click, and I pretend to be so absorbed by the opening credits that I don't notice. I might miss stuff sometimes, but I'm not completely clueless. A movie he's seen before that's supposed to be super romantic and fun with gay characters, on a Tuesday evening... this is a movie he really likes, maybe even loves. So we're watching it.

It takes only a few minutes before he's fully absorbed in

what's happening on the screen. I mentally pat myself on the back, then let myself enjoy the movie.

We barely move for the next ninety minutes, and it's getting close to the end when something clicks in my brain. "Oh my god, this is where that sound on TikTok came from!" I hit pause so we don't miss anything, then turn to Lee. "Right? Perry's going to give Sawyer this big I-love-you speech and then sing, right?"

Lee's lips quirk. "I could tell you, but that would be a spoiler."

My elbow connects with his ribs, and he yelps. "I don't think it's a spoiler when I've heard the sound used fifty billion times already." I gesture to the screen. "Plus, they're at a karaoke restaurant, and there's only ten minutes left in the movie. Singing I-love-yous are almost guaranteed."

He laughs. "He doesn't actually sing the 'I love you,' but yeah. This is where the TikTok sound came from."

I un-pause the movie but watch his face instead of the screen. The way he's smiling, the softness in his expression... he loves this. I'm so glad I insisted we watch it.

His gaze flicks to me. "What?"

"Nothing." I turn my attention back to the big scene.

When the credits roll, Lee closes the laptop, puts it on his desk, and straddles my lap. "Thank you."

I fill my palms with his ass and sigh happily. "For what? I liked it."

"Yeah, but that's not why we watched it." He leans in to kiss me. "So, thanks."

"Well, you know..." I shrug, trying to be nonchalant. "It seemed like you wanted to watch it."

"I did. It's my favorite movie, and I've seen it about fifteen times already."

Fifteen? It hasn't even been out for a year. "Then I'm really glad we watched it."

The smile he gives me is soft and makes me feel all warm. "You deserve so much sex." He glances at his smartwatch. "We don't have time to fuck now, but I'm going to make you come your brains out before we go."

"Oh yeah?" Not gonna pretend I don't like that idea.

He doesn't answer, just leans in and kisses me, a wet, openmouthed, NSFW kind of kiss that sends my dick from mildly interested to statue-stiff in mere seconds. Lee breaks the kiss, and when I whine and try to pull him back, he tsks at me. "We're on a tight timeline. You gotta sit back and just take it." His hand drops to rest on my crotch, and I swallow hard.

"Way to twist my arm," I croak.

He grins and opens the fly of my jeans. "Lift your hips."

Together, we wriggle my jeans and briefs down to my thighs, which leaves my cock and balls exposed but my legs trapped together. It's weird and totally hot. Even hotter when Lee leans over and licks the head of my dick, then blows cool air across it.

My cock throbs, and I shiver. "Lee..."

"Sshh, I'm busy," he says, not looking up. He closes his hand firmly around my shaft, leaving the swollen red head peeking out the top, then wraps his soft lips around it and *sucks*.

I'm pretty sure I make a noise, but I'm too busy desperately trying to keep my eyes open so I can watch to be certain.

Lee sets a fast pace, his hand twisting repeatedly in a

strong milking motion while he alternates sucking and tonguing my slit, and the stimulation is amaaaaazing. I let my head fall back and feel the tension build, my balls tightening more and more with each passing second—

He stops.

His hand disappears.

I jerk my head up in bewilderment to find him watching me. His lips are puffy and wet, and all I can think is how they should still be on me. "What—"

"I need your full attention," he declares. "We're running out of time."

"I'm not going to come if you stop," I point out, pouting.

He grins, then bends his head again and this time takes me deep, all the way to the back of his throat, and oh my god, I think I might die.

The rhythm he sets now is slower, more torturous. He keeps a tight seal around my cock with his goddamn blowjob lips, like a vacuum as he pulls almost all the way off, then slides back, enveloping me in the hot, wet heaven of his mouth. He can't get quite to the base, but he's damn close, and I stare down at his flushed face stuffed full of my dick, lower lashes damp where his eyes are watering, and the breath stutters in my chest. Without thinking, I lift my hand and tangle it in his hair, wanting that extra layer of connection.

He withdraws again, making eye contact as the cool air whispers around my wet cock. This time he pulls all the way off, licking his lips and whispering, "Happy Birthday, Charlie," before he sucks me back inside, his tongue pressing along the vein that runs down the underside. My sac is so tight, it almost hurts, but I don't want this to end, don't—

Fuck... "Coming," I gasp in warning, but he doesn't pull away, just eases back a tiny bit and continues to suck, and I take that image with me into the dizzying burst of my orgasm.

The next time I blink, every muscle in my body is relaxed, including the one Lee's easing out of his mouth. He glances up at me and smiles, a little uncertainly. Fuck that. Nobody gets to make him feel insecure, not even him. I tighten the hand that's still in his hair and tug him toward me.

"C'mere," I mutter. It comes out hoarse.

He rises to meet me, and I kiss him, wrapping my other arm around him and pulling him close.

Happy Birthday to me.

Liam

"Twenty-one shots for the birthday boyyyyyy!" Charlie's friend Carson hollers as he sets a tray down on the table a bunch of us are sitting at. Charlie blinks at it blearily. He's already had a few shots—quite a few. More than he'd planned —so his judgement isn't at peak performance, but I can still see him calculating that twenty-one more are a bad idea.

"Thanks, Car!" he shouts, then begins passing the shots around the table. Carson laughs at him and takes one in each hand.

I grab one for myself and one for Lila, who I met a couple weeks back, and we clink glasses to the birthday boy, who's already downed his shot and is now climbing shakily onto his chair.

"Uh-oh," Lila says, but she's grinning.

"People! People. This is an important day. A *great* day. The day I no longer have to choose between drinking soda or hoping the bartender isn't going to look too closely at my shitty fake ID."

There's a round of cheers and laughter.

"But on this day twenty-one years ago, a woman suffered. She suffered *greatly*, for twenty-five whole hours, with no epidural because she let her idiot sister-in-law convince her it was better that way, and by the time she wised up, it was too late."

"He's going to regret this," Lila predicts, laughing.

"Only if his mom hears about it. Which... is anyone filming?" I glance around the table and see that several of Charlie's besties are capturing the moment. Good. That means I can just sit back and enjoy it.

"That woman was my mom," he announces gravely, as if none of us have guessed. "And her suffering that day was to bring me into the world."

I reach for another shot. I think I'm going to need to be drunk to deal with him later.

"In honor of my mom and what she went through twenty-one years ago, I'm gonna sing a song from the album she was listening to when she pushed me out."

The shot goes down the wrong way, and I cough and sputter like a moron.

"Lee? Is Lee okay?" Charlie tries to take a step toward me, and it's only the quick thinking of two of his more sober friends grabbing him that keeps him from stepping right off the chair. "Whoops! That could have been bad. Lee, you're not dying, are you?"

"Not dying," I rasp out, waving for him to continue as Lila thumps me on the back. "What's the song?"

Charlie holds up his hands, palms out, fingers splayed, and announces, "I present to you the music of the incomparable Alanis Morissette."

"Oh my god, this is going to be amazing," Lila breathes. We both lean forward.

He takes a deep breath and launches into a very off-key rendition of "You Learn," a song my own mother loves and which I therefore know all the lyrics to. Charlie does not. Or maybe he's just too drunk to remember them. Either way, he definitely doesn't have a career as a singer in his future, unless it's people paying him *not* to sing.

He puts all his energy into it, though, and as always, his charm is irresistible, and by the time he gets to the second verse, we're all singing along with him—to the bits we know—and the rest of the bar is split between joining in and staring at us like we're lunatics. He nearly falls off the chair one more time, and Brax, one of the bartenders, yells from behind the bar for him to get down.

We stumble to a close on the song, and Charlie lifts an empty shot glass and yells, "To my mom!"

"To Charlie's mom!" we yell back.

Then Brax comes out from behind the bar and heads toward us, and we scramble to get Charlie off the chair.

"What the hell, guys?" he demands.

"Hi, Brax," Jake says brightly with his winningest smile.

"Hi, Brax," the rest of us chorus.

He doesn't look impressed. "Don't make me throw you out," he warns, crossing his arms. It really adds to his dark, bad-boy look.

"It's my birthday!" Charlie announces. "Can I buy you a birthday drink?"

The busboy clearing the table snorts. "Yeah, Brax, want a birthday drink?" he teases. I found out earlier that his name is Ty and he's apparently a big deal on the lacrosse team, which I vaguely remember hearing about. He winks at Brax, who rolls his eyes and... slaps Ty's ass? I guess this is a friendly workplace.

Lila must see my confusion, because she leans over to whisper, "They're dating."

Ohhh.

Brax's frown has turned into a chuckle, though, and that's all I care about. "Just tone it down, okay? And stay off the furniture."

"He'll only sit on it from now on," I promise—recklessly, since I have no idea how I'll make Charlie do that.

Brax looks unconvinced but goes back to the bar with Ty, their heads bent together.

"My hero!" Charlie declares, sprawling across the two people between us to plant a sloppy kiss on my cheek.

"That's a stretch," I mutter, but he's already distracted.

Lila eyes me. "Are you and Charlie...?" She wiggles her brows, and I snort. "What? I know you weren't when we met, but it's been a few weeks since then, and he seems really into you."

"He's not... in that way. We're just friends."

"Well, if you change your mind about that, I think you'd be a great couple."

"Who'd be a great couple?" Jake drops into the empty seat that's just opened up beside Lila.

"Liam and Charlie," Lila says. "They'd be cute together, but Liam says they're just friends."

Jake makes a choking noise and leans in close to her. "Lila, babe, I could not agree with you more. Let's discuss it some more. Somewhere quieter, maybe?"

She lightly shoves him back and laughs. "Don't hit on your friends, dumbass. You forget that I've seen you so drunk, you pissed on your clothes because you forgot to hold your dick. You'll never be sexy to me now."

He sighs mournfully. "Yeah. That was a bad night. Okay, well if I'm not going to hook up and I'm not going to drink more, I should probably go."

Lila checks her watch. "Me too. Class tomorrow." She glances over at Charlie. "Who's in charge of the birthday boy?"

I raise my hand. "That would be me. And I think now is a good time for him to stop drinking, since he blew past his limit about an hour ago."

"Charlie!" Jake yells, and Charlie spins in a full circle before his gaze finds us. "Time to go, buddy."

"Is my birthday over?" His mouth turns down, and I'm so tempted to give in and let him stay until closing.

But... class. For both of us.

"Nope, but you have a special surprise present at home," Jake announces, and like it was choreographed, everyone at the table turns to listen.

"I do?" Charlie's brows draw together, and then his face lights up. "Oh! I do! Time to go."

My face is burning hot, and I hope if anyone notices they just assume it's from the alcohol and not the fact that Charlie and Jake just announced that we're having sex tonight. Not that we are, with Charlie drunk like this. And not that Jake would be part of it.

Charlie's goodbyes last forever, mostly because he keeps forgetting who he's already said bye to and everyone finds it hilarious that he's gone around the group three times for hugs. Then he insists on saying goodbye to Brax, who eyes him and asks me if I need help getting him home.

Finally, though, we're walking through the cool evening air back to campus. He chatters the whole way, first about what a great night he's had, then about how much he'll regret it tomorrow—"but not *true* regret, Lee, because it was so much fun and now it's a *memory*"—and then when we get to his dorm room, he looks at the bed and sighs.

"I'm so sorry, Lee, but I don't think I'm going to be any good at sex tonight. You'll have to do all the work."

I bite my lip to hide a smile as I close the door and take off my jacket. "I'm kind of tired too. Why don't we put sex on hold until morning?"

His smile is sweet and beautiful. "You have the best ideas."

Ten minutes later, cuddled against me in his bed, he murmurs, "I'm so glad I got to spend my birthday with you."

"Me too," I whisper, and just for a second let myself imagine it means more.

CHAPTER TWELVE

CHARLIE

THE WEEK AFTER MY BIRTHDAY, I WHISTLE AS I GET ready for class, and Artie glances over at me, grinning. "You're in a good mood."

"What's not to be in a good mood about? I'm not failing any classes, the weather is great, I know who my friends are, and in two weeks we'll be on break."

"I guess when you put it like that, it makes sense," he agrees. "But it's like you've been in an extra-good mood lately. A lot. Almost like you're in looooove or something." He draws out the last bit teasingly.

I blink. "In love? Why would you think that?"

It's his turn to look confused. "Well... I just thought you and Liam... I mean, you spend every weekend in his dorm room, and he's here any night I stay with Mia. Plus you guys hang out together all the time. You see him more than me, and we live together."

What's he trying to tell me? "I thought you liked Lee?"

"I do! He's great. But... you know what, never mind. I do like Liam. I think he's a great... friend for you." He turns back to shoving stuff for the day into his bag, and I frown. I can't help feeling like this is one of those times where I'm missing something.

I grab my phone and text Lee. He's good at explaining shit to me without making me feel like an idiot.

Charlie: Artie's being weird.

Liam: Weird how?

Charlie: I dunno? He thinks I'm in an extra-good mood. What does that even mean?

Liam: That your mood is good? Maybe he's thinking about how down you were a few weeks ago.

That's a good point. It's nice to have friends who notice my moods and are glad when I'm happy.

Charlie: Lunch today?

Liam: I can't. Last-minute study group before midterms.

My mood is instantly soured, but I get it. Lee's got his life all planned out, and the first step is getting his bachelor's degree and master's at the same time. That means actually studying.

Charlie: But we're still going shopping tonight, right?

It took me a while to pin him down on this. If it had been up to me, we would have hit the mall weeks ago. He kept making excuses, and since some of them were along the lines of "I can't go shopping because I have to suck you off," I didn't argue too hard.

But my mom's hosting a fundraiser this weekend that she wants me to attend, and since she used her mom voice when she asked (told? It didn't feel like I could say no) if I was coming, I'm driving up to LA on Friday night. Per Mom's instructions, I asked Lee if he'd come with me. Mom really wants to meet Lee. Ever since I told her he was helping me, all those weeks ago, she always asks about him.

Lee was reluctant to come at first, because studying and work and "I thought charity fundraiser balls were just something that happens in fiction. I definitely don't belong there." But I begged and rimmed him, and he gave in. So tonight we're hitting the mall to get him a suit, and I have a devious plan to convince him to let me pay for it.

Liam: If we really have to.

I try to think of something encouraging to say.

Charlie: When you're a professor and need to schmooze rich people to fund your research, you'll need a suit.

At least, that's what TV and movies have taught me. Who knows if it's actually true.

Charlie: And you'll probably need one when your friends get married. And for funerals.

Liam: Are you trying to tell me there are a lot of funerals in my near future?

Charlie: Who knows? Probably not, but does it hurt to be prepared?

Liam: Okay, I'll buy a suit to prepare for many hypothetical funerals.

Charlie: I wonder if that's what doomsday preppers do.

Liam: . . .

Liam: Uh, no. I don't think doomsday preppers stock up on funeral clothes.

"Charlie, you're gonna be late." Artie's voice breaks my concentration, and I glance up from my phone to find him on his way out the door.

"Coming," I promise, grabbing my bag with one hand and texting awkwardly with the other.

Charlie: Gotta go, but I'll see you later. Can't wait to make the most of your killer bod!

I make it to the front of the dorm before my phone chimes again.

Liam: Now I'm fucking terrified.

Ten hours later, Lee stares at the entrance to the men's clothing store I picked with a deer-in-headlights expression. I give him a nudge.

"Come on, this won't be bad."

He shakes himself, then narrows his eyes at me. "You're planning something."

"What?" I try to look innocent. "I'm not planning anything. Just helping you pick a suit."

"Oh?" He crosses his arms across his chest. If he wasn't wearing an ugly, shapeless sweater, I'd be able to see his biceps press against the fabric of his sleeves. That's my goal for later—a sweater that shows off his hot body.

But first, the suit.

"What else could I be doing?"

"Do you remember me telling you I had a budget for this suit?"

I nod. "Of course."

"And you remember me telling you what that budget was?"

"Sure." I shrug and meet his gaze.

"Are you honestly going to tell me that this store sells suits to fit that budget?"

"Um... maybe?"

He lifts a brow, and I take a second to wish I could do that. It looks so cool.

"Okay, so what I'm thinking is that I can pay for the suit and you can spend your budget on a couple of other outfits. There's a Target here; we can go there next."

He turns around and takes two steps before I catch his arm.

"C'mon, Lee, please? A better-quality suit will last you longer, and since you're only coming to this thing as a favor to me, it's the least I can do. Plus, I really want to update your wardrobe, and I can't do that if you blow all your money on one suit. Pleeeeease?"

He points a finger at me. "I do *not* appreciate all this sneakiness."

"I won't do it again," I promise.

Looking at the store reluctantly, he asks, "Do they rent suits?"

Oh hell no. I want to buy him one. "I'm not sure. But seriously, Lee, I owe you this. You're still helping me with my friendship development even though I'm not paying you anymore."

"Because we're friends!"

"And friends can do each other favors. You help me with stuff and agreed to come to this party, and I'll pay for the suit. It's not an equal exchange, but friendship isn't about keeping score, so I'm sure you'll forgive me for not pulling my weight."

For a long moment, he just stares at me like I've lost brain cells, but then he laughs. It lights up his face and makes his interesting features warmer, more approachable. "Fine," he agrees. "You can buy the suit. But I get the final say on which one," he adds, probably thinking he'll pick the cheapest.

"And we go buy you some other clothes after," I bargain, earning myself a snort.

"Let's see how this goes first." He marches past me into the store and looks around, then heads to the nearest rack of suits. I join him as he fishes out the price tag from a sleeve, looks at it, and drops it like it's covered in itching powder.

Before he can move on to the next rack—or say anything —a trendily dressed salesclerk who looks around our age comes over with a polite smile.

"Good evening, gentlemen. What can I help you with today?" He clocks Lee's jeans and sweater, and his smile fades a little before rallying when he sees what I'm wearing. And it's not because I'm in designer wear—I'm wearing Levi's and a Franklin U hoodie over a plain white tee—but he can obviously sense that I have style and appreciate clothing. Which Lee does not.

"He needs a suit," I volunteer before Lee can say we're just browsing. "Classic style, plain color." I know him well enough to understand he'll never let me buy him something trendy. "Dark gray, maybe."

The clerk scans Lee up and down again. "Sure thing. Size thirty-four pants?"

Lee blinks. "Uh, yeah. Usually."

"I got you. Come this way. I'm Blaise. Is this for a special occasion?"

Lee trails after him with a deeply suspicious look on his face. "It's for a party, but I want to be able to wear it for other stuff too."

"You're a practical man," Blaise says, grabbing a suit off a rack. "How do you feel about this one?"

Lee and I study it. I'm pretty sure that to Lee it's just charcoal-colored fabric with sleeves and legs, but I can see it's a plain cut that won't date but in a slim fit, which will flatter him. The fabric is also decent quality. While I'd love to get him into something more interesting, I know a losing game when I see it.

"I like it. Try it on, Lee," I urge.

He reaches for the tag dangling from the sleeve, and I sigh. To my surprise, he pulls his hand back. "Fine, I won't look," he says. "But promise this isn't going to cost an insane amount of money."

"Nothing here has an insane price," Blaise assures us.

Lee looks doubtful, but he follows Blaise to the dressing room, muttering about different definitions of "insane." I smile after him.

Blaise comes back while I'm browsing around the store for any other options that might be good for Lee.

"Your boyfriend is going to look great in that suit," he says casually.

"He's not my boyfriend," I reply automatically, looking at a display of shirts and wondering if I can convince Lee it's part of the suit. "But yeah, he will."

"Oh... sorry. I just assumed you were together." There's a note of glee in his voice that makes me look up. Blaise is staring in the direction of the dressing rooms. "I should check how he's doing."

"He can manage putting on a suit," I counter, resisting the urge to roll my eyes. He just wants to see if he can catch Lee in his underwear. Which reminds me... he needs better underwear. "Do these shirts come in a slim fit?"

Reluctantly, Blaise drags his gaze away from the dressing rooms and helps me sort through the shirts to find the fit and size I want. We're debating what color will flatter Lee and the suit best—he thinks a medium gray, whereas my vote is for deep, dark blue—when Lee's voice interrupts us.

"I think it's too tight."

I look up... and nearly swallow my tongue. I've seen him naked. I know what a great body he has. But seeing him in clothes that fit properly... clothes that are designed to flatter rather than just cover nakedness... wow.

"It's not too tight," Blaise breathes, and I accidentally slam my shoulder into his as I walk toward Lee.

"It's not too tight," I repeat to Lee, but my tone is reassuring and not pervy like Blaise's was. "Can you do this?" I lift my arms, elbows bent and pointed outward, and Lee mirrors me.

"I guess? Not a lot of freedom of movement, though."

"You're not going to be doing backflips or whatever in this suit," I remind him. "Turn around."

He scowls at me but obeys, and I admire the back view.

"The fit looks good," Blaise says professionally, arriving at my side. "Uh, the waist might be a little loose? Could you take off the jacket for a sec?"

With the jacket off, it's clear the waist is loose. Because Lee has the most amazing ass known to man, and while it fills out the pants to perfection, there's a gap at the waistband.

"You definitely can't go down a size," Blaise observes, his eyes on Lee's bubble butt. "We can take the waist in for you, though. And... did you bring the shoes you plan to wear? We should check the length of the pants too."

Lee's panicked gaze darts to me, and I guess immediately

that he doesn't have dress shoes. Fortunately, the store has a small selection on display.

"Oh, we forgot to grab your shoes," I say as nonchalantly as I can manage. "Why don't you get new ones to go with the new suit? It really all goes together, like a package deal."

His eyes narrow, but Blaise, opportunist that he is, leaps on the opening. "Definitely. And I'll grab that shirt as well—do you prefer gray or blue?"

"What's wrong with white?" Lee asks, and Blaise pats his arm, his hand lingering.

"It's a party, not a business meeting. Leave it with me. What shoe size are you?"

As he swans off to collect the shoes and shirt, Lee turns to me. "Even I know shoes are not part of a suit."

I shrug. "Kinda they are. And a good pair of dress shoes will last even longer than a suit. Plus you can wear them with other outfits. And really, this is an investment for me."

"How do you figure?" There's a tiny smile playing on his lips.

"I want to dance at the party, which means you dancing with me. And you can't do that if you don't have shoes. So... for me to dance the night away, I need to buy you shoes."

He laughs. "You're so full of shit. But fine. You can buy me shoes as well."

"And the shirt." From the look he gives me, I'm pushing my luck. "What? You can't wear a T-shirt under the suit."

"People wear T-shirts under suits all the time," he argues.

"Not when they look like yours. Trust me on this."

He rolls his eyes. "Why do you hate my clothes so much?"

"Because they're ugly. Wait." I hold up my hand when he opens his mouth to reply. "Try on the shirt so I can prove it."

"Trying on a shirt I'd never buy for myself is going to prove that my usual clothes are ugly?" he asks skeptically, and I nod.

Blaise comes back with both the gray and blue shirts and a shoebox, and Lee strips off his T-shirt. He doesn't notice the noise Blaise makes, but I do, and I glare at him. What kind of professionalism is this? Sure, Lee looks hot in those close-fitting pants and nothing else, the muscles of his six-pack rippling as he reaches for one of the shirts—the *blue* one, fuck you very much, Blaise—but that's no reason to perv on him like a creeper.

I lick my lips as he buttons the shirt. What is it about watching someone get dressed that's so sexy?

He tucks the shirttails neatly into the pants and spreads his arms. "Well?"

"Look." I spin him to face the mirror. "Your usual clothes are ugly, and that's the proof."

He studies himself. "I mean... I guess these fit better. And it looks... neater?"

Sighing, I let my shoulders slump. "You just don't get clothes, do you?"

"They keep me warm and stop me getting arrested." He pats my shoulder. "I like how much you like clothes, though."

"That shirt fits perfectly," Blaise interrupts. "But if you put the shoes on, I'll pin the pants for the tailor."

Lee does as directed, then stands still while Blaise feels him up in the guise of pinning his pants. Okay, so maybe he doesn't actually feel him up, but he might as well be, the way he kneels in front of him and touches the fabric at his waist.

When he finally stands up again, it's way too close to Lee. I mean, have some fucking respect for personal space and take a step back. Then he hands Lee the jacket and suggests he try it on again. I try not to whimper at the finished product.

"You think it looks good?" Lee asks me, still studying himself. "I mean... I know it fits and all, but if I'm going to get a suit, it should suit me, right?" He pauses. "Suit me. God, that's a bad pun."

"It looks good," I assure him. "Even with the pun. You look totally fuckable."

He spins to look at me in horror. "What? No, this is supposed to be a suit I can wear to work functions and funerals!"

"What?" Blaise asks.

"Could you give us a minute?" I direct a plastic smile his way, and he reluctantly backs off and makes himself busy putting the gray shirt away. I turn back to Lee. "You can wear it to work functions and funerals," I say earnestly, wondering if maybe I put too much emphasis on the funerals this morning. "You're allowed to look good at those things."

He scoffs. "The only people who should look fuckable at work functions are sex workers!"

"That's very small-minded of you," I chide. "Are you trying to tell me I don't always look fuckable? Because I *try* to, you know."

His jaw drops, and then he laughs. "You're right." He turns back to examine his reflection again. "It does look good."

"It does," I agree, then hesitate.

"What?"

"Well... how do you feel about a haircut?"

His face shuts down fast, and he shakes his head. "No, short hair doesn't suit my face."

I think he's wrong—I've seen him in the shower, with his hair plastered to his head, and without the shaggy locks to hide it, the structure of his face is compelling. He's not conventionally handsome by any stretch of the imagination, but there's definitely something attractive about the sharp bones and planes. I don't argue, though. This isn't about making him uncomfortable in his own skin or changing him.

"It doesn't have to be short. Just tidy it up, give it some shape. Some style."

He doesn't look convinced. "Maybe."

I don't push him—I've done a lot of that already tonight, and honestly, who cares if he'd rather not have a stylish haircut? I'm glad he agreed to new clothes, but even that's not important. "Go change, and we can get out of here."

He's back dressed in his ugly clothes a lot faster than I would have thought possible, and I sigh sadly at the sight. At the register, Blaise rings everything up and bags the shirt and shoes. "The suit will be ready tomorrow night, since the alterations are simple," he says. "If you pick it up just before we close, maybe I can take you for a drink after?"

Lee says nothing. Which, okay, doesn't break my heart, but it's kind of rude, and Lee's not like that.

"Lee?" I say. He looks at me, and I tip my head toward Blaise, who's watching us expectantly.

"Do you want to get a drink with me?" he repeats, looking Lee right in the eye, and Lee starts.

"Uh... me? You mean me?"

Blaise smiles like that's the cutest thing anyone in the history of the world has ever said. "Of course I mean you."

"Oh. Um..." He slides a sideways glance toward me, his cheeks pink. "Sure. Yeah. That sounds... great."

"Great!" Blaise beams at him, and Lee smiles back, a little more confidently now.

"Great," I echo. Guess this means Lee and I aren't hanging out tomorrow night. Not that we had plans or anything, but... it's fine. I have other friends. Lots of them, in fact.

Blaise announces the total, and I hand him my credit card before Lee can have a coronary and change his mind. They both frown at me, Lee because he's still struggling with the idea of spending that much money on clothes, and Blaise probably because "just friends" usually don't spend that much money buying each other clothes. Or so I've learned in the past few weeks, anyway. I still think that's dumb, but whatever.

We leave the store, and I glance sideways at Lee as we walk toward Target. He's totally lost in thought. "So..." I clear my throat. "Productive night for you. New suit *and* a date, and we've barely started shopping."

His frown is fierce. "Do *not* get carried away with the shopping thing," he warns. "You're not going to get away with what you did back there again." Before I can protest my innocence, he sighs. "Is it weird?"

"That you're allergic to fashion? I mean, I wouldn't say weird. People like different things. It's outside my personal experience, though." I *love* fashion.

He chuckles. "No, I meant the date. Is that weird?"

"It's a little unprofessional, but that's not your fault. And as long as he didn't make you feel uncomfortable, I don't think it's worth making a fuss over. Why? Do you not want to go?"

His hesitation lasts just long enough to worry me. "It's not that. Exactly. Blaise is cute, nice, and he was into me. At least it seemed that way?"

"He was," I confirm. Even I can hear the edge in my tone, but Lee's too wrapped up in his insecurities to notice.

"So, yeah, I'd be an idiot to turn down a date. And it's a real meet-cute, right? Went in to buy a suit, came out with a date... if things worked out, it'd be a great story to tell our grandkids."

I stop dead. *"Grandkids?"* Is he really that into Blaise?

Lee grabs my arm and pulls me along, getting me moving again. "Relax, I'm not planning a wedding. I'm just saying it's a cute story if things go well. I'm a romantic; I think of things like that."

"Okay," I agree cautiously, still not over the whole grand-kids thing. "So what's freaking you out?"

"I'm not *freaked out*, just... isn't it weird? Me going on a date with us... you know." He gestures from himself to me awkwardly, and I finally get it.

"Oh! Yeah, well... you're still allowed to date. I don't think he'd expect you to be exclusive on the first date, you know?" It suddenly strikes me that there's a lot of shit that can happen on a first date. Is Blaise going to give Lee the kisses he loves so much? Are they going to fuck?

I'm weirdly not okay with that.

Shaking off the uncool possessiveness—Lee isn't mine. He makes his own decisions—I muster a smile for him. We're friends, and he needs me to be his friend right now.

"Yeah," he says, then repeats, more strongly, "Yeah. It's just a first date. You're right. And this is what I've wanted, right? Someone to be interested in me." He nods decisively. "Thanks, Charlie."

"You're welcome," I reply brightly, even as I wish he'd stay home and watch a movie with me instead.

CHAPTER THIRTEEN

LIAM

I WISH I COULD SAY THIS IS THE WORST OR MOST awkward date ever, because at least that way I'd have a reason for leaving. I could go home, get into my sweats, and dream about finding a man who actually sees me and wants me anyway.

But the truth is, the date is... fine. Blaise is funny, nice, and genuinely interested in what I have to say. Conversation hasn't lagged. We've been at this trendy bar for two hours and four stupidly overpriced drinks, and I'm having a good time.

There's just no spark between us.

At all.

And I'm afraid we're going to get to that point in the date where he makes a move, and I'll have to either say "no, thanks" or go for a no-strings orgasm. Which I'm not usually opposed to, but for some reason it feels wrong right now.

Yes, I know what the reason is. But denial is a powerful tool. If I admit I might have feelings for *someone*, I'd be obliged to act on them and put distance between us. And I don't want that.

So... yeah. I'm probably going to have to blow off Blaise, and that's a shame, because we could be friends.

As though reading my mind, Blaise smiles at me and says, "You're not attracted to me at all, are you?"

"What? No!" I sputter. "I mean, yes, of course..." He tilts his head, smirking, and I sigh. "It's not that you're not attractive. I find you attractive, and I really like you."

"Just not sexually."

I grimace and shake my head. "Sorry."

He sighs. "Thank fuck. Because you're great, and your body is fucking hot, but it would be like fucking my cousin." He bites his lip consideringly. "Maybe if we'd met at a club and just blown each other without talking first."

"You're saying that getting to know each other killed the attraction between us?" I grin. "Wow, that's so flattering."

"Not good for either of us," he agrees. "Although I think maybe you're already hung up on someone."

The denial sticks in my throat. "It won't go anywhere," I say instead, picking at the cuff of the sweater Charlie selected for me last night. I left Target with three complete new outfits that he assured me were "mix and match," and Charlie all smug about the total being under budget.

"Why not?" Blaise asks. "Now that we're not gonna fuck, let's be friends. Unload all your troubles on me."

I snort. "Yeah, not happening."

"No, seriously." He leans forward. "It's the guy you were with last night, right? Charlie? Because if it is, I think you've got a chance."

I shove down the ray of hope that leaps into being. "I don't think so. He's pretty set on not dating right now, and we're friends. He's had, uh, issues with his friends wanting to date him in the past, and I could never betray his trust by doing that to him."

"If you're upfront about it, would he really care? Just tell him you're down to fuck if he wants and see where it goes."

My face gets really hot, and Blaise does that head-tilty thing again. "Oooh. So you guys are already fucking."

I pick up my glass and drain the last of my drink to avoid having to say anything, and he laughs. "That totally explains the vibe last night. I thought you were together, but then he said you weren't, so I took a shot."

"We're not together," I mumble.

"Friends with bennies?"

I nod, and he does too.

"Cool. For what it's worth, I don't think it would take much effort on your part to make it more."

I open my mouth to disagree, but my phone vibrates in my pocket, and I seize on the excuse. "Since we're friends now and this is no longer a date, do you mind if I check my phone?"

He flips his hand. "Go for it. Gives me an excuse to check mine. Since I'm not getting any from you tonight, I'm going to find someone else."

"Great plan." Glancing down at my lock screen, I'm surprised to see messages from both Jake and Artie. I have their numbers because Charlie started a group chat last week, but we've never directly texted each other before. I swipe to read them.

Artie: Hope your date is good! Please come home before I kill Charlie.

Jake: Holy fucking shit, Liam, you must have a magic cock, because Charlie is fucked up about losing it. I can't take his whining anymore!

I stare at the messages in shock. Charlie is whining? I send them both the same text back.

Liam: Is Charlie ok? What's going on?

Jake: He won't be ok for long if he doesn't shut up

Artie: We're at Shenanigans with Jake. Charlie's had a few and is chatty and sad

Artie: Please say your date is nearly over

Jake: Could you please text him so he'll stop saying you've probably forgotten he's alive? Please. I know you're on a date but I'm begging.

What the actual fuck? I'm still blinking at that last message when Blaise clears his throat. "So, uh... I just matched with that guy over there. Are you about ready to take off, do you think?"

"Go," I tell him. "Have fun. Wait, give me your number first." We exchange numbers, then he strolls purposefully toward a cute twink at the bar, and I flip back to my messages. What the hell is going on?

I message them both again.

Liam: Charlie's drunk? Take him home.

It seems like common sense to me, but I get replies almost instantly.

Artie: He won't go. Says the memories are too strong there.

Jake: He wants to swap dorms with me save me please

Memories? And he wants to swap dorms with Jake?
I do the only thing I can.

Liam: OMW

Shenanigans is only half-full when I get there. It's a Thursday, late, in the lead-up to midterms, and most people have other stuff on their minds. I find Charlie and his friends easily enough, sitting at a table in the corner with two empty beer pitchers. Charlie is slumped over the tabletop, resting his head on his arms, and at first I think he might have passed out. But as Artie exclaims in relief at the sight of me and Jake springs up to give me a heartfelt hug, Charlie groans and lifts his head.

"Lee?" he mumbles, squinting. "Am I dreaming? Life is so cruel to me."

Ooo-kay. I drape the garment bag containing my new suit over the back of the empty chair, then go to kneel beside him.

"Charlie? You feeling okay?"

He blinks at me for a few seconds, then says, "You can talk?"

I shoot a concerned look at Jake and Artie. "How much did he have?"

"Well," Artie begins, "I had two glasses."

"I had three," Jake adds.

We all look at the empty pitchers.

"So he drank a whole jug himself?" That's not enough to get him like this.

Jake winces. "And he had some shots when we first got here."

"Lee?" Charlie latches onto my arm, lunging toward me and nearly sending us sprawling to the floor. "Lee, you're real!"

I pat him. "I am. Please breathe in the other direction." I turn back to Artie. "So tell me again why you didn't take him home?"

"I couldn't go back there," Charlie explains earnestly before Artie can open his mouth. "All the *memreeeees*." The weird emphasis and drawn-out last syllable on "memories" gives me an inkling of what he's put his friends through. "I thought you'd gone for-ev-errrr. That I'd lost you and you forgot me."

This is too weird. "We literally had dinner together four hours ago," I remind him. "And we're going to LA tomorrow."

"But you were with himmmmm."

Yeah, okay. "It was a date, Charlie. One you told me to go on, remember? But if it makes you feel better, Blaise and I have decided to stick to being friends." My heart is pounding dizzyingly fast, and I want to scream "What does this mean?" but he's been drinking, and everyone knows alcohol is a mindfuck. It could just be that he's gotten used to me being around to support him as a friend and the booze is turning that into some kind of abandonment thing. I'm not reading into anything he says while he's drunk.

"Weally?" He perks up, hope filling his voice. "I can be his fren too. We can all be frenz together!"

"We sure can. Why don't you put your head down and rest while I talk to Artie and Jake?"

He nods happily, but when his head just continues bobbing, I guide it back down to the table. He cushions it on his arms and burps.

Standing, I pinch the bridge of my nose and wonder what the fuck is the best way to get him home.

"I hope you didn't blow off your date because of Charlie," Artie says softly, and humiliation snakes through me. Am I really so transparent? Can everyone see that I'm falling for him? And oh my god, these two must think I'm the worst person ever, since Charlie literally paid me to help him identify and let down friends who wanted to date him, and now I'm his friend who wants to date him.

"No, we just didn't hit it off that way," I mumble. "Uh, how are we going to get him back?"

"I know it's wrong, but thank fuck," Jake declares. "I could *not* have dealt with Charlie moping like a baby over you having a boyfriend."

"He's just drunk," I protest. "It's not like that."

They exchange glances. "You didn't hear him before," Artie ventures, but I cut him off.

"He's drunk. And he relied on me a lot last month, when everything happened. It all got mixed up in his head. You'll see; when he sobers up, he'll be mortified, and we'll laugh about this."

Jake looks doubtful, but Artie nods. "Sure. Well, he needs to sleep it off to get sober. Are we taking him back to yours? It's closer, and it's Thursday. He usually stays with you on Thursday."

I hesitate. That's all true, but usually we're fucking like bunnies. It's wrong to sleep in the same bed with him when he's drunk.

"I don't think we have a choice," Jake says. "We need him awake enough to walk, and once he's conscious, I don't think he'll willingly let Liam go."

"Let's get him up and moving and see how we go," I decide. "My dorm's on the way to yours, so if it seems like we can't get him farther, we'll stop there."

They agree, and we turn to the next task: getting Charlie on his feet.

"Are we going somewhere?" he mumbles, prying his eyes open and swaying. He's standing, but only just.

"Time to go home," I announce in that mock cheery tone that comes so easily around drunk people. He turns his head toward me, and his face lights up.

"Lee! You're here!" He lunges at me, and it's only with quick help from Jake that we stay upright. Draping his arms over my shoulders, Charlie rests his head against the top of mine. "Lee."

"Right here. Come on, let me go so we can get you home."

His grip tightens, and he snuggles closer. "Just one more minute."

Artie tries to pry him off me, but he's got a surprisingly strong hold for someone who can't even stand up straight. In the end, it takes both Artie and Jake, with me working from within the embrace, to free me.

"Go!" Jake orders as Charlie looks around in confusion and tries to sit down again. "Look, Charlie, it's Lee! Oh no, Lee's leaving! Let's follow Lee!"

"Lee?" Charlie's head snaps around, and he reaches for me. I grab my suit bag and back away hastily, getting out of arm's reach. He pouts. "Lee, don't go!"

"Come with me," I cajole, taking another two steps back, and sure enough, that does the trick. He stumbles forward, supported on each side by his friends. Slowly, we make our way out of the bar and start the journey back to campus. I've never considered it to be far before, but tonight it feels like miles. Charlie stumbles to a stop every few yards, and I have to get his attention and make sure I stay out of his reach to keep him moving. Each time, he's so excited to see me and eagerly chases after me—in a shambling, weaving, kept-upright-by-friends way—for a bit before forgetting what's going on and trying to sit or lie down right in the middle of the sidewalk.

It becomes more and more ridiculous as we go, and by the time we reach the edge of campus, I know there's no way we're going any farther than we have to. Charlie's crashing with me tonight.

"So tiiiiiiired," he whines, stopping again.

I sigh. "Charlie!" I call. "Are you coming? Follow me."

"Yeah, Charlie, follow that sweet, sweet ass," Jake says, and I turn around to give him a flat look.

"Don't objectify me just because you're jealous of my ass." I give it a little shake.

"No bejectifying my Lee!" Charlie shouts, shaking his

friends off and lumbering toward me. He's surprisingly fast, given how long it's taken us to walk a couple of blocks, and I take a few quick steps to stay in front of him while the others catch up.

"Okay, I'm sorry," Jake hastens to assure him as he grabs one arm. "I won't, uh, 'bejectify' Liam."

"I am never letting him hear the end of this," Artie mutters. "At our thirty-year reunion, I'll be all, 'Hey Charlie, remember the night you were a total loser?'"

"We should be videoing this," Jake adds.

"I got some before, when he said Liam going on a date was the greatest tragedy to ever occur in the world."

"How many shots did he have, exactly?" I demand. I've been drinking with Charlie before. Hell, I was there at his twenty-first. He usually holds his liquor pretty well.

Artie seesaws a hand. "It depends how you count."

That makes no sense at all, but I'm afraid to ask him to clarify.

Finally, we make it to my dorm. I swipe us in, and then we head for the elevator I only used when moving in. It's small, slow, and always smells like feet and cheese. But there's no way we're getting Charlie up the stairs.

"Something's wrong!" Charlie declares in alarm as the elevator jolts into motion. He lifts his head and looks around with wild eyes. "The world is moving! We're trapped in a box! Oh no, they have us! The machines rose up!" He struggles upright from where the guys propped him against the side wall and starts stabbing all the buttons on the control panel. There aren't many, but we manage to stop him before he hits the emergency stop or the phone line button.

"It's fine, Charlie," I say in my most soothing voice,

keeping a tight grip on his hands as Jake and Artie wrestle him toward the back wall.

His eyes focus blearily on me. "Lee! They got you too? Oh noooo. I wanted to save you."

"I know. Uh... you can save me now? You just need to keep still for a minute so we can, uh, do the plan."

"Do the plan?" Artie murmurs. I don't have a hand free to flip him off, so I settle for glaring.

"The plan! Yesssss. We'll do the plan." Charlie nods enthusiastically, then turns pale. "I don't feel so good."

"If he pukes on me, I'm leaving him here," Jake threatens.

"He's not going to puke." I really hope. "Deep breaths, Charlie. Slow, deep breaths."

He starts puffing just as the elevator stops and the door opens—thankfully on my floor. We get him out and down the hallway with minimal fuss, since all his focus is now on breathing, and the second I open the door to my room, he shakes us off and flops facedown onto my bed, burying his face into my pillow.

"Lee, you smell so good," he mumbles.

"Thank fuck that's done." Jake exhales deeply, then looks at me. "Are you good with him?"

I study the long body sprawled on top of my duvet, already snoring softly, and sigh. "Yeah. He can sleep in his jeans. Thanks for helping."

They say their goodbyes and leave, and I hang up my new suit, wrestle off Charlie's shoes, and move the trash can to right beside the bed. Then, after a moment's consideration, I grab my towel and lay it on the mattress beside him, just in case he's not awake enough to make it as far as the side of the bed. At least he's not on his back and I don't have to worry about him choking on vomit.

And with that pleasant thought, I strip down to my fancy new underwear—that I had to buy individually instead of in packs—and get into the other bed. Chris, my roommate, won't mind, especially if I change the sheets for him, and it saves me from feeling like a creeper for crawling into bed with a drunk guy.

I stare across the room at him. With his face mushed mostly into the pillow, all I can see is part of his profile and his half-open mouth. He's definitely not at his hottest, passed out and snoring, but still my heart gives a little clutch. Because he's in my bed, taking comfort in my smell, after an evening where he missed me.

Denial's not really working for me anymore. And that scares the crap out of me. Because what do I do now?

CHAPTER FOURTEEN

CHARLIE

I wake up feeling like death has stomped all over me and then decided I'm too damaged to take. Groaning, I try to lift my head and instantly regret it. No. Nope. Nuh-uh. I'm just going to have to lie here forever.

Although... where is here? I have vague memories of drinking at Shenanigans with Artie and Jake, although most of the night is fuzzy. But they would have gotten me home safely, right? I'm not lying naked on the floor of the bar bathroom, am I? If a guy can't rely on his roommate and his bestie to take care of him when he's trashed, then there's something truly fucked-up about this world.

They probably took embarrassing pictures, though.

I seem to be lying on a bed, at least, which means I'm not at the bar. With one hand, I pat down my body to see if I'm wearing pants. To my great relief, they're still in place. So with crisis averted, I can go back to sleep.

Except... I'm pretty sure this isn't my pillow. Mine is ergonomic memory foam that Mom bought and that I'm low-key in love with. This is just an ordinary pillow. And it smells a lot like Lee.

Lee... who went on a date with that smarmy salesman last night. How did I end up in his bed? And where is he?

Bracing myself, I crack open an eyelid, just a sliver. The room is dim, the blind closed, so I open both eyes—well, mostly—and try to look around without moving my head.

The first thing I see is the neon pink sticky note on the pillow right in front of my face. I pick it up and angle it so I can read the words.

Aspirin and water on desk. Trash can beside you. Phone charging. Text me when you wake up so I know you're still alive.
Liam

Aww, he's such a good friend. See how he takes care of me, even though I apparently passed out in his bed and have no idea how I got here? The least I can do is what he asks.

I grit my teeth and slowly drag myself into a sitting position. My head spins, my stomach lurches, and for a second I contemplate diving for the trash can.

Count it out, Charlie. One... two... three...

The nausea subsides, and I take a cautious breath. Okay. I'm upright. What was I doing?

My gaze lands on the bottle of water on the desk beside the bed, and I become aware of the absolutely gross taste of my own mouth. Blech. Moving cautiously, I grab the water and take a few sips, then when my stomach doesn't object, a larger swallow. The aspirin Lee promised is there too, along with a power bar, and I wash down the pills and make myself take a bite of the cardboard-tasting bar. What I really want is a greasy egg-and-bacon sandwich, but that will have to wait.

Okay... this is good. I'm making progress. Now to text Lee.

Except my phone is on the other side of the desk.

I sip my water and stare at my phone for a while. It's clearly not going to get up and come closer to me on its own, but maybe if I concentrate hard enough, I can move it with the power of my mind. I mean... who knows what really happened last night? Maybe the reason my memory is so fuzzy is because aliens abducted me and performed experiments that developed my tele... something ability. Telepathic? No, that's to talk from brain to brain. Tele... motion?

I'm pretty sure that's not right either.

Whatever it is, it's not working no matter how hard I stare and silently order the phone to come to me. I'll actually have to get up.

Setting the water bottle down, I slowly swing my legs over the side of the bed. Every movement makes me want to whimper. Whyyyy did I do this to myself?

My leg knocks over the trash can, and I gaze down at it, wondering if I can bend that far to pick it up. It's probably not worth the risk. Instead, I focus on levering myself to my feet and taking the step that will bring my phone into reach.

It's fully charged, and I unplug it and check the time first. Fuck! It's nearly noon. I've missed my morning class, and I'm probably going to have to skip bringing Lee his lunch. He's told me every week since I started that I don't need to, but I can't stand the idea of him eating a power bar when I have the time to bring him something decent.

I take the phone back to the bed with me and unlock it while I sip more water.

Charlie: I'm alive. Kind of. What happened last night? How'd I end up here?

Lee starts typing so fast, he must have had his phone in his hand.

Liam: You don't remember?

Charlie: I remember going to Shenanigans with the guys. We were drinking, but what made me get so wasted?

This time there's a long pause. The ellipsis appears and disappears a few times, which I think means he's typing and deleting.

Liam: You'd have to ask the guys. I only came in at the end. My place was closest, so that's where you ended up.

I feel like there's a lot more to this story, but I'm not sure how to ask. And what to ask.

Charlie: Ok. Thanks for the water and aspirin and not letting me choke on my own vomit.

Liam: Did you hurl in my bed?

Charlie: No. But would you forgive me if I had?

Liam: Not sure. Probably not.

Rude.

Charlie: Lucky I didn't, then. Hey, how was your date?

My stomach churns while I wait for his response. Is he going to gush? Is he going to dump me for the weekend because he wants to spend time with Blaise? Is he going to end our FWBs arrangement? I hope not. I want Lee to be happy, but I want me to be happy too, and it's been so good getting sex and cuddles while I'm relaxed with a friend.

Liam: Good. We're just going to be friends, though.

Happiness surges through me, but I tamp it down. What if he's disappointed? Lee's feelings about this matter more than mine.

Charlie: Whose idea was that? Do I need to go down there and glare at him?

Liam: Why would you glare at him?

Charlie: For hurting your feelings. I'm against violence, so I can't beat him up. But I can glare like a champion.

Liam: Hahahahaha don't make me laugh. You'd start to glare, then worry that it might upset him and end up bringing him coffee.

Charlie: Fuck you, I would not.

Would I?

Charlie: Anyway, do I need to?

Liam: No. It was a mutual decision and I think we really will be friends.

Liam: Thanks for the offer, though. Maybe someday you can show me your championship glare.

Charlie: I get the feeling you're not taking me seriously, and you SHOULD.

Liam: Uh-huh. Going now. I'm in class. Remember we're leaving at five thirty. Are you going to be ok to drive?

Um. Maybe?

Charlie: Of course. But let's say I hypothetically wasn't. Can you drive?

Liam: Are you asking if I can or if I will?

Charlie: Hypothetically, both.

Liam: Hypothetically, yes. But the idea of driving in LA or even adjacent to it makes me nervous. So look after yourself today.

Charlie: Don't worry, I'm fine! Enjoy class.

I flip across to another message thread.

Charlie: Hey! Why the fuck did you let me drink so much last night?

My phone rings in my hand, and I wince. That's waaay too loud. I answer it quickly.

"Hello?" Wow, I sound like a two-pack-a-day smoker.

"You sound like shit, man," Jake declares, and I wince again.

"Quietly, please. Use your inside voice."

The fucker laughs. Loudly.

"Aww, not feeling too good? Nobody deserves it more."

That... does not sound good. "What happened?"

"You got shit-faced and then moaned about Liam being on a date for hours. That's what happened."

What? "No, seriously."

He scoffs in my ear. "Seriously. We had to call him to help us shut you up and get you home."

"You called Lee to help get me home? Two of you couldn't manage it alone?" I'm not that big of a guy.

"You have no idea what a chore you were last night, man. You're lucky we didn't just leave you there to end up in the drunk tank."

I still think he's got to be exaggerating, but on the other hand, I did wake up this morning without any memory of getting home, so... "Thanks?"

"You owe me," he says. "Like... huge. I learned way more about Liam last night than I ever wanted to know."

Horror strikes me. I don't believe in kissing and bragging, and I hate the idea that alcohol stomped all over the boundaries I set myself. "Like what?"

"Well, he's the best kisser in the world," Jake replies, heavy on the sarcasm. "He's got the body of a god."

Okay, that's not too bad.

"He makes you feel all tingly when he smiles."

Embarrassing for me, but not a disaster...

"The thought of losing him to someone who can't tell blue suits him better than gray breaks your heart."

"Anyone could have seen that the blue shirt goes better with his skin tone!" I argue.

"You're missing the point. Also, you need to up your game. It's not good when your boyfriend thinks you're just in it for sex."

I blink, trying to understand the change in subject. I must still be a little drunk. "What boyfriend? I don't—do you mean Lee? We're not boyfriends." Something pangs in my stomach, and I wonder if I'm going to hurl up the two bites of power bar.

"You're kidding, right?" Jake's disbelief is loud, and I wince.

"Uh... no?"

"Charlie, fuck off, I had to listen to you last night going on and on about how crap things would be if Liam dated someone else. You can't tell me you don't have feelings for him."

"Of course I do! We're friends," I defend. "I care about all my friends and their relationships."

He audibly takes a deep breath. "Are you even serious or are you fucking with me? You spend more time with Liam than with anyone else. You sleep over with him every week-end. You guys are always texting."

I frown. That's all true... and when he says it like that...

"But he went on a date with someone else. If he wanted to be more than friends, he wouldn't have done that." Right?

"You said last night that you told him to!"

Oh yeah. I did do that.

I scrub my hand through my hair, my head pounding. "Look, Jake, I can't think straight right now. Maybe there is more between me and Lee than just being friends who fuck." Something inside me clicks as I say it, but I push that aside to think about later. "But since he's the one I usually ask if my friends are into me, I'm in a tough spot."

"You're such an idiot."

"Probably," I agree, then remember why I texted him in the first place. "Hey, can you do me a favor? I'll owe you even more than I already do."

He sighs. "What is it?"

"It's going to be a while before I can move much without crying, so can you grab lunch for Lee and meet him between classes?"

The silence lasts so long, I check the screen to see if the call dropped out. "Jake? Hello?"

"I'm here," he says. "Let me get this straight. You want me, your friend, to go buy and deliver lunch to Liam."

"Yes." He's come with me to get it a few times, so he should be able to handle it. "I can text you what he likes if you don't remember."

"Did, uh, did Liam ask you to bring him lunch?"

"No, of course not." Why is this such a big deal?

"So you've just randomly decided to bring lunch to your 'friend.' Do you not see how boyfriendly that is?"

"Jake, he's got back-to-back classes all day—"

"So did I, last semester. You never brought me lunch. Because that's not something you do for people who are just friends."

Oh. "It's not?"

"No." The *dur* is implied heavily in his tone. "Turkey and cheddar with veggies, right?"

The sudden change of subject makes my head spin. "Uh, yeah. You'll get it for him?"

"I will, because I think you guys would make a great couple and I want to weight the odds in your favor."

The call drops out before I can reply. I pull the phone away from my ear and stare at it. Did he just hang up on me?

I don't have the energy to care. He's going to get Lee's lunch, and that's all that matters.

Wait...

Charlie: Don't forget the coffee. He likes hazelnut lattes.

He responds with an emoji flipping me off.

I slump back against Lee's pillow, my head spinning. Is Jake right? Am I already dating Lee in all but name?

This is something I have to give careful consideration, because if I fuck it up, I'll lose Lee. And that's not okay.

It takes a very long, very hot shower, two bottles of Gatorade and another bottle of water, three shots of espresso, and a disgustingly greasy egg-and-bacon sandwich before I feel human enough to pack for the weekend. Truth be told, if I hadn't promised Mom I'd come—she was bummed about missing my twenty-first—I wouldn't have left Lee's bed at all, just waited for him to come home and take care of me.

But I did promise, and anyway, I think Lee needs this break. He works super hard, between his coursework and Mr. Romance, and this party will be fun. Well... it will be when he experiences it my way. Though maybe I won't drink much.

There's a knock on my door, and I glance over from where I'm stretched out on my bed. "Come in."

Lee pokes his head around the door, sees me, and grins. "Still feeling crappy?"

"You don't have to be so happy about it," I grumble.

He comes into the room with his backpack and garment bag. "You have no idea how much work it was to get you home last night. Laughing at you now is the least I deserve."

"Yeah, yeah." I eye him. "Where's the rest of your stuff?"

He blinks at me. "What rest? My shoes and change of shirt and underwear are in my backpack."

I sit up fast. "You packed for two nights away, including a fancy party, in just your backpack?"

"I mean, there's this too." He jiggles the garment bag, but I'm already standing and prying his backpack away from him. "Charlie, hey!"

The situation inside isn't as dire as I worried it might be. He's rolled all his clothes up neatly, which, if he's done it right, should cut down on wrinkles. His shoes and toiletries are at the bottom, which is also a good sign.

But he's only packed the bare minimum. Like... underwear, a clean tee, and a sweater. "Where's your shirt that goes with the suit?" I ask, and he jiggles the garment bag again.

"I put it in here. Are you seriously judging how I packed?"

"Not how as much as what. Where's the rest of it?" I nod to where my overnight bag sits beside the closet, clearly full. And we're going to my home, where I have a closet full of clothes. He does a double take.

"We're only going for the weekend, right? Is there another party or something you forgot to tell me about?" A worried frown creases his forehead.

"No, but..." He's right. Just because I like to have outfit options doesn't mean he does. And what he's brought is fine... as long as he doesn't spill something on the jeans he's currently wearing.

"You said your parents were casual," he accuses. "If I need to bring nicer clothes, tell me now."

I'm such a dick. Abandoning his stuff, I go and wrap my arms around him and kiss his frowning lips. "It's fine. They are casual, and everything you've brought is great. I just never travel without a range of clothes."

He relaxes into my embrace, turning his face into my neck. "Okay. Can we get going, then? Are you driving?" He pulls back and studies my face.

I grimace. "I probably shouldn't. My head's kinda fucked."

He sighs. "Fine. But you owe me. Just like you owe Jake for bringing me lunch today." He shakes his head. "Thanks again, but you really didn't have to make him do that."

"He was happy to do it," I declare, which isn't exactly a lie. "We'll stop at a drive-through somewhere for dinner, so you needed a decent lunch." I repack his backpack and hand it over, then put on my shoes. "Let's hit the road."

CHAPTER FIFTEEN

LIAM

Despite my worst fears about driving in the Greater LA area all being true, we make pretty good time and get to Charlie's family home just after nine. It's in Brentwood Park, which meant nothing to me until I was driving through it and realized that Charlie doesn't just have money, he has *money*. I'm afraid to google what these houses are worth, but it actually makes me fall for him a little more? Because while I always knew cash wasn't an issue for him, he's never acted the way I would expect a mega-rich asshole to act. And we have a few of those on campus, so my expectations aren't unrealistic.

Charlie's mom must have been watching for us, because the second I stop the car in the driveway—in front of the kind of house I thought only existed in movies—the front door swings open and she comes running out.

At least, I think it's his mom. I turn to ask, but he's already halfway out of the car, and I watch through the windscreen as he meets her with a huge hug. I get out too, just in time to hear her say, "I can't believe my baby's twenty-one!"

Definitely his mom, then. I stand patiently as she launches into an inquisition, demanding to know exactly what he did for his birthday, and Charlie tries to squirm out of telling her about his drunken musical tribute to her labor. Then she must notice that he's still a little hungover, because she grabs his head and studies his face up close.

"You must be Lee," a voice says, and I turn—and nearly fall over.

I'm looking at Charlie in thirty years.

It's uncanny how much he looks like his dad. If not for the fine lines and graying hair, I'd say they could be mirror images. Which means his dad is totally hot too, in an older-guy kind of way.

"Uh... hi. Yeah. Liam. I'm Liam Rigby." I pull myself together and stick out my hand. "It's nice to meet you, Mr. Martin. Thanks for letting me stay this weekend."

He shakes my hand, smiling warmly, and oh my god, Charlie's got his smile too.

"You're very welcome. Charlie talks about you all the time, and we wanted to meet you. But please call me Warren. Mr. Martin makes me feel old and boring." Before I can reply, he looks past me and calls, "Alle, are you seriously going to do this on the driveway in the cold with only the garden lights? Where's the hospitality you're apparently famous for?"

I glance over my shoulder in time to see Charlie's mom flip his dad the bird, and I bite back a grin. Charlie might look like his dad, but I've seen that exact expression currently on his mom's face on his more times than I can count. It changes to a smile when she sees me.

"Lee? It's so good to meet you at last." She lets go of

Charlie and comes over to hug me. "Come on inside out of the cold."

I refrain from mentioning that it's not really that cold. "Thanks, Ms. Martin. I'll just get my bag."

"Charlie and Warren can get them," she says, smirking at her husband. "And please call me Alle, or Allegra if you want to be formal." Wrapping her arm around mine, she turns me in the direction of the house. "Now tell me, how's Charlie really doing after that whole disaster last month? He says he's fine, but..." She trails off and shrugs as we walk up the three steps and through the front door.

"He's okay," I assure her, trying not to gawk. It's not that the inside of the house is flashily decorated. It actually looks very welcoming and lived-in, with keys on the console table beside the door and a pair of shoes abandoned on the bottom step. But it's just so big and... I don't even know what word to use. It looks like a high-end hotel. "He's uh, still a little bummed about losing some friends. And he doesn't like that he has to think about whether a gesture is appropriate before he acts on it. But he's gotten a lot better at picking up those social cues." I'm not sure if he told her about the sugar daddy incident or any of the other details, so I leave it at that.

She sighs, steering me into a living room. It's got long, plush leather couches facing a big fireplace with a fire crackling in it. The ceiling is high, and I get the feeling that during the day the wide windows give a killer view of the garden. "He's always had such a big, giving heart. I never had to tell him to share. If I'd known how it was going to come back to bite him in the ass, I might have tried to make him be selfish sometimes."

I shake my head as we sit on one of the insanely comfortable couches. "He's perfect the way he is." It's not until she smiles broadly that I realize how that sounded. "I mean, he's the kind of friend everyone wants." Annnnd that makes it sound like I'm only his friend because he's so generous. Shutting up now.

"He's a good boy, but he's far from perfect," she counters. "I lived with him for eighteen years. I know exactly how annoying he can be."

"You better be talking about Dad," Charlie says as he and his dad come into the room. He drops his overnight bag by the door, then bounces over the back of the other couch and sprawls on it. "Ahhh. I miss having a living room at school."

"So you say every time you come home," his dad says dryly. "Move your feet, please." He sits in the space Charlie just pulled his legs out of. "If you want a living room, you can always move off campus. We'll find you an apartment, or a house if you want a few roommates."

Charlie shakes his head. "I like being in the dorms near everyone."

I look down at my lap, smiling. That's such a Charlie thing. He really does like being surrounded by people—he knows more people in my dorm than I do.

We talk for a while, Charlie's parents asking us both questions about school, and I'm surprised by how relaxed I am. I was low-key dreading this weekend, but his parents are decent, and this couch is the best thing I've ever sat on... including Charlie's face. It's easy to forget they're apparently richer than god while I'm staring into the fireplace that could be in anyone's house, really.

Charlie yawns big, and his dad pokes him in the side, making him laugh. "Not getting enough sleep?"

"I had a... rough night," Charlie mumbles, pink-cheeked. "An early bedtime might be what I need."

"Me too," his mom agrees, standing. "I need to be up before five tomorrow to get the last-minute details organized before the party. Charlie, your suits have all been dry cleaned, but I didn't know which shirt you wanted to wear."

It somehow doesn't surprise me that Charlie has multiple suits. I'm kind of looking forward to seeing what he decides to wear tomorrow night.

"I'll check and make sure there's time for Marc to press it if necessary," he says. "Or I'll do it myself."

Alle nods. "Do it yourself. Marc's got enough to do tomorrow." She looks at me. "Marc runs the house and cooks for us. He works Saturday mornings, so you'll see him at breakfast, but then he's off from noon until Tuesday morning. And we won't take advantage of his kind nature during his time off," she says pointedly to Charlie.

"When have I ever?" he demands dramatically. "Marc's my bestie! He used to sneak me cookies and help me with my homework."

Both his parents laugh. "Helping you with homework... he deserves a raise for that," Warren muses fondly. "That was the most frustrating thing I've ever done in my life."

"Do you remember the time," Alle starts, and Charlie leaps to his feet, cutting her off.

"I'm beginning to remember why I love being at school so much," he says. "Come on, Lee. Let's leave my parents to pick apart my childhood in peace."

I obediently get up, but then glance sideways at his mom. "Tell me later?"

She cackles while Charlie howls about betrayal.

As I pick up my bags and Charlie grabs his, he asks, "What room have you put Lee in?"

Her smile vanishes. "Oh. I... thought he'd stay with you."

My face gets hot. I don't know what Charlie told his parents, but I may just have to kill him.

Charlie, damn him, misses the elephant in the room completely. "I mean, sure, that works, but you've always got a room ready for my other friends." Warren pinches his brow and shakes his head, and Charlie glances around at us in confusion. "What?"

"Give me fifteen minutes," Alle declares, moving toward the door, but I put out a hand to stop her.

"It's fine. Charlie and I have shared before." And this way, neither of us will be sneaking through the halls in the middle of the night.

She eyes me worriedly. "Are you sure? It's no trouble. I'm so sorry for assuming—"

"It's really fine," I assure her, then flick a glance at Charlie. "I'm sure you had a solid reason for assuming." He still looks completely blank, and I can't bring myself to be angry. "C'mon, Charlie. Let's get you to bed."

We wish his parents goodnight, and then I follow him upstairs and along a hallway to a bedroom that's the size of my aunt's whole apartment. It's definitely Charlie's room— signs of him are everywhere—but it still manages to look classy. And the king-size bed is calling to me like a magnet.

Charlie puts his bag on a bench at the end of the bed, unzips it, and begins taking out clothes and neatly putting them away. "I don't get why Mom didn't have Marc get a room ready for you," he says, frowning. "Not that I don't want to share—I do, and this makes it easier—but I don't get it."

I wander over to one of the two doors in the wall and peek inside. Bathroom. Hopefully that means the other one is... yep, a closet. I hang my suit bag up with Charlie's legions of clothes, then step back into the bedroom.

"She thinks we're sleeping together," I explain patiently. "Which we are, but I didn't think you'd tell your mom that."

"I didn't!" He frowns. "Do you think she thinks we're... you know... boyfriends?"

My heart freezes in my chest. I clear my throat. "I don't know. What did you tell her about me?"

He opens his mouth to reply, then closes it and shakes his head. "Never mind. You sure you don't mind not having a room to yourself?"

I push aside my curiosity—what was he going to say?—and smile. "If we were at school, I'd be sharing with you this weekend anyway. And we wouldn't have a bed that big." I nod toward the acres of mattress.

"True." He grins. "This is my chance to show you my best work."

I eye him as he prowls toward me. "Are you up to it? Because no offense, but I don't want you hurling in the middle of sex." He stuck to just fries for dinner because, in his words, "a hangover, a long car ride in traffic, and a burger don't mix."

"What, you wouldn't lovingly mop up my vomit?" he teases, and I try not to gag at the thought. "Okay, fine, I promise not to hurl. But that means you don't get a blowjob tonight, because I don't trust my gag reflex right now."

If I wasn't a horny twenty-year-old, I'd pass on sex after hearing that.

"Fine, no bj," I say instead. "But you'll owe me."

"I'll give you one in the morning," he assures me. "It can be your very own personal wake-up call." He drapes his forearms over my shoulders and links his hands at my nape. "You'll drift out of sleep and it'll feel so good, you'll think you're still dreaming."

I snort. "You've got a high opinion of your skills." He's not wrong, though.

"Is that a challenge?" His brow quirks, and I lean up to kiss him.

"If you want it to be. But not until your gag reflex is under control again." Ducking out of his hold, I head for the bathroom.

When I come back out, he's turned off the overhead light and the bedside lamps cast a warm glow over his bare skin as he bends over the bed. The globes of his ass flex as he widens his stance, giving me a peek at his pucker.

"Wow. This is what I call hospitality," I manage, and he chuckles, peering over his shoulder at me.

"At your service."

"I like the sound of that. What—"

The knock gives us a split-second of warning before the door starts to open, and Charlie drops to the floor and frantically yanks the quilt from the bed.

"Boys, is there any..." Alle trails off as she pokes her head in. Probably because I'm standing in the middle of the room with a boner she hopefully can't see while her son is a quilt-covered lump on the floor. "Uhh." She bites her lip, and I wonder what she's thinking. She looks from me to the Charlie lump and back, then says, "Do you have everything you need?"

A lock would probably be good, but I don't say that, just nod. "Yes. Thank you." I'm too embarrassed to say more. Thank all the sex fairies that I'm still fully dressed and she didn't come in thirty seconds later.

"Okay. Well, goodnight." She smiles, but it's tight. She's probably going to hate me now.

"Uh, goodnight." My return smile is also strained.

"Goodnight, Mom," the lump says, his words muffled. Alle bites her lip.

"Night, spawn." She backs out and closes the door.

There's a moment of dead silence before I hear her laugh.

Then it gets worse.

"Boys still up?" Charlie's dad asks.

"Do *not* go in there," Alle says, and I bury my face in my hands.

"Why? What did you see?" Warren sounds amused, and footsteps approach the door.

"They're making a blanket fort."

I snort, dropping my hands and looking at Charlie. He's inched the quilt back so his face is visible, but it's still wrapped around the rest of him.

"A blanket f—? Ohhhhh, a *blanket fort*. Right. I don't need to say goodnight." The footsteps recede, and Charlie and I wait until the hallway is completely silent.

"Oh my god," I say.

"That was... yeah. I guess Mom has another embarrassing story to tell." He snickers. "It could have been worse."

I try not to think about that.

He throws back the quilt, revealing his naked body sitting on the floor. "Let's get this back on track."

I stare. "Are you nuts? We can't have sex now. Your parents..." I shudder, unable to finish the sentence.

He clambers to his feet. It's completely unsexy, but my cock still twitches as I watch. "They won't come back, and their room is at the other end of the house. There's three bedrooms and two and a half baths between us."

I look at his hard-on, standing stiff and proud. "How can you still be that hard when your mom almost caught us?" I ignore the fact my own dick is still half-hard and getting harder with his gorgeous body displayed before me.

"She didn't see anything, and she's gone now, and I really want you." He gives me a pleading look.

"Charlie—"

"Pleeeease? You can lie back and I'll do all the work. And we'll keep the quilt over us so if someone does come in— which they won't—they won't see anything."

That's ridiculous, but also, I don't think I'll be able to sleep beside Charlie tonight if I don't get off first. And I can't say no to him. So I pretend to give in reluctantly. "Fine."

His smile lights up his face, and he turns to arrange the quilt on the bed while I strip and put my clothes on the chair in the corner.

When I turn back to the bed, he pats the mattress, and I join him there, unable to resist stealing another kiss.

"If you really don't want to, we don't have to," he murmurs, and I draw back enough to look at his face. He's smiling hopefully, but his gaze is steady.

"Of course I want to."

The smile beams full-force, and he pushes my shoulder.

"Lie down, then. I'm all prepped, but you need a condom still."

I recline against the pillows and watch fondly as he tries to find the condom he'd apparently put on the bed before his mom came in. It's disappeared, so he grabs another one, bends over to give my cock one good suck, then rolls the condom on.

"I love your mouth," I tell him.

"Tomorrow," he promises. "Wake-up call. It'll be epic." He rises onto his knees and straddles my hips. "Ready?"

I reach out and take hold of his dick, pointing so eagerly at me, and give it a pump. "I am now."

He positions himself over the head of my cock and slowly eases down. I try not to let my eyes roll back in ecstasy. "Your ass is a fucking miracle."

He seats himself fully and gives me that blissed-out, sex-drunk smile I love so much. He's so incredibly responsive. "Shhh, I'm busy using your body for my pleasure."

My laugh is choked off when he starts to move, rising, then sinking down again. He sets a swift rhythm, and I lie back and lose myself in the sights and sensations. Soon sweat sheens his skin, muscles working as he fucks himself onto me, his brown eyes closing as he throws his head back. Just looking at him like this is enough to bring me to the edge, and the way his ass milks me is too much...

I tighten my grip on his cock and begin stroking in earnest, loving the sound he makes as my thumb swipes over the flushed, leaking head.

"Lee," he moans, and shock thrills through me.

"Shh," I hiss, glancing at the door. "You gotta be quiet."

He laughs breathlessly and speeds up, then drives down,

burying me as deep as he can, his ass clenching tight around me as he cries out and comes all over my chest.

I cling to sanity, wanting to hold on just—

He opens his eyes and smiles at me, panting. "You're so amazing."

My orgasm explodes through me.

Lying in the dark, I stare at the ceiling and listen to Charlie's even breathing. He's cuddled up against my side the way he always does when we sleep together. I thought it was because the beds at school are so small, but there's literally feet of space on the other side of him, and he's still glued to me. He really does love cuddles.

And it's killing me.

The cuddles. The kisses. The texting. The constant togetherness. I love it all, but knowing he thinks of me as just the buddy he bangs is... painful. I have nobody to blame but myself, though, and I can't bring myself to let him go.

I turn my head and softly kiss his cheek where it lies beside mine on the pillow, and he stirs.

"Lee?" he murmurs, still mostly asleep.

"I'm here. Go back to sleep."

He rolls onto his side and tucks his face against my neck. "So glad you're here."

Aww. He's such a sweetheart. "I am too."

"Need you always."

I close my eyes. If only he meant that the way I want him to.

"Lee?" He sounds more awake now.

"Yeah?" My voice is hoarse.

"Don't laugh at me... or leave. Really don't leave. Please."

"I'm not going anywhere."

"You're the only person who really gets me and likes me anyway. Aside from my parents. But they don't count, 'cause, like, they're obligated to love me."

Through my breaking heart, I say, "They'd love you even if they weren't obligated. You're a loveable person." It's the closest I can get to admitting how I feel—even to myself.

"Maybe. But I'm still so glad I have you."

I bite my lip, trying to think of a response, but a second later he adds, "And I'm kinda worried how they'll be if I fuck up the company."

I freeze in the dark. "What?"

The sheets rustle, and his shoulder moves against my arm, as if he's shrugging. "I'm supposed to join Dad at the company when I graduate, but you know me. I manage okay with my schoolwork, but I'm not exactly passionate about warehousing and distribution. And I don't think 'managing okay' is the standard my dad sets at his Fortune 500 company. There's a pretty good chance I'm going to end up tanking the whole thing, trashing generations of work, destroying thousands of people's livelihoods, and disappointing my parents."

Whoa. I swallow hard, then fumble around for his hand and grip it tight. "I don't think so. I think you're too conscientious to ever let that happen. You ask for help when you need it. But you're underestimating yourself anyway. You might not love your schoolwork, but you're not stupid, Charlie. And you're amazing with people. You'd be the kind of boss people genuinely love and feel comfortable talking to when there are problems."

He doesn't say anything for a long moment, then squeezes my hand and whispers, "I don't want to be that boss. I mean... I don't want to be the boss of that company." His voice cracks a little.

I don't know what to say. He's never talked about this before, never even mentioned it. I never even thought about what he'd be doing after we graduate, but it's obviously something that weighs on him. "What do you want to do?" I ask, hoping I don't say the wrong thing.

He sighs. "I don't know. It would be so much easier if I did. My parents are great—you met them. They won't make me chain myself to something I hate. But they won't just let me do nothing. Not that I want to do nothing. The boredom would kill me. If I go to them and say I don't want to work for the company, I'm almost positive they'd be fine with it, but they'll ask what I want to do instead. And if I say I don't know, they'll suggest I start working there just until I work out what I do want. And the next thing I know, I'll have been there for thirty years and feel like I can never leave because it's my legacy."

I wince, glad he can't see me. "There's time still," I say, wishing it didn't sound so weak and clichéd. "We can think about what careers might make you happy."

Charlie raises my hand to his mouth and kisses it. "See? You get me. You accept me. Nobody else knows me like you do. If you think it's going to be okay, I believe you."

Words catch in my throat, and I lie there in silence as his breathing evens out again. Nobody's ever had that level of trust in me.

Maybe I should stop overthinking this and just go with it. Bask in his affection, enjoy the sex, the kisses, his company. There's only a couple months left until the end of the school year, and who knows what will change over summer? By next year, this might all be just a fond memory for both of us.

CHAPTER SIXTEEN

CHARLIE

THE SOUND OF LEE'S VOICE LEADS ME TO THE KITCHEN on this lovely Saturday morning. Waking up alone wasn't my favorite thing in the world, but hearing Lee's chuckle and smelling bacon and waffles makes up for it.

I hover in the doorway, watching with a smile as Marc and Lee laugh together. "Care to share the joke?" I saunter in and take the stool next to Lee at the breakfast bar. I really want to lean over and kiss his cheek, but since Jake's little speech yesterday and then Mom's assumption about Lee not needing his own room, I'm not sure if that would be too boyfriendly or not. Part of me is starting to think I don't care, that maybe I want Lee to be my boyfriend, but our situation is kinda awks. Plus, no way do I want to risk that he's not interested in that and might dial back our friendship.

He grins over at me, and my chest tightens. "Marc was telling me about the time—"

I hold up my hand. "Nope. Enough said. Whatever it was, I don't need to relive it."

Lee chuckles again, and I get up and walk around the island to hug Marc from behind. "Didja miss me?"

The combination groan/laugh is a familiar sound from my childhood, as is the way he taps the tongs against my hand. "Like a hole in the head. Get out of my way before you set the kitchen on fire again."

"You set the kitchen on fire?" Lee asks. I kiss the side of Marc's head before returning to my stool.

"Just one time. It was an accident. Nobody told me that metal can't go in the microwave."

"Aw, you were a little kid still."

"Not as little as you'd think," Marc says, sliding loaded plates in front of us, then raising a brow at me. "Coffee?"

"Yes, please." I don't suggest getting it myself. Marc was the one who taught me to use the coffee machine, but he doesn't like people touching things in the kitchen when he's there.

A minute later there's a steaming cup of heavenly goodness in front of me and I'm digging into my bacon. Marc leans against the island with his own coffee and talks to us while we eat. He knows all about the scene in the café—Mom told him, and then his nephew showed him the TikTok—and he's curious about Mr. Romance and whether Lee's coaching is helping me to be less oblivious.

Finally, Lee sits back, his plate empty. "That was amazing. Can I do the dishes?"

"That's nice, but no," Marc declares, his voice firm. Lee hesitates, then smiles.

"Thank you, then. I'm going to grab a shower."

"I'll be five minutes," I promise. There's not much left on my plate.

"I think I can cope," he assures me dryly, and Marc laughs. As soon as Lee's deposited his dishes in the sink and left, Marc reaches over and smacks me upside the head.

"Ow! What did I do?" I shove in some waffle and rub the sore spot.

"You didn't text to tell me you have a boyfriend. I changed your shitty diapers and helped with your algebra homework, kid. That means you have to tell me what's happening in your life."

I squirm. "Lee's not my boyfriend."

Marc folds his arms across his impressive chest and just *looks* at me.

"He's not. We're friends."

One eyebrow slowly rises, and I sigh in defeat.

"Okay, fine, I think I want him to be my boyfriend, but it's complicated. I'm not sure if he likes me that way."

He stares at me, then buries his face in his hands.

"Stop being all dramatic," I chide, scooping up the last of my bacon.

Running his fingers through his hair, he eyes me. "Okay. I'm gonna let you work this one out on your own. He's a good friend to you?"

"The best," I assure the man who helped raise me. "I know I can trust him with anything." I think about our conversation in bed last night. I'm still low-key worried about what my future holds, but knowing that Lee's got my back and will help me sort out my life takes away a lot of the stress. If he thinks we can work it out, then it's all good.

Liam

The fundraiser is a revelation to me. It's being held in the ballroom of a fancy hotel, and from the moment we step inside, it's like we've entered another world. Uniformed servers circulate with trays of drinks and canapés, and there's so much sparkly jewelry on display, the crowd seems to glitter. I felt instantly out of place.

That lasted only until Charlie shoved a drink in one of my hands, a bite-sized morsel of deliciousness into the other, then dragged me halfway across the room to talk to a man who geeks out with him about the suit some actor wore on the red carpet at the BAFTAs. I only know what the BAFTAs are because Charlie made me watch the red carpet with him, but they're so enthusiastic in their reminiscences of clothes that I can't help enjoying myself. Then they notice I'm there and Charlie introduces me. Turns out the man is such a big-time TV producer that even I've heard of him. I can't be nervous after that—not after seeing someone so rich and powerful be so normal.

We move from group to group, and the tone is always the same. Charlie knows almost everyone, and the few times he doesn't, he introduces himself with a smile and a self-deprecating "I'm Allegra's son." People welcome him warmly, ask him about school, and listen when he weighs in on whatever's being discussed. He makes it a point to include me as well, and I've gotten to speak to some really interesting people. Before we move on to the next group, he finds a casual and non-pushy way to remind people of the cause being supported and how much their contribution can help.

Because even though this is a five-thousand-dollar-per-plate event, people are expected to make a donation as well.

When dinner is announced and people start making their way to their tables, Charlie smiles over at me. "Not as boring as you thought, right?"

"Not even close," I admit.

"After dinner and the speeches, there's gonna be dancing. Mom likes to get bands that people are talking about but haven't had a big break yet. Two of her previous finds got record deals after playing one of her fundraisers."

Charlie might look like his dad, but he thinks so much like his mom. I can totally imagine him coming up with an idea like that. This whole time he and I have been mingling, his parents have been doing the same, with Allegra swooping into groups, getting them smiling, then coaxing promises of money before moving on.

We wander toward the tables and find our places. Charlie already warned me that we wouldn't be sitting with his parents, but I'm surprised to see that we're sitting with several A-list actors from one of the decade's biggest movie franchises.

"Charlie," one of them greets warmly. "Your mom said you were coming tonight."

"Wouldn't miss it," Charlie assures him. "This is my friend Liam." He goes around the table introducing everyone to me, even though half of them need no introduction. I manage not to fanboy like an idiot.

"Great to meet you all." My smile feels a bit stiff, but I don't think anyone notices.

I keep quiet during the appetizer course, letting the conversation flow around me and observing the way Charlie interacts with everyone. He's completely natural, even though I know he's a crazy fan of this movie franchise. He talks about school, about the country one of the actors was just on location in, about the economy, about private schools in LA... I knew he was a people person, that he's highly social, but I didn't realize until now how far that goes. He truly has the ability to fit in with anyone. More, he likes people. He likes chatting to them, and he makes an effort to show interest in the things that interest them. When he doesn't know about something, he asks, then listens intently to the response and follows up in a way that shows the speaker he's engaged.

For all that we say he's oblivious and misses cues, it doesn't show when he's in "work" mode. And that's very much what this is. Allegra clearly trusts him to make these people comfortable and ensure they enjoy themselves enough to donate big, and Charlie's making it happen.

I let myself be drawn into conversation with the actress on my right side about the differences between Southern California and Wisconsin, where we both happen to be from, but I can't shake the idea forming in the back of my brain.

The music starts, and Charlie leans toward me. "Dance?"

I smile at the actress. "Excuse me? I've been promised dancing."

She laughs. "That sounds like a great idea."

In the end, most of the table joins the exodus to the dance floor. The first few songs have an upbeat tempo, and I let myself relax into the music. Charlie's a good dancer, and the band is a lot better than I expected.

Then the music changes, the beat slowing, and Charlie

gives me a questioning smile. I move closer and loop my arms around his shoulders.

"Having fun?" he asks, putting his hands on my hips. His long fingers graze the sides of my ass.

"Surprisingly, yes. Your mom throws a good party."

"And it's all for a good cause. You're earning karma points just by being here."

I laugh, and he draws me a little closer.

"Thanks for coming with me. And for being you." The serious note brings my gaze to his face, and I search his expression. There's a hint of vulnerability there. Is this about what he said last night?

"Thanks for inviting me. And for being you." I hesitate, then add, "There's nobody else I'd rather be with."

He sighs and closes the last bit of distance between us, leaning his head against mine, and I let myself drown in the moment.

CHAPTER SEVENTEEN

CHARLIE

Lee's acting weird.

I think it started on the weekend, but I can't be sure. He got on great with Mom and Dad—and Marc—which I knew he would, and he even enjoyed the fundraiser. I mean, that might be because I made him dance with me most of the night. Gymnasts have awesome dance moves. Everyone there was jealous of me for being his partner.

But since we got back, he's been... strange. I wanna say distant, but what does that even mean, really? We still spend as much time together, so there's no distance between us. And yet somehow there is.

I skip class to go to pre-gym lunch. I don't always go and watch Lee be a hot gymnast, and when I do, I don't usually have lunch with them first. Lee's kind of a stickler for going to class. He doesn't actually say anything when I skip, but he works so hard on his own coursework that I know he thinks it's important. And hey, if I'm going to be a valuable part of the family business after I graduate, I should be trying to learn everything I can, right?

I try not to cry at the thought.

Anyway, since Lee's being weird, I want to spend more time with him, so I'm skipping class for lunch and gym with him and his friends.

Ian and Matt are already in the dining hall, so I wave at them and get food for me and Lee.

He comes in just as I'm heading for the table, and I know he's seen me when he frowns. Is he really that upset that I'm skipping class? I wait for him to join me.

"I got you salad," I point out hopefully. "And I asked someone to take notes for me in class."

The frown fades a little. "Are you okay? Nothing happened?"

Oh. He's worried about me!

"I'm fine," I rush to assure him. "I just wanted to spend some time with you."

If anything, that brings the frown back. "Come on, then."

I follow him to the table, sulking a little, and we sit. Matt and Ian are arguing about something and barely notice us.

"I'm telling you, it means I don't have to go. If anything, I should go to Illinois instead. Which I won't," Matt says, jabbing his fork in the air for emphasis. Lee grabs his hand and lowers it.

"Try not to stab any of us today, please."

"Except yourself," Ian snaps, glaring. "If I have to go, you have to go. Gabe even said you should go. So you're going. Don't make me get on that plane alone!"

I shoot a glance at Lee. Is this about spring break?

"Flying cross-country beside a walking bag of vomit isn't fun for me, dude!"

"How do you think I feel about it?" Ian's voice rises in pitch, making him sound near-hysterical.

"Let's all chill," I say in my best soothing voice. "What's the problem here? Aside from Ian's vomit."

"My brother can't make it for spring break after all. He has to stay in Illinois because the ga— He has to work. So I said I may as well not go either."

Got it. "Man, no. Ian might be a walking bag of vomit, but he's your bro and he needs you. Plus, it's a trip to JU. You should be all over that."

They exchange glances. "You like Joy Universe?"

I shrug. "What's not to like? Disneyland is closer to home for me, but we always went to JU because we like it better." I frown. "They did have some problems a few years back, but that seems to have been cleared up."

Ian looks at Lee. "You don't have plans for spring break, do you?"

He shakes his head. "Maybe building a new website for Mr. Romance. And I might take up running. If Matt stays, he can come with me."

"Or you can come with us," Ian counters, then adds, "Both of you."

"What? To JU?" I've never heard Lee sound so confused. I, on the other hand, am pumped.

"Yes! We'd love to."

Lee turns to me, eyebrow raised. "We would?"

I nod emphatically. "We definitely fucking would."

"It'll be fun," Ian coaxes. "Kieran got us the whole VIP package, and the resort we're staying at kicks ass. Plus all the parks and shit. Since Gabe can't come, his room will be empty."

"It's cool of you to ask, but it's not in my budget," Lee says firmly, and I pout.

"It probably is, though," Matt counters. "Kieran got a huge discount because he used to work there and apparently they still love him. Plus, you guys could split it. Let me call and find out how much Gabe's room would cost." He whips out his phone. Lee starts to protest, but I elbow him, then lean in close.

"Would it hurt to find out the price?" I murmur.

He turns to look at me, his face close enough to kiss. "And what about the airfare? And food?"

"Actually," Ian interrupts, eavesdropping shamelessly, "it's an all-inclusive package. Meals are included."

Lee flips him off without looking.

"Let me ask you something, and then we'll never discuss this again," I promise. "Wait to see what Matt says, and then decide if you really can't afford it or if you're just pinching pennies. Because you deserve a break, Lee. You work so hard. And you're taking classes over the summer, which means you won't have a break then either." I hesitate, then add, "I want to go on vacation with you, and I can pay for it if need be. Do this for me, please?" I know it's playing dirty, but the only way to get him to take time off is to get him away from school.

He doesn't look happy with me, and I brace myself, but finally he just nods. "I'll wait to see what the total cost will be, and I'll think about it."

Victory! I try not to grin.

Matt ends his call and says, "He's going to email me the info. I'll forward it to you."

"Great, thanks," Lee says. "I'll check on flights and stuff and let you know."

"It would be awesome if you came," Ian begs, and Lee throws a napkin at his head.

I smile. This is nice.

Sitting with my knees drawn up to my chest, I watch Lee run down the mats and spin his body through the air. I'm not sure what he's doing, exactly, but it looks amazing. He's not using the equipment today, just doing stuff on the mats... Floor Exercise, he called it, and it definitely looks like exercise. When I was a kid I could do a mean cartwheel, but it's been a long time since I tried, and I wouldn't want to lay any money on whether I can still manage it. The way he flows through the air is just amazing. And he's always so happy and relaxed after gym time. I want to watch him do this always.

I sigh. All the time. Forever. After what Jake said last week and Mom's mix-up on the weekend, I'm starting to wonder if maybe I've missed something important. Maybe they're right, and Lee and I *are* more than just friends. But how can I know for sure?

Duh. Google.

I pull out my phone, open a browser window, and type *how do you know if you're more than friends?*

A shocking number of results pop up. I guess that means I'm not the only dumbass on the planet who can't always read social cues. I browse through the first few, but the one thing they definitely have in common is that they're talking about friends who aren't already having sex, so things like "it seems like they want to kiss you" or "their hugs linger" are on the lists. Those don't apply to me and Lee, since we already kiss and hug. So I change my search to *how do you know if you're more than friends with benefits?*

Again, a whole lot of results. This must be a really common problem. Yay for me.

I click into the first article and skim the first item on the list. *He calls you baby.* Okay, that's a no. I'm pretty sure neither of us have ever called the other "baby." So far, so good.

My smug smirk drops as I continue down the list. *Friends know his name... hang out, no sex... spend the night, get brunch...* We do all those things. We also know things about each other's lives, talk and text on the phone, and... well, he hasn't lent me a book, but he bought me one—I think that counts. *And* it was a book I liked a lot. I bought myself the rest in the series. So that covers off the item about knowing each other's likes and dislikes. Fuck, there's one about knowing things about family members—he's *met* my parents.

I go back to the search results and find another article, but that one's just as bad.

"What are you frowning about?" Ian grabs his water bottle and chugs.

"I think Lee and I are unofficial boyfriends."

He chokes, and I scramble up to thump him on the back. It's weirdly satisfying.

"Thanks, I'm good," he wheezes, waving to Matt and Lee when they look over to see if he's okay. "You think... Why do you think that?"

I eye him. "Can you keep a secret? At least until I work this out?"

He sits down beside me. "Yes. As long as it won't hurt Liam."

"I would never hurt Lee." I shake my head vehemently. "That's why I need to talk about this."

"Okay, hit me."

I explain everything that happened last week, then show him the articles I looked at. "What does this mean? You introduced me to Lee so he could help me avoid friends falling for me, and now I might be his friend falling for him."

Ian stares at me. "This is the weirdest thing ever. And I have a lot of experience with weird things."

I pout. "Are you going to help?"

He nods. "Yep. For starters, those articles are written by bored interns and designed to be click-bait. Don't take them as law. They did make some good points, but the only people who can know if you're more than friends with benefits are you and Liam."

"But I *don't* know," I whine.

"You probably do. For example, friends don't get blind drunk and whine about a friend going on a date like you just told me you did."

Frowning, I say, "I'm not sure the two things are connected, though. Maybe I just got drunk for no reason."

Oh look, Ian's perfected his "you are such a dumbass" look. "Okay, so it would be fine with you if I set Liam up with this super-hot guy in one of my classes? He's smart, sexy, and thinks Liam is amazing after only talking to him for two minutes."

"He is amazing," I defend. "I guess that would be okay." My stomach churns.

"Great!" Ian pronounces. "And you won't care when one date turns into three, and they get serious enough that Liam ends your friends with bennies arrangement. And then his boyfriend will come with anytime you guys hang out—which won't be as often, because they'll be spending so much time together. Touching. Having sex. Talking. Making plans for—"

"Okay, fine, shut up." I clamp my hands over my ears until his mouth stops moving. My whole body feels sick and gross just at the thought of Lee being with someone else like that. "I think I have feelings for Lee."

Ian raises a brow. "You think?"

I sigh. "I'm butthole over nose in love with him."

"Butthole ov— Dude, what the fuck?"

"It's an expression," I defend. "Stop picking on what I'm saying and help me!"

"I thought I just did. You've realized your feelings for Liam." He dusts his hands together. "Job done."

"Not job done. Remember, he helped me solve the problem of friends wanting to date me, and now I'm his friend who wants to date him! He's going to hate me. Or worse, he's going to let me down gently and then distance himself from me until we barely ever talk. Either way, I lose him."

"Oh my god," Ian mutters. "How is this happening to me? I should have just let myself dehydrate. Who cares about dizziness and muscle cramps, really?"

I look over at him anxiously. "Are you dizzy? Do you need me to get you more water? Here, lie down."

Holding up both hands, he declares, "I'm fine. But thanks." His smile is sheepish but warm. "You're a good friend, Charlie. I promise you, Liam won't hate you if you tell him how you feel."

"You can't make promises like that."

"I can. He's not going to hate you."

Hope wars with worry in my chest. "What about distancing himself from me? Is he going to do that?"

"Charlie, you need to have this conversation with Liam, not me."

I sigh. I know he's right, but I'm terrified of the risk involved. So many of the possible scenarios end with me losing Lee. "I want to get used to the idea of being in love with him first. Maybe bask in it for a while. Just in case."

It's his turn to sigh, and for a minute, we both watch Lee work his magic on the mats.

"What's he doing?" I ask, eyes following the almost effortless way he hurls his body through the air.

Ian waits for Lee to land, then says, "Round off, backflip, back sault."

"Those words mean nothing to me."

"Then why did you ask?"

I shrug. "Shouldn't I know stuff like this about the guy I love?"

He laughs. "Dude, you should know stuff like his favorite movie and how he likes his coffee. The names of gymnastic elements he only does for fun, not so much."

Damn it. "I have a lot to learn about being in love."

Lee's been in the shower for two minutes when I decide the boyfriendly thing to do is to join him for a surprise blowjob. Maybe I can ease him into the whole idea of us being in a real relationship by doing all the things boyfriends do, and then when he's lulled into a false sense of security, I can be all, "Surprise! We've been boyfriends this whole time!"

I run into the first problem when I get to the bathroom and realize I can't just join Lee in the shower stall. Whose fucking idea was it to make them lockable from the inside? How's a guy supposed to give his boyfriend a surprise shower bj if he has to knock first?

I lean against the stall door. "Lee?"

There's a pause, and then Lee says, "Um... yes? Charlie, is that you?"

"It's me. Let me in."

"I'm showering. What's wrong?"

"Nothing's wrong. I need you to let me in."

"Uhhhh..." The voice behind me has me turning to see Dean, whose room is down the hall, blinking at me. "You know there's more than one shower, right?" He points to the other stalls.

Maybe Dad was right about me getting a place off campus. Lee and I can live together and have shared showers all the time without interruptions or stupid locking stalls.

"It's all good," I assure him. "I just gotta talk to Lee about something."

He opens his mouth to say something, hesitates, then closes it again. "I'll, uh... go. I can use the bathroom at my friend's place."

"Have a great night!"

The look he gives me is just plain weird. "You... too." As he stumbles out, I turn back to the stall door.

"Leeeeeee. Let me in."

"Jesus Christ, Charlie, what the hell?" The lock clicks, and I almost fall into the stall as the door swings open. Lee's on the other side, suds in his hair, looking pissed off and also hot as hell all ripped and wet. I crowd in, make sure the door is closed and locked, and then kiss him.

"What—"

I cut him off with another kiss, backing him toward the still-running water. "Surprise! Time for a blowjob."

"Charlie, wait—you're still wearing clothes!"

Am I? I look down, and yep. Ooops.

Fortunately, it's just jeans and a tee, nothing that will be ruined by the water. I do take a second to kick my shoes off and into the "dry" part of the stall. They're Vans, so a bit of water won't hurt them, but still.

He starts to laugh. "Seriously, what are you doing? Go back to the room. I'll be done in a minute."

I set my jaw stubbornly and drop to my knees. "No. This is a surprise suck. Relax and enjoy it." He's blocking most of the water, but as it streams down his body, some ends up on me. I look up at him and see a combination of hunger and... something. Sadness? Why is he sad? I don't ever want him to be sad. This has to be a happy bj.

I blink away water and focus on his cock, which is only half-hard. "Hello." I stroke a finger along the length, and it perks up. "It's good to see you too."

"Charlie..." Lee sounds exasperated, but when I look up, he's smiling.

"Shh. This is between me and your dick. We need some alone time." I wrap my hand around his cock and enjoy the way he shudders. He's a little longer than me but not as thick, and he's got this fucking awesome bend to the left. Trust me when I say you haven't lived until you've been fucked by a guy with a curved dick.

"Can you get on with it before the water goes cold?"

I scoff, slowly jerking him to fully hard while I think about how I want to do this. "There's a bottomless water heater. Nice try, though."

Coming to a decision, I let go, put my hands behind my back, then swallow him down as deep as I can.

"Fuck!" Lee's cry echoes off the tile, giving me endless satisfaction. His hands come to my head, not pushing or controlling, just resting there, and I look up at him. The blissed-out expression on his face just makes me want to work harder.

I draw back until only the head is in my mouth, then wriggle my tongue into the slit the way I know he likes, and his hands clench in my hair. Oh yeah, baby, that's it.

For a few minutes I stick to that, alternating taking him as deep as I can with working just the head, and it's not long before he's panting.

Time to step it up.

Slowly, I bring my hands back into play, first sliding them up the front of his thighs, where the rock-solid muscles are trembling. I stay there for a moment, letting him get used to the touch... letting him become complacent.

Then I move one hand to cup his sac.

The sound that bursts from his throat is raw and fucking hot.

And loud.

"Uh, you okay in there?" someone calls, and oh shit, I didn't hear them come in. Lee's fingers dig into my scalp, and I give him my best puppy-dog eyes.

He clears his throat. "Fine," he manages. "Um... just... remembering how bad... um..." He yanks my hair, and I realize I'm still lightly sucking his cock, and that's probably not helping right now.

Oops. Too bad.

He glares at me when I shrug, then coughs and finishes, "...I bombed a test."

"Really?" Whoever the guy is, he sounds like he's laughing. Over the sound of the shower, I hear a flush. "Because it sounds like you're jerking it and having a great time." Water runs in one of the sinks as Lee sputters, then the guy calls, "Have fun!" and seemingly leaves.

We wait a beat, but he's really gone.

"I'm going to kill you," Lee promises, but his dick is still hard as a spike in my mouth, so I ignore him and walk my fingers back between his legs, trailing lightly over his taint and between his cheeks. One finger circles his pucker, and air explodes from him. "After," he adds, letting his head drop back.

Happy bj for the win! I settle back in, determined to make this a good memory despite the interruption. Lee hardcore loves ass play, so it's not going to take him long to come now. Steady suction on his cock, one hand on his balls, and a finger teasing his hole...

"Get off, I wanna come on your face," he gasps, and oh fuck yeah. I pull back, replacing my mouth with my hand, jerking him in steady strokes, and his whole body goes tense right before cum spurts from him. I close my eyes as it paints ribbons over my lips and cheeks and Lee moans.

It's the best sound in the world.

A second later, he frees himself from my hold, and I open my eyes as he drops to his knees in front of me. The shower spray, no longer blocked by his body, rains over us both.

"You're such an idiot," he chides, then leans in to kiss me, tasting himself in my mouth. "Thank you. This was a great surprise." His hand goes to the soaked front of my jeans. "Get these off and let me take care of you."

"That's not what this was about," I protest, but don't stop him. I might be clueless sometimes, but I'm not stupid.

"But I want a turn."

Well, then... doesn't being a good boyfriend mean giving your man what he wants and needs? Time for me to step up and show what great boyfriend material I am.

CHAPTER EIGHTEEN

LIAM

I don't know what's gotten into Charlie lately, but he's been super clingy. Part of me loves it—any excuse to be with him is great, right? But then times like this, I want to strangle him.

"Charlie, let it go," I say again, as patiently as I can manage. A little less patiently than the first time, but hey, I think I should get points for having any patience left at all. "It was not the end of the world that we couldn't sit together on the flight." In fact, it might have been a good thing that I got put across the aisle, because Ian really is a walking bag of vomit. And he likes to share his misery—even with the distance between us, I could hear his whining.

To be fair, he's entitled to whine. It's a four-hour flight and he puked six times. I'm surprised he had that much in him, considering he's been fasting since last night in an attempt to reduce the vomiting.

But as if Ian's whining isn't enough, Charlie's been pouting that we were separated. Ian couldn't sit alone, what with needing to be looked after, and Matt couldn't because

Ian's a big baby who insisted his "surrogate brother" had to be the one to look after him. Charlie tried to get the airline to rearrange our seats so he and I could sit together, but the flight was full and it wasn't going to happen. I'm not sure why this is such a big deal to him, since we're going to be sharing a room for the next week. Isn't that enough togetherness?

Apparently not, since we're still on the airbridge and he's complained about it twice. That's not even counting the times he whined before we left San Diego.

He carries our cabin bags—all four of them—while Matt and I help a sick, dehydrated Ian. The airline offered a wheel-chair, but that would have meant waiting for everyone else to deplane first, and Ian just wanted to "get off this flying remnant of a hell dimension" as soon as possible. Matt assured us all that he'll bounce back quickly now he's not in the air, and that all he needs is electrolytes. From the looks of him, that's wishful thinking, but they've been through this before, so they probably know best.

We emerge into the gate area, and a whistle catches my attention.

"There they are," Matt says, turning us in that direction. We walk toward two men, one of whom is an older version of Ian—only hotter. His full tattoo sleeves are on display in the tank top he's wearing, though I can't make out the designs. The guy with him, presumably the boyfriend who scored us this amazing deal (because yeah, it really is) is also good-looking, but in a more polished way. His red hair is neatly combed, and he's wearing chinos and a polo shirt.

Ian's brother comes forward to help us with him, and we maneuver him into a seat. "Here." The redhead offers a bottle of Gatorade and packet of Saltines, and Ian takes them grate-fully. They clearly knew what to expect.

While Ian sips and nibbles and takes deep breaths, his brother hauls Matt into a tight hug. "I've got orders to crack your ribs with hugs," he says, and visibly squeezes. Matt yelps and beats at the back of his head.

"Con, need... breathe!"

Laughing, Con lets him go and turns to us. "I'm Connor, Ian's smarter and better-looking older brother. You must be Liam. We've heard a lot about you."

I shake the hand he offers. "Hi. Thanks for letting us tag along."

He flips a hand. "The room was there, and I like meeting the boys' friends. Honestly, I like knowing they even have friends. Gabe, Matt's brother, was half convinced they made you up."

Matt makes a sound of protest. "Just for that, I'm going to feel up your hot boyfriend."

Said hot boyfriend laughs, still sitting beside Ian and gently rubbing his back.

"This is Charlie," I say, more to move the conversation forward than anything else.

"Hey!" Charlie smiles winningly. "Great to meet you."

"Good to meet you too. My hot boyfriend's name is Kieran, in case you were wondering."

Kieran rolls his eyes. "Could you stop calling me that, please?"

Connor winks. "But it's your name."

"Ugh, stop before I puke again," Ian interrupts. "I'm feeling better. Can we get out of this waiting room for purgatory?"

Kieran stands and pulls him up. "Yep. We'll grab your checked luggage, and there's a driver waiting for us. He dropped us off and went to park."

"Woohoo! Joy Universe, here we come!"

We all look at Charlie, and he drops the arms he was pumping in the air. "What? I don't understand why you're not more excited."

Kieran slings an arm around his shoulders and steers him into the main concourse. "People like you were my favorite guests when I worked here."

I smile, grab my cabin bag, and follow.

As our butler closes the door behind him, I turn on Charlie. "Exactly how big of a discount did Kieran get us?" The rate in the email Matt sent me was reasonable for a week in a hotel, meals and park passes included, even for tightfisted me. But there's no fucking way it covered this nice of a hotel and butler service. Butler service! What the hell are we going to need a butler for?

Charlie shrugs, flopping down on the immaculately made king-size bed. "Dunno. It must have been a lot, though."

I bite my lip and study him. I'd accuse him of having subsidized my half of the room, but Matt forwarded his brother's email directly to me. There's no way Charlie had the opportunity to doctor it.

Guess I'll just have to accept this amazing opportunity and have fun.

Charlie pats the mattress beside him. "How do you feel

about a nap?" The wicked gleam in his eye tells me sleeping is the last thing on his mind.

"We won't have time," I remind him. "Remember? Ian wants to hit Planet Joy for dinner and Joy Bear's Magical Parade." I thought he was joking when he suggested it, but apparently not.

Charlie's pout lasts only for a second before the lure of childhood memories pulls him off the bed. "Okay! Then kissing during the fireworks. But after that, we're going to christen every inch of that bed."

My mouth goes dry. Kissing during the fireworks? Since I told Charlie I liked kisses, he's gone out of his way to provide them often. But this... this is a movie romance moment.

I suck in a deep breath and force a smile. "Let me just check my email. I need to do Mr. Romance stuff once a day."

He nods. "I know. Your work ethic is one of the sexiest things about you."

Kill. Me. Now.

I boot up my laptop while Charlie does something on his phone. I think he's checking out the JU guest app, because every so often he'll talk about a ride or show he wants to do. I mostly concentrate on what I'm doing and reply with "Mm-hmm."

"Oh my god. Lee. *Lee.*"

I look up, the urgency in his voice getting my attention. "What?"

"Look!" He turns the screen toward me, but since he's halfway across the room, that's not helpful.

"I can't see it, Charlie. What is it?"

"We can have lunch on the restaurant set from *Gay-timatum!*"

Butterflies erupt in my stomach, and I get up to go see. "The karaoke restaurant?"

"Yep!" He bounces on the mattress. "The one with the big I-love-you speech and then the song!"

I take his phone and read, and yep, there's a lunch experience on that set, including the chance to sing on the karaoke stage.

"We have to do it," he declares, taking the phone back. "That's your favorite movie. I'll tell the others."

"They might not want to," I begin, even as I wonder if they'd care if I ditch them.

"Pffft. It's lunch and karaoke. They'll be up for it. And if they're not, just you and me will go. It's your favorite movie, Lee. I'm not going to let you miss it."

Aw. "Okay then. Thank you."

It's actually shocking to me how much I'm enjoying this trip. I figured we'd fuck around at the parks for a couple days on the rides, but mostly just hang out. Instead, Charlie and Ian have insisted we go to just about every show, experience, and attraction the parks have to offer, and it's been a shitload of fun.

Now on day three, I get dressed feeling more refreshed and relaxed than I have in ages. Between the sun, time out in the fresh air, amazing food, and hours of sex every night, all my stress is gone.

"Charlie, come on!" I call through the bathroom door. "We're going to be late." I'm tempted to go in, but I know if I do that, we'll just end up fucking in the shower. And then we'll definitely be late.

The water goes off, and he calls back, "Five minutes. Please don't be wearing your ugly clothes when I get out."

I laugh and glance down at the shorts he hates so much. When he picked my new outfits, he didn't bother with shorts. He regrets that now—I know because he's said it several times. But since the Joy Universe complex only has high-end retail and licensed clothing for sale, he'll just have to deal with it.

When he emerges from the bathroom a minute later in a cloud of steam, buck naked, he takes one look at me and sighs. "You're the only person on the planet who's worth having to look at those shorts for."

My whole body warms, and I try to hide my happy smile. When he says stuff like that, it makes me feel incredible, seen and accepted, even for the parts of me he doesn't love. When Charlie looks at me, I feel attractive. I'm sexy. I'm not the short, ugly, romantic weirdo. I'm Lee, and Charlie wants me in his life.

I just wish he saw me as more than a friend he fucks.

Sometimes I think he might. There's no way to escape the fact that we act more like boyfriends than anything else. But he's never said anything to show he *thinks* of us that way, or that he wants more, and let's face it, the ball's in his court. I can't be his friend who wants to date him, not after the way we met. If he doesn't feel the same, it would shatter his trust and our friendship, and I can't do that to him.

He gets dressed in record time, and even though he's wearing shorts, a T-shirt, and sneakers just like me, he somehow manages to look like he stepped off a yacht somewhere. We grab our wristbands, which get us in everywhere and access our food credits, and our phones, and leave the room. Initially, I planned to take water bottles and snacks when we hit the parks, but when we arrived and Kieran explained exactly what was included in our package, I let that idea go. I've never had this level of VIP treatment before, and I can't say it sucks.

In the lobby, we spot Ian and Matt right away. They're talking to Connor and Kieran and an older blond guy I don't know—he's wearing a shirt and tie, though, so my guess is he works here. Who else would come to JU and wear a tie?

Charlie and I go to join them.

"Here they are," Kieran says. "Guys, this is Derek, who used to be my boss and is the one responsible for arranging our stay. Derek, Liam and Charlie."

Derek smiles, and any awkwardness I might have felt melts away. "Great to meet you both. I hope you've been enjoying yourselves."

His effortless charisma kind of reminds me of Charlie, except where Charlie is completely loveable and sweet, this guy has a sharper edge. "Hi. Yeah, this has been an amazing trip."

"Totally epic," Charlie adds. "So... you used to be Kieran's boss?"

"He was actually my boss's boss. I was just a lowly assistant resort manager, and Derek here is an assistant director. He's the boss of everyone."

Derek laughs. "One fifth of everyone," he corrects. "There are four other ADs."

"But you're one of the big guys?" Charlie persists. "One of the biggest guys?"

We all look at him.

"What? I was just wondering." He shoves his hands in his pockets. "Could I have like five minutes of your time?"

"Charlie," Kieran starts, no doubt about to tell him exactly how valuable five minutes of Derek's time is, but Derek lifts a hand to stop him.

"Five minutes? Sure, why not? Fair warning, though, whatever you're going to ask, I can't promise I'll say yes."

Charlie grins confidently. "That's okay. I won't know for sure until I ask." He turns to us. "You guys can go ahead; I'll catch up."

I don't feel good about any of this, and Matt and Ian must feel the same, because we all hesitate.

Derek laughs. "Guys, I promise I'm not going to have him arrested or thrown out, no matter what he says. I'm trying to lure Kieran back here. Ruining his family vacation won't help with that."

Ian turns on Kieran. "You're going to leave your job at Mannix Estate?"

"No," Kieran and Connor say together, then exchange a glance.

"I swear, I'm not going to say anything bad," Charlie promises earnestly, and we reluctantly leave.

"What was that about?" Matt asks as we step outside the hotel. We're staying at the Chateau, which I've learned is the fanciest place in the complex. It's just a short walk to Planet Joy, the flagship theme park, but to get to Joy Visual Studios, which is where we're going today, we'll have to either take the shuttle or a boat.

"No idea," I reply. "He's been a bit... weird lately. I think something's bothering him, but he hasn't said what."

"Did you ask?" Ian asks. He's staring intently at me in a super creepy way.

I shrug. "No. If he wants to talk about it, he will. I don't want to pry."

"Yeah, but maybe he just needs to know you'd be *open to it*. Like, if you ask, he'll know *you want it* as much as he does. To talk. He'll know you want to talk."

"Why are you being creepy and weird?" Matt asks him, and Ian sighs.

"I just think Liam needs to give Charlie a sign that he's open to talking about... stuff."

I have no idea what he's babbling about, but I nod. "I'll tell him he can talk to me about anything."

Ian doesn't look happy but lets it go.

"Meanwhile, why would he want to talk to Kieran's old boss? Do you think he wants a job or something?" Matt asks dubiously.

My stomach flips at the thought. Could Charlie really want to work at a theme park and resort complex in the middle of nowhere? Unlike Disney, JU wasn't built near a big city. Instead, it has a town nearby where all the employees live. A college campus was recently opened there, but it's still not exactly a thriving metropolis. And he might love it here, but working in the offices probably isn't that different from what working with his dad would be.

Not that it matters to me, of course. Just because I'm hoping to do my doctorate in Southern California doesn't mean Charlie has to stay there too. College friendships often become long-distance after graduation.

"I guess," Ian says. "Maybe he's thinking of an internship for this summer, with the hope that they might have something for him when he graduates. It's not dumb. He really loves it here."

That's true. Charlie's open, friendly personality fits right in at a place where the goal is making people happy.

Before I can weigh in, Charlie joins us. "I thought you'd be gone," he says, slinging an arm around my shoulders. I lean against him.

"We got distracted." Matt looks over his shoulder. "But I think I see a boat coming. Are we ready?"

"Onward!" Charlie shouts, and I laugh and shake my head.

We hustle over to the line and then onto the boat, and it's only when we're all sitting and enjoying the breeze as the boat cruises along the canal that I remember to ask, "So what did you want to talk to that Derek guy about?"

For a second, Charlie doesn't reply, seemingly enraptured by a mama duck and her ducklings on the far back. They are pretty cute, but we've seen about fifty ducks since we got here, so I don't think he's all that fascinated.

"Are you thinking of getting a job here?" Matt adds.

"Maybe," Charlie says vaguely. "Just short-term. It would be good experience for when I join the family business."

Since he's dreading even the thought of joining the family business, that answer is complete bullshit, but this is clearly something else he's not ready to talk about, so I let it go.

"Cool. Did you guys make our lunch reservation?" I ask Matt and Ian, changing the subject. I've been looking forward to the *Gay-timatum* lunch experience since we got here, and I'm excited that the guys are into it too.

"Done," Ian assures me, and I sit back happily.

Matt and Ian start arguing about which non-reservable sideshow experience we should line up for first, but I tune them out. We'll end up doing both anyway, so who cares which is first? I'm getting the thing I want most, and in the meantime I get to cruise down a canal with Charlie by my side, the sun shining overhead. What more could a romantic gay boy ask for?

After a morning filled with set tours and "behind the scenes" revelations, we line up at the entrance to the *Gay-timatum* set. I try to stay cool. First, I don't want my friends to see me being all fanboy. Not that I think they'd mock me—much—but it's not worth the hassle. On top of that, there's every chance the set is going to be a total letdown. I'm not an idiot—I know production companies do a lot of work with camera angles and lighting to make sets look amazing. So when I walk in, it might look small and poky. Or tacky—the colors too bright, the fabrics cheap. The walls might be obviously fake without the camera lens to buffer them.

So I keep telling myself to expect a movie *set*, not a movie *moment*. That scene might be one of my favorites ever, but this set isn't what made it magic. There's no reason to be disappointed, no matter what. Today is going to be great anyway.

Two employees come out of the set and wave for attention. "Good afternoon, everyone! Thanks so much for coming to the *Gay-timatum* lunch experience here at Joy Visual Studios. We're just about to open the doors, so here's what we need you to do so we can get you seated and enjoying yourselves as fast as possible." She goes on to ask us to have our wristbands or reservation numbers ready, reminds us that this is an adults-only experience, and promises we'll all get the opportunity for a photo op and a turn singing on the karaoke stage, but that we need to wait to be invited up.

"What song are we singing?" Ian asks as she stops talking and turns to ask the people at the front of the line for their reservation.

"No."

Charlie turns big eyes on me. "No karaoke?"

I sigh. "Fine. But no dumb songs."

Matt and Ian immediately begin squabbling over song choices, but Charlie studies me. "You don't have to if you don't want to. This should be fun for you, not annoying."

I smile at his sweet face. "Nah, it'll be fun. These two just get really into karaoke. But they're not drunk, so we probably won't be kicked out this time."

The line moves swiftly, and we're nearly at the front when Matt turns to me. "You need to cast the deciding vote. 'Call Me Maybe' by Carly Rae Jepsen or 'Mr. Perfectly Fine' by my girl T Swift?"

"Of all Taylor's songs, why'd you pick a heartbreak one?" I hold up my hand. "Never mind. I vote Carly Rae. This is a good day, and we're singing a happy song if it kills us."

"Yessss!" Ian pumps his fist.

"Why would a happy song kill us?" Charlie asks. Fortunately, we reach the host stand before I need to think of an answer.

It takes only a minute for our wristbands to be scanned, and then we're ushered through to the set. I half want to close my eyes, just in case it's a disappointment, but that's stupid.

We walk across the threshold, and my anxiety falls away.

It's not perfect. It looks smaller, the props tackier. But it's still amazing, and I'm so glad we did this. As we follow the host to our table, I almost give myself whiplash trying to take everything in.

Once we're settled with menus, the song list, and the promise that someone will come to take our order soon, I finally let myself grin wide.

Charlie whips out his phone. "Say cheese!" He points it at me, and I hold my closed menu with the restaurant name in front of me and smile wide for the camera. I'm going to want to remember this.

It gets noisier as more people are seated, and our server comes over to get our order.

"Y'all are number seven on the karaoke list," she says, tapping her tablet. "Every table is allocated a turn, and then if there's still time before this sitting is over, you can put your hand up for another turn."

"How likely is it that there will be time leftover?" Matt asks.

She shrugs. "Pretty good. Not every table wants to get up and sing. Have you picked a song yet? We usually ask that you have two ready in case someone before you uses your first choice."

"We got two," Matt says, gleeful that he might get to sing Taylor after all, and our server smiles and walks away.

"Well?" Ian asks me. "Worth it?"

I look around the room again. There's the table Sawyer sat at when Perry serenaded him. It's been blocked off, presumably so nobody can whine about other people being seated there. And over there is the hallway to the bathrooms, where their friends stood to spy on them. It's so surreal to be sitting in the middle of it all.

"Yep. Thanks for indulging me."

All three break out into wide grins and high-five each other.

"So, is this something you'd sell as Mr. Romance?" Matt gestures to the room. "A reenactment?"

"You mean have one person serenade the other during a meal?" I bite my lip. It's an expensive date to plan, since you'd need to either be staying at JU or a local. Plus park passes, the meal reservation... It might work best as a package for someone wanting a romantic vacation. "It's doable, but you'd want to be sure your date doesn't get embarrassed by having people gawk. And that they like the movie."

Charlie snorts. "Imagine if you went all out doing the big speech and song, and then come and sit down and your date's all 'I hated that movie and I'm judging you so hard right now.'"

"Or your date leaves halfway through," Matt adds.

"Or, or!" Ian points a finger in the air. "You're in the line to get in and they ask why you're here, they hated the movie and have no interest in the lunch experience."

I join the laughter. "I really hope that never happens on one of my dates." It never has so far, but all it would take is some bad intel.

"It won't," Charlie assures me.

"Oh, they're starting! We're seventh, right?" Ian's looking at the stage, and I turn my head in that direction. One of the staff is stepping up to the microphone.

"Welcome, everyone, to the karaoke showdown at Mouth

Café! As you all know, the prize for today's winner is out of this world!"

I look over at Ian. "There's a prize?"

He shrugs. "It said there was when I booked, but it didn't say what. Or how the winner would be picked." He glances around. "Do you see anyone who might be a judge?"

"Dude, you're not going to win," Matt advises. "I've heard you sing many times. Let the dream go."

Ian sniffs and turns back to the stage, where the people from table one are milling around with microphones in hand. The music starts, and they launch into a very pitchy rendition of Queen's "Somebody to Love." Within thirty seconds, I've winced twice. Ian leans in and says, "I'm better than that, at least!"

Matt seesaws his hand.

Queen gives way to Springsteen, then Rihanna, then Gayle's "abcdefu," which gets the whole room singing except for a few shocked-looking older people.

But when the opening chords begin for table five, Ian groans. "Nooooo. They stole Carly Rae."

"Yes!" Matt shoots both arms up, and I drag one down.

"Having fun here?" It's our server, back with our food.

"We're gonna sing Taylor," Matt tells her happily.

"Sweet. Swifties unite, right?" She passes our plates around. "Do y'all need anything else?"

We assure her we're good, and then set to eating as much as we can in the song and a half left before our turn. No point letting good food go cold.

"Table seven, please join us!" The emcee leads the room in a round of encouraging applause as table six (who sang

Justin Bieber) leaves the stage. We abandon our food and take our places.

The music starts, and I sing along but mostly hang back and let the others ham it up. They're having so much fun that I can't help smiling. I wish Matt had picked a different Taylor Swift song, though. These lyrics are hitting too close to home. Is this how I'm going to feel when Charlie inevitably moves on from my life? I mean, he's not cruel, not insincere, definitely doesn't expect the world to revolve around him, but when he meets someone he wants to be with, things will change for us. I'll be left behind, heartbroken, and he'll be moving on, perfectly fine.

This got depressing fast.

Charlie glances over at me, and his grin fades into a frown of concern. I instantly paste a smile on and throw myself back into the song. I'm not going to ruin this for him or myself by moping over something that hasn't happened yet.

CHAPTER NINETEEN

CHARLIE

I watch Lee carefully for the rest of the song, but he's back to his normal self. I'm not sure what he was thinking that made him look so sad.

We finish to thunderous applause—well, applause, anyway—and leave the stage, panting from the effort of giving the song that Taylor flair.

"We killed it," Matt declares, then kisses his fingers and raises them to the ceiling. "Did you proud, Tay Tay."

Even I think that's weird.

Back at the table, while the others shovel in food and argue about how awesome our performance was—super awesome or just plain awesome—I surreptitiously check my phone. That Derek guy said he'd text me as soon as he got everything teed up, but it's been hours. He was sure he could make it happen, but maybe he can't?

Maybe the idea is just stupid.

As though the universe can hear me and is responding, my phone vibrates in my hand, a message popping up from

Derek JU. This is it. I check to make sure the others aren't watching me, then tap on it.

Derek JU: All set. Tonight at nine. You can have 30 minutes.

Yesssssss! Even if it is a stupid idea, knowing I can do it makes me feel a lot better.

Charlie: THANK YOU! You won't regret this. Anytime you need a favor, let me know.

Derek JU: You're welcome. Sending you the details of your contact. He'll be waiting.

That's followed by a contact profile for someone called Grant. I save it into my phone under Grant JU and send Derek another thank-you. He really came through for me.

Now I just have to make sure I don't fuck it up.

When dinnertime rolls around, Ian decides he's tired. "We should go back to our resort and have room service in our pajamas," he suggests.

I panic. If we go back to the resort, what excuse will I give to get Lee to leave it again later? "What are you, ninety? You just need coffee. Let's grab some while Lee and Matt decide where we're having dinner."

They all look surprised. "Coffee? Right before dinner?" Matt asks, as though it's unheard of.

"Sure. They do it in Italy all the time." Maybe. Someone must, anyway.

Lee purses his lips. "I don't know, Charlie. Room service dinner sounds kind of good."

Oh no. No no no no no. This can't be happening.

"You'll have the rest of your life for room service dinners," I proclaim as dramatically as I can. A few passersby glance over. "You're twenty and in one of the best theme parks on earth! How can you willingly give up the chance to—" Fuck, I need inspiration. We've done almost everything this park has to offer. "—the chance to—" I glance around desperately. "—the chance for a twilight viewing of *Space Reivers*."

Matt's jaw drops, but Lee's suspicious. "What?"

"*Space Reivers*! They're having a twilight viewing on the lawn. How can you not want to see that?"

"Because it's an animated movie about space pirates where a bunch of kids and animals save the day?" Ian says.

"It's a classic from our childhoods," I insist.

"I never saw it in my childhood," he argues, "since I was thirteen when it released."

I grab his arm and pull him away. "Coffee! You guys pick somewhere for dinner," I call over my shoulder, even as Ian protests. "Shut up!" I hiss. "You're going to ruin it."

His mouth snaps closed, and he eyes me. "Ruin what? And if you say *Space Reivers*, I'm gonna hurt you."

"*No*, not that stupid movie." We get in line at the coffee cart. "What do you think I am, five? But we gotta stay in the park until nine. Please, Ian, help me."

That got his attention. "Why?" He glances around and lowers his voice. "You can tell me."

I hesitate. What if he thinks it's stupid? But if I'm going to pull this off, I'll need his help. "You know how I'm in love with Lee?"

"Yep."

"And how you said I should tell him?"

His eyes widen. "You're going to?"

"Is it a bad idea?"

"No! It's a great idea. You should absolutely do it. Now would be good."

I shake my head. "Not now. Tonight. At nine...ish."

He frowns. "Why at nine? And... are you planning to do it *here*?" His doubtful tone fills me with dread.

"Not like, *here* here. I thought at the *Gay-timatum* set restaurant. Derek, this morning? He's arranged for me to have access after it closes. Just me and Lee. And I thought I could—"

"Serenade him? Like in the movie?"

Actually, I have a bit more planned than that, but I nod. "Yeah."

Ian stares at me for so long, I start to wonder if he's stroking out. Then he smiles. "Dude, that's fucking perfect. It's the romantic movie moment he wants without the cringe of having other people there."

I let out a breath of relief. I originally thought of doing it at lunch but figured Lee would hate having strangers watch. "So you don't think he's going to hate it? Or hate me? Or that I'll need to find somewhere else to sleep tonight because he's not into me that way?"

"No to all of those." He rolls his eyes, then steps up to the coffee cart. "Hey, how's it going? Do you have decaf?"

The teenager at the cart smiles disinterestedly. "Sure do."

"Great, 'cause my idiot friend said I wanted coffee even though I definitely don't. So I'll have a decaf Americano." He glances at me. "What do you want?"

Uh... nothing. But I should order, since I'm the one who said coffee before dinner is a thing. "Same. And a decaf hazelnut latte. Should we get something for Matt too?"

"Cancel that latte," Ian tells the kid before he can write on the cup, then shakes his head at me. "Are you nuts? Liam doesn't want coffee. Don't piss him off just a couple hours before you tell him you love him. Dumbass."

Oh. Good point.

Panic rises again. "But he wants to go back to the resort and I'm going to make him watch *Space Reivers* to keep him here." My voice cracks. "He's already going to be pissed off and he'll *hate me*."

Ian pays for our coffee, and as the guy starts making them, he turns to me. "Stop being a drama queen. Liam's not going to hate you. Let that go. He might be a bit pissed off about the movie, though, so let's see if we can think of a way to keep him here that he'll actually like."

I got nothing. And the more I try to think of something and can't, the more panicked I get. From the look on Ian's face, he's not exactly rolling in ideas either.

"Can I make a suggestion?"

My head snaps eagerly toward coffee guy. "Yes. Please. Help me."

His smile this time is genuine. "Sorry for listening."

"We weren't being quiet. Don't worry about it," Ian assures him. "As long as you don't tell Liam, we're cool."

"I'm Charlie," I feel compelled to add. "He's Ian."

"Jordan. If you want to kill a couple of hours here in the park, you should check out the computer animation studio. It's kind of pricey, though."

"That's fine," I say. Ian elbows me.

"What even is it? I didn't see it on the map."

"It's only open by reservation, and it usually books out months ahead. But my friend who works there told me they had a cancellation for tonight because someone had heatstroke—do you want me to see if it's still open?"

"Yes," I say. Ian jabs me again.

"But what is it, exactly?" he asks.

"Basically, you pick a thirty-minute animated script, and then the techs take pictures and video and create an animated version of you. Then you read out the script, and at the end, you have a half-hour cartoon with you in it."

My jaw drops.

"Yesssss," Ian breathes. Then he shakes himself and says, "How much is it, exactly?"

Jordan opens his mouth, but I interrupt.

"Forget that. I want it. How do we see if it's still available? And we have to be done by nine. Is that possible?"

He shrugs and hands us our coffees. "Sure. It takes about two hours all up, so you should just make it. Let me check with them." He grabs a walkie-talkie thing from his belt and half turns away from us to talk into it.

"Dude, are you sure?" Ian asks quietly. "This is going to be expensive. We'll chip in some, but—"

"I'm sure," I insist. "I want to do this because it's fucking awesome. You all just have to come along because friendship obligates you."

He snorts.

Jordan turns back to us. "It's still available, but they need you there in fifteen minutes. And I need to give them your name and the resort you're staying at."

"Charlie Martin, at the Chateau." What I love about this place is that my personal profile in their system—which is linked to my wristband—has my credit card attached. So I can charge things back to my profile and not worry that maybe the charge ended up on the reservation credit card, which is Kieran's. "Can we bring food? We haven't eaten yet."

"I'll double-check, but it should be fine."

While he passes on my details, I say to Ian, "Here's the plan. We go back and tell them surprise! I was trying to arrange this but didn't know if it would happen, and that's why I didn't want to go back yet."

He nods. "That's actually a good plan."

Jordan turns back to us. "You're all set, and yes, you can bring food. Got a map? I'll show you where to go."

Ian whips out his map, and Jordan marks the studio location, then makes another X where we are now. "If you go down here, then cut behind here, that's the fastest way. And it'll take you right past the food trucks too."

"That's right near the restaurant set," I blurt, and he nods.

"Yep. Most of the working sets and studios are in the same part of the park. They're going to need to see ID and your wristband."

I pat my pocket where my ID is—in case I wanted a beer

with lunch—and glance at my wrist to make sure the wrist-band is still there. "No problem."

"Have fun!"

We thank him and then head back to the others, who look grumpy.

"Why did we just watch you talk to the barista for five minutes?" Matt demands.

"He was helping us out—my surprise came through!" I announce.

Neither of them is impressed, so I race through a garbled explanation.

"Wait, so we act out the cartoon, and the characters will look like us?" Lee grins. "That's pretty cool."

"It's *awesome*," Matt declares. "I'm going to be an epic cartoon character."

"We gotta go, though." I check the time. "Like, now."

We hustle through the park. As we pass the food trucks, we pick the only one with no line (smoothies and salads) and grab a bunch of things to eat.

The studio has no signage. I'm pretty sure I'm in the right place, though, because this is where Jordan marked the map, and the buildings around us all have signs announcing what they are. I try the doorknob—locked—then see a discreet buzzer and hit that instead.

"Yes?"

"Hey, I'm Charlie..." Shit, do I actually have a reservation on the books? Or is there just one person expecting us?

"Come on in." The door buzzes open, so my name must have been recognized.

Inside is just a small boxy vestibule with a door on each

side wall and a corridor opposite the entry. It's empty, and we crowd in and look around.

"Um... are we about to be mugged?" Matt asks. "Like, were we lured here for—"

One of the doors opens, and a smiling woman comes out. "Charlie?"

I lift a hand. "Hi. That's me."

"Good to meet you. I'm Tala."

I introduce the others, and she smiles at them all.

"Come on through, and we'll get started."

"Jordan said it was okay for us to bring food," I say as we follow her, and she nods.

"Sure. This first bit has to be done one at a time, so the rest of you will have plenty of time to eat."

We go into a decent-size room that's split in half. One side is furnished like a living room, and the other side looks like a movie studio, with a green screen against the wall and green flooring in front of it. There's a big, professional-looking video camera and a console with a bunch of screens and stuff.

"Take a seat and get comfortable. I'll grab the scripts, and Charlie, we're going to need you to sign for the package."

"No problem." I sink onto the sofa and pull Lee down beside me as Tala goes through a door on the other side of the room. "So this is fun, right? Better than room service?" *Please don't hate me.*

He leans over and kisses my cheek. "This is incredible. I wish you'd mentioned it earlier."

"Yeah, uh, I was on the cancellation list and didn't want to get your hopes up." I avoid his gaze. "We should eat."

Tala comes back with an armful of folders and an older

man. "This is Steve. Steve, say hi to the guys." She introduces us, getting all our names right, and Steve flips us a casual wave before heading over to fiddle with the camera.

"These are the scripts you can choose from." Tala lays the folders on the coffee table, then grabs one and flips it open. "As you can see, they just have Character 1, Character 2, and so on. Once you've picked the one you like, we'll input your names and pronouns and print each of you a copy to use during recording and then take home."

Ian picks up one of the scripts and flips it open. "Oh, hey, there's a little summary thing at the front. That makes it easier."

While the guys look at scripts and argue about them, Tala turns to me with a clipboard. "Let me talk you through what's included tonight." There are three sheets on the clipboard, and she goes through them in a lot of detail, but it's basically what I already knew. Except for the price. Jordan wasn't kidding when he said it was pricey, but honestly, this is an incredible experience, and I can afford it.

But Lee must never know how much it cost.

I sign, she scans my wristband, and then she gets me a receipt, which I shove deep into my pocket. When I go back to the guys, they've narrowed it down to two.

"You pick," Lee says, and I look at them both.

"This one. And Lee and I get the romantic plotline."

Lee gives me a sideways glance. "We do?"

I nod firmly. "Yep. Because I wanna do the pining." Also, how perfect is it? He'll already be thinking of me as his love interest, and then I'll take him to the restaurant and sweep him off his feet!

"Pining it is."

The next hour is more fun than it should be. Steve and Tala have us stand on the green flooring one at a time and walk, run, jump, skip, turn around, reach in different directions, crouch down, lean over... the works. Apparently this builds a profile for how we each move, which the animation software will replicate. They also have us make faces—happy, sad, mad, bored, annoyed—smile, laugh, speak, and sing. And while each of us has a turn, the others eat and heckle from the couches.

Then, when our profiles are logged, we crowd around the console and watch the computer develop our characters. This shit is amazing—we not only look like animated versions of ourselves, we stand and move like us.

Once we've approved the characters, Tala leads us through to a sound studio. "Get comfy on the stools. We'll do a sound check, then you just read the script through. If you make a mistake, like saying the wrong word, just correct it and keep going. We'll fix that at our end. We don't have time to stop and start or do multiple takes, so don't take it too seriously."

"You clearly haven't been paying attention if you think we take things seriously," Ian says, and she laughs.

"Just have fun with it."

And it *is* fun. We flub a few lines, our acting is terrible, and the script isn't exactly award-winning material, but it's still super cool.

"...give me this chance, and our love will last forever, through all hardships, onwards and upwards," I say, sneaking a peek at Lee. This is our big romantic scene, and I want to see if it's affecting him.

There's a tiny smile on his lips, but that could just be

because this scene is super cheesy, and he loves that. He doesn't seem to think my words are anything more than part of the script. They *are* part of the script, but I was hoping to see some... I don't know. Longing? Just an indication that he wished what I was saying was true.

I'm starting to get nervous now. What if I make my big gesture, give him a romantic moment, and he's not interested? Ian says he won't hate me... but that doesn't mean things won't change.

What I don't know is how.

CHAPTER TWENTY

CHARLIE

It's ten minutes to nine when we finish recording, and I'm trying not to watch the clock—and failing. At least we don't have far to go. If we had to cross the whole park, I'd be screwed.

"Okay, let's take a quick look at the first few minutes," Tala says. "There's a lot of work that needs to be done, but this should give you an idea of what it'll be like."

We go back into the other room and crowd around the monitors again. Steve taps on the keyboard, and our cartoon comes up.

It's freaking awesome.

Animated me talks with my voice while animated Matt puts up a sign about a party, and then we have a conversation about the people who are coming.

"Whoa," Ian breathes, grinning wide.

Steve hits a button, and the screen goes black. "I'll clean it up tomorrow, and you'll get download links by email."

"If you prefer a DVD or a flash drive, both those options are available," Tala adds.

"Download is fine," I assure them. "Although, could we have a flash drive as well?" Just in case.

"No problem. We'll deliver it to your resort by the end of the day tomorrow," she assures us, walking us out.

Outside, the spring night air is cool but not uncomfortably so, and I breathe in deep. This part of the park is practically abandoned, since all the attractions here have already closed for the night, and it's oddly peaceful.

"I'm wiped," Matt says. "I can't believe our break is nearly over already. We should spend more time with Connor."

"Let's go do that now," Ian says, seizing his arm. Matt yanks free.

"Right now?"

"Yep. Let's go."

Before Matt can reply, I jump in. "I've got a stop to make first. Come with me, Lee? We'll see you guys tomorrow."

Lee frowns at me. "You've got a stop to make? Where?"

"Yeah, where?" Matt looks from me to Ian, then opens his mouth again, only to close it when Ian takes a step out of Lee's line of sight and slashes his finger across his throat. "Uh, you know, I think seeing Connor tonight is a good idea. See ya!"

They walk off, heads bent together, with Lee staring after them and sputtering in bewilderment.

"Come on, it's this way," I say, not giving him time to think about what's happening.

"What stop?" he asks again, falling into step with me. "Where are we going?"

"It's just around this corner..." I deliberately keep it vague, although that's the actual truth.

He mutters something about me getting too much sun, and I try not to laugh. As if I could get too much sun. I'm a born and bred California boy.

We round the corner, and the entrance to the restaurant set is just ahead. A tall, dark-haired man is standing out front, looking at his phone.

"Hi!" I call. "Are you Grant?"

He looks up and smiles at me. "Hey. You must be Charlie."

"Yep, and this is Lee. Thanks so much for this. I can't tell you how much I appreciate it."

"It's no hassle at all. We love this stuff around here. And I had to come back in to pick up my stepson after his shift, anyway." He pulls a swipe card out of his pocket and unlocks the door. "The lights and equipment are on. I'll be back in thirty minutes."

"Thank you. Can I buy you a coffee or something?" I can tell Lee's dying to ask me what the fuck is going on, but manners are manners. This guy's done me a solid.

"I'm good, but thanks." He steps back from the door, and I grab Lee's arm and tug him inside.

"Charlie," he hisses as the door closes behind us, "what the actual fuck?"

"I know this is weird, but I asked that Derek guy if we could have access to the set in private, and he arranged it. I know how much you love this movie, and I thought you might enjoy it more without strangers here." That's half the truth, anyway.

Lee says nothing, just looks at me and then around the room. There's nobody else here, but the tables are set for tomorrow's lunch, and the lights are on. Soft music plays in the background, which I'm pretty sure means the karaoke equipment is also running.

"That's really thoughtful of you," he says at last. "He arranged it just because you asked?"

Uh. There was also the fact that Derek turned out to be a romantic. "Well, maybe I begged a lot. And he's trying to get on Kieran's good side." Not that Kieran even knows me that well or cares. "Let's have a look around." That's something we couldn't do earlier, what with the dozens of other people and employees filling the place.

We wander around the set, checking things out up close, then peek through doors. It's so weird to see them leading nowhere. Like... on one side, there's this detail-perfect restaurant, then you walk through the door that supposedly leads to the kitchen and bam! Nothing. Just an unfinished space in a warehouse. And turning to look at the wall beside you and seeing it's just plywood and two-by-fours, when you know the other side is supposedly brick... Trippy.

Back on the set, I lead him to the roped-off table, the one where Sawyer sat while Perry declared his feelings. "Why don't you sit over here?" I say as casually as I can manage. He sits in Sawyer's chair without my prompting, and I take two steps back. "I'm just going to check on something."

Before he can ask me what, I book it off set to the alcove where we found the sound system. I was relieved to see how idiot-proof it is, and I set it up to play "the" song in exactly five minutes. That should give me enough time. Then I take a second to settle my nerves, square my shoulders, and walk back out to the set.

Lee's taking video of the room, panning slowly around, and when he sees me, he smiles. "Say hi for the camera."

"Hey." It comes out kind of squeaky, and I clear my throat.

"In case I forget to say it later, this is the best surprise ever. Thanks for thinking of what I'd really like, Charlie."

Oh god. He's still filming, so I put on a smile and say, "I'm not done yet." I walk toward the stage, wondering if I should tell him to put his phone away. I mean... if this goes badly, he's not going to want his video of "the best surprise ever" to be tainted by it. But if it goes well, he'll have his romantic moment immortalized forever.

Screw it. He can always edit the video if he needs to.

I step up to the microphone at the front of the stage. It's not a real mic, just a plastic prop, but this is where Perry stood to give his speech, and since there's nobody else here, Lee should be able to hear me without any issues.

"Are you going to sing?" he asks, a thread of laughter in his voice as he points his phone camera at me. "Didn't get enough already today?"

"We haven't known each other very long," I say, starting the speech, "but it's safe to say we fit into each other's life like we've always been there."

His smile slowly fades as he recognizes the words, the phone dipping slightly. "Charlie, what—"

"I've been looking for something that doesn't exist, and in the meantime I've overlooked the thing I really need. Really want. The thing..." Fuck. *Fuck.* What comes next? "The, uh, thing..." I can't remember the next word. Hell, with Lee staring wide-eyed up at me, I can't remember any of the damn speech. I should have written it on my hand.

I sigh and scrub my hands over my face and through my hair. "I'm sorry. I wanted to do this for you, give you the

perfect romantic moment, but I've fucked it up like usual."
Three steps bring me to the edge of the stage, and I jump
down, then stand there like an idiot, not sure what to do.

Lee puts his phone down on the table and gets up but
doesn't come closer. The six feet between us feels like six
miles.

"I don't understand," he says. "What's going on,
Charlie?"

Great. As if I haven't already made an idiot of myself,
now I have to explain it.

"I love you. I know that's not what we're supposed to be
about, but I couldn't help it. You're the best friend I've ever
had and so much more. I can't imagine wanting to be with
anyone else like this, ever... I would rather spend five minutes
in silence with you than an hour doing anything else in the
world. I-I thought... You talked about wanting a romantic
moment. A cupcake moment. Someone who could think
about what matters to you, what you want, and make it
happen. And this is your favorite movie, and you love this
scene, so I thought... But I didn't want to do it while there
were other people here, because you'd hate that." I stumble to
a stop.

Lee blinks at me. Once. Twice. Then he takes a step
forward.

"You wanted to give me a romantic moment?"

I nod, then say, "Yes."

"Because you... love me?" Does his voice shake a little?

"Yes. I love you."

He takes two more steps and stops right in front of me.
"So you arranged this to tell me you love me?"

"Yes." It's a whisper. Is he going to hit me?

He grabs my face and kisses me hard, then stumbles back. "Wait, no, I just... have to make sure. You love me?"

Hope sits up and dances inside me. "I love you. I want to be your boyfriend."

He closes his eyes, and when he opens them, he's grinning. "I love you too."

As he steps into my arms, the song starts playing, and I sing him the first line as our lips meet.

EPILOGUE
LIAM

"...I LOVE YOU." I SMILE TO MYSELF AS I LISTEN TO THE recording. This is one of my favorite things to do when Charlie's not with me—play back the video from that night at the restaurant set. I was so flustered when I put my phone down that I forgot to stop recording, so his whole speech—both the rehearsed and unrehearsed parts—got captured for posterity. The first thing I did when I realized was back it up to three different cloud services. I'm keeping this baby forever.

It still feels surreal sometimes, that Charlie and I are truly together now. Not that there's any way I could doubt it. He takes great joy in proclaiming me his boyfriend to anyone who so much as speaks to him. It's gotten to the point that our friends are keeping track of it and allocating points to the people who hear it most. I'm not allowed to join in, but I've been nominated as the judge.

As if to punctuate the thought, a message alert pops up. I hit pause and flip screens.

Jake: He did it again.

I laugh even as another message appears in the group chat.

Ian: No way—stop cheating! It only counts if it's genuine.

Jake: Swear to god. The girl in line behind us at Bean Necessities asked where he got his shirt. He told her, then said "my boyfriend likes it."

Artie: hahahahahahahaha he's getting worse!

Matt: Spill your coffee on the shirt

I should probably step in.

Liam: Don't wreck his shirt or he'll be whining all night. That counts. One point for Jake.

Ian: Noooooooo don't let him win!

Jake: suck it!

Another message alert pops up, and I change screens. It's my friend Spencer.

Spencer: Definitely moving next semester. Can't wait to get out of the dorms!

I frown, remembering our conversation from a while

back. I've been meaning to tell him he might not find the Living & Learning house as quiet as he thought.

Before I can reply, the door opens, and I look up as Charlie comes in. He spots my phone and huffs.

"Dammit, he already texted, didn't he? It just slipped out!"

Because yes, Charlie knows about the contest and has been actively trying to screw everyone out of points but just can't help himself.

"C'mere, boyfriend." I open my arms, and he joins me on the bed and crawls into them, pouting. I kiss the side of his head as he wraps himself around me. "You know I love it when you call me that," I murmur, and he nods, his breath warm against the side of my neck.

"That's why I don't try harder," he admits. "Who cares about their stupid game when I have you?"

The warm feelings inside threaten to overwhelm me. I can't believe I'm this lucky, to have a guy who randomly says things like that. Who cares so much about me that he asked his dad to mentor me over the summer so I can get a better idea of how to run my business as I expand it. Who brags about me to anyone who might listen. We've been officially together for only four weeks, but there's already been a fifteen percent uptick in Mr. Romance inquiries, and I'm putting that down to Charlie's big mouth.

And there's never any doubt in my mind how he feels. He's openly affectionate, more than when we were "just friends," taking every chance he can to touch me, even if it's just a brush of fingertips. He says he's not a romantic person, but he really is—it shows in the way he always thinks of me and what I might want.

In the way his gaze always slides my way in a group setting. The way he brags about me. The way he brings me lunch when I have back-to-back classes and always remembers what I like.

"I did a thing," he mutters against my neck, and I sigh. Because that's code for "I bought you something."

"Charlie, I don't love you for the presents," I remind him.

He untangles himself from me and sits up. "I know. But I was all stressed and shit, and you know shopping calms me down. I wasn't going to get you anything, I swear, but then I saw it, and I *had* to."

"Are you still worried about talking to your parents?" I take his hand in mine, rubbing my thumb along the back, and he visibly relaxes.

"No. Maybe just a bit. I know they'll be okay with it, but the anticipation is killing me. Maybe I should just send them an email." I say nothing, and he huffs. "Yeah, fine, I know I can't send an email. But... what if they really want me to learn to run the company?"

I bite my lip. I've met Charlie's parents twice now—they came down to visit after Charlie told them we were together —and spoken to them on the phone a few times, and I'm almost positive they don't expect Charlie to ever run the company. They know he'd hate it. His strengths lie in other areas, and his parents love him enough to recognize that and accept it. I think they've just been waiting for him to tell them what he really wants to do.

He slides a glance at me. "If you were anyone else, I'd say you were quiet because you think I'm too dumb to run the company."

"I don't think that, and it's not true," I say sharply. "Who called you dumb?"

"No one." He shrugs. "But I know people think it. I'm not exactly setting the world on fire."

"You're doing fine. And now that you've worked out what you want, you can concentrate on achieving that."

"If Mom and Dad go for it." His mouth turns down in a frown.

"They'll love it," I assure him, trying not to sound exasperated. The idea first came to me when we were in LA for the fundraiser, and since then I've just become more and more convinced. When I finally suggested it to Charlie, he stared blankly at me for ten seconds, then lit up like a Christmas tree. "It's perfect for you, and you and your mom get on like a house on fire. She's going to love having you work with her to build awareness of domestic violence and fundraise for women and children who need help." He's going to be amazing at it, too. His natural charm is going to work wonders in getting people to donate money, and he's never met a stranger he couldn't tell all about his favorite cause. What he's done for Mr. Romance is a great example. "Do you want to go up and talk to them this weekend instead of waiting two weeks for school to finish?"

He thinks about it. "Will you go with me?"

"Of course."

"Then yes. Let's get it over with." He leans in to kiss me, and I meet him halfway. We topple to the mattress, and he pulls me closer, sliding his hand into my hair. What's left of it, anyway. I got it cut last week, and with my permission, the stylist went pretty short. I don't need to distract from my face anymore—not when Charlie loves everything about me. If he can love me, why shouldn't I? Everyone else can go fuck themselves.

He pulls back, and I make a sound of protest.

"Your present!" He climbs over me and off the bed.

Rolling onto my back, I say, "I'd rather have a fuck."

"You can have both," he assures me as he digs into his backpack. "But I want you to have this first." He comes back to the bed with a small paper bag, and I sit up. There's no printing on it, nothing to indicate where he bought it, which is a relief. One thing I've learned since meeting him is that the more expensive stores always put their name on their packaging.

I unfold the top and tip the contents into my palm.

It's a luggage tag. Which... random. Although, mine did break on our trip, so I kind of need one. The side I'm looking at has the clear plastic window for me to slide in a card with my name on it, so I flip it over to look at the other side.

And laugh.

Black-and-white letters against a bright blue background proclaim "This Is My Flipping Bag," and below that is the outline of a gymnast doing a handspring.

"Thank you." I lean over and kiss his cheek. "I love it. It's perfect for me."

He smiles at me. "So Jake was wrong? He told me I should get you a romantic present, but I said the romance is in the details."

This time I kiss his mouth. "I'll turn you into a romantic yet."

Because the romance is absolutely in the details.

Thanks so much for reading *Mr. Romance*! If you're curious about Spencer and Cory, you can grab their story, *Bet You* by Neve Wilder.

For more Kieran and Connor (and to see Ian and Matt), check out the Ghostly Guardians series.

And if you were intrigued by Joy Universe, Derek's book is *I've Got This.*

Coming next from me is *Conspiracy of Dragons*, the final book in the Here Be Dragons series.

MEET ALL THE COUPLES OF FRANKLIN U!

Brax and Ty's story:
Playing Games
Marshall and Felix's story:
The Dating Disaster
Charlie and Liam's story:
Mr. Romance
Spencer and Cory's story:
Bet You
Chris and Aidan's story:
The Glow Up
Cobey and Vincent's story:
Learning Curve
Alex and Remy's story:
Making Waves
Peyton and Levi's story:
Football Royalty

HI FROM LOUISA!

Hey folks! I hope you enjoyed *Mr. Romance*! Make sure to read the books by the seven other incredible authors in this series - you won't regret it! I'm so grateful to Saxon James and Riley Hart for inviting me to take part in this project.

This book was so much fun to write, and you may have noticed that it's a veritable basket of easter eggs, with crossovers from two of my other series (Ghostly Guardians and Joy Universe) and a mention of a third (Hidden Species). If you're curious about any of those books you can check my website www.louisamasters.com or Amazon.

For those of you wondering if Ian and Matt will get their turn in the spotlight, all signs point to yes! I have Plans for them (with a definite capital P), but I'm giving them some time to grow up first. In the meantime, my next book will be the final Here Be Dragons installment, *Conspiracy of Dragons*.

And don't forget to join the fun in my Facebook group RoMMance with Becca & Louisa.

Hugs!
Louisa xx

ALSO BY LOUISA MASTERS

Franklin U
Mr. Romance

Ghostly Guardians
Spirited Situation
Vortex Conundrum

Here Be Dragons
Dragon Ever After
The Professor's Dragon
The Dragon Experiment
Conspiracy of Dragons

Hidden Species
Demons Do It Better
One Bite With A Vampire
Hijinks With A Hellhound
Sorcerers Always Satisfy

Met His Match
Charming Him
Offside Rules

A Christmas Chance (novella)

Between the Covers (M/F)

Joy Universe

I've Got This

Follow My Lead

In Your Hands

Take Us There

Novellas

Fake It 'Til You Make It (permafree)

One Golden Night

O Hell, All Ye Shoppers

Out of the Office

After the Blaze

ABOUT THE AUTHOR

Louisa Masters started reading romance much earlier than her mother thought she should. While other teenagers were sneaking out of the house, Louisa was sneaking romance novels in and working out how to read them without being discovered. As an adult, she feeds her addiction in every spare second. She spent years trying to build a "sensible" career, working in bookstores, recruitment, resource management, administration, and as a travel agent, before finally conceding defeat and devoting herself to the world of romance novels.

Louisa has a long list of places first discovered in books that she wants to visit, and every so often she overcomes her loathing of jet lag and takes a trip that charges her imagination. She lives in Melbourne, Australia, where she whines about the weather for most of the year while secretly admitting she'll probably never move.

http://www.louisamasters.com

CPSIA information can be obtained
at www.ICGtesting.com
Printed in the USA
BVHW092050090922
646659BV00007B/753